"Ross

She went to him. ...s around him, her ...baby— pressing into his.

He held her tightly. She leaned into him and cried.

"I thought I'd be able to hate him for the rest of my life," he said.

They stood like that for a moment, frozen, and then he kissed her. This kiss was nothing like their kiss nine years earlier. Nothing like the one the other night. No romance, just raw need, and her body responded instantly.

"Jennifer," he said.

A statement and a question rolled into one, and she knew what he needed. Knew she needed it, too.

Yes, she said, not with her voice but with her hands and lips.

He took her upstairs and undressed her. Made love to her slowly and reverently, worshiping her. And he held her and he wept.

I *love him*, she thought. I *always have*....

Dear Reader,

After my daughter's birth I understood something about my own parents. Though I'd felt quite clearly that they loved me, I hadn't grasped how much. We'd gone through the usual ups and downs and I knew they'd made plenty of mistakes, as all moms and dads do. I knew, too, that a parent's love for a child is supposed to be one of the most powerful you can experience. But did I really, truly get it? No. Not the way I did when I had a baby of my own. *Oh, I thought, this is what it's like*. And it blew me away.

Although her baby hasn't yet been born, Jennifer Burns has an inkling of the intense protectiveness and devotion she'll feel. Already she's determined to do whatever it takes to give her child the best possible start in life—which includes a relationship with the father. As you read, you'll learn why this is so very important to her. You'll also watch her definition of a "real" father evolve throughout the book as she realizes Ross Griffin may be the best man for the job. Though he's not the biological dad, he has the most important qualification—a deep capacity to love and cherish her child.

I'd enjoy hearing what you think of *Her Baby's Father*. You can write me at P.O. Box 1539, Eastsound, WA 98245.

Best wishes,

Anne Haven

Her Baby's Father
Anne Haven

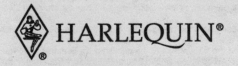

HARLEQUIN®

TORONTO • NEW YORK • LONDON
AMSTERDAM • PARIS • SYDNEY • HAMBURG
STOCKHOLM • ATHENS • TOKYO • MILAN • MADRID
PRAGUE • WARSAW • BUDAPEST • AUCKLAND

If you purchased this book without a cover you should be aware that this book is stolen property. It was reported as "unsold and destroyed" to the publisher, and neither the author nor the publisher has received any payment for this "stripped book."

ISBN 0-373-71078-X

HER BABY'S FATHER

Copyright © 2002 by Anne Ha.

All rights reserved. Except for use in any review, the reproduction or utilization of this work in whole or in part in any form by any electronic, mechanical or other means, now known or hereafter invented, including xerography, photocopying and recording, or in any information storage or retrieval system, is forbidden without the written permission of the publisher, Harlequin Enterprises Limited, 225 Duncan Mill Road, Don Mills, Ontario, Canada M3B 3K9.

All characters in this book have no existence outside the imagination of the author and have no relation whatsoever to anyone bearing the same name or names. They are not even distantly inspired by any individual known or unknown to the author, and all incidents are pure invention.

This edition published by arrangement with Harlequin Books S.A.

® and TM are trademarks of the publisher. Trademarks indicated with ® are registered in the United States Patent and Trademark Office, the Canadian Trade Marks Office and in other countries.

Visit us at www.eHarlequin.com

Printed in U.S.A.

For H.H.T., because you kept your daughter's letters.

ACKNOWLEDGMENTS

Many thanks to Kristen Bernard and Jharna Morrissey
at River Valley Midwives, for their inspiration
and guidance with firsthand research;
to Kim Bressem, for looking after The Bean; and to
Donna Miller, for proofreading and emotional support.
I'm also indebted to Dr. Robert Weitzman,
for answering medical questions;
to Sam Thoron, my father-in-law,
for also helping with research;
and to Joshua Wolk, for his consultations on arm breaking.

Any technical errors in this fictional work are mine.

Bev Sotolov is an incredible editor
and I feel privileged to work with her.
Ruth Kagle has been a supportive and diligent agent.
Thanks also to Annelise Roby and to everyone at Rotrosen.

Finally, I must acknowledge that this book would not exist
without the help of my husband, Joe Thoron,
whose contributions are too numerous to list.

CHAPTER ONE

BUCK UP, HONEY. Time to be strong.

Jennifer Burns repeated the words as she slowed her dusty old station wagon in front of Ross Griffin's house in Portland, Oregon. She parked at the curb, cut the engine and sat. Cupping her rounded stomach, she fortified herself with thoughts of the new life inside her.

She was doing this for the baby's sake. That made everything worth it.

Jennifer studied the large Victorian where Ross lived. It sat on a hill above the city, with a sloped front lawn and a low hedge lining the walk. The house was pale yellow, the trim painted in darker shades of peach, giving it a warm glow in the pre-dusk June evening. A blue Camry sat in the driveway. A flower pot hung from the roof of the porch.

Ross's home appealed to her. She wondered what his life there was like.

And wished the reason for this reunion could be anything other than what it was.

The car door gave its usual creaky groan as she opened it. Stepping out onto the smoothly paved road, she eased her body to a standing position. Her limbs felt stiff from the two-day drive and her lower back ached dully. As she crossed the front yard she was strongly conscious of her pregnancy, of her unmistakable waddle and the ripeness of her curves—so different from the last time she'd seen Ross. She'd been seventeen, a kid, still scrawny.

This was going to be quite a surprise.

Jennifer hadn't been able to bring herself to call him. She'd tried three times and had always hung up before dialing the last digit. It was silly and illogical and she knew it. But after what had happened with his brother, she didn't know what to expect from Ross. Their past—the friendship she and Ross had once shared—might not mean a thing to him. And they hadn't parted under the best circumstances. He could try to brush her off. He could hang up on her.

No, she'd told herself, better to show up in person. Better to have this conversation face-to-face. It was too important.

Reaching the porch, she used the handrail for stability as she climbed the steps. A woven jute welcome mat sat in front of the door, and as she walked up to it she felt her heart rate quicken. Staving off another attack of nerves, she raised a hand and knocked.

ROSS WAS STANDING in the living room, staring at the shredded foilage and potting soil scattered across the middle of his new rug, when someone knocked on the front door. Frank, the three-legged female Chihuahua who'd attacked and killed his last fern, yipped twice, turned in a circle and scampered under the sofa.

Ross shook his head as he walked to the front hall. Dog-sitting. And he'd agreed to a week of this. She was cute enough, but her passion for his house-plants—not to mention her sensitive stomach—made her a difficult guest. Next time Kyle and Melissa and little Emily left town, they could stick Frank in a kennel.

He opened the door and saw a pregnant woman standing on his porch.

No, not just a pregnant woman. Someone he'd known in another lifetime.

"Jennifer Burns? Is that you?"

"Hello, Ross."

Nine years slid away to the summer she'd dated his younger brother. To one of the few times he'd ever been jealous of Drew.

Ross remembered the long walks he and Jennifer had taken. The animated conversations. Lounging on the deck behind his parents' house on warm eve-nings. Being a twenty-one-year-old kid who thought he knew anything about anything.

He stared at this new version of Jennifer Burns. The shorter, chin-length cut of her dark-blond hair suited her features, which had matured very well. Her face was fuller, with a healthy pregnant-woman's glow. A splash of bleach marked the sleeve of her pink maternity shirt. She wore cropped jeans with deep creases across the upper thighs, as if she'd been sitting a long time. He could see her ankles, slightly swollen, above a pair of inexpensive white sneakers.

Pregnant. On his doorstep. Looking anxious but determined, as if she had a very important purpose for being there.

He knew what it meant. The knowledge came swiftly and effortlessly. Like a needle stick. Not so much painful in itself, but a single, simple moment containing a world of consequences.

The wave of anger surprised him. Anger at her. At his brother. At himself, for caring even the slightest, when he hadn't seen her in almost a decade.

She fidgeted under his gaze. "I need to talk with you. May I come in?"

Ross didn't trust himself to speak. He stood back, let her enter, then motioned through the archway between the front hall and the living room.

Frank's mess on his floor and a pregnant Jennifer Burns in his house. Not what he'd planned for the evening.

"Excuse me," he managed to say. He left her in the living room and went to the hall closet for a whisk broom and a hand-held vacuum, then to the kitchen for the trash can. Frank's mess, at least, could be fixed.

Rejoining her, he set to work on the fern's remains without offering an explanation. The brown glazed planter had broken into several pieces and he swept it up along with the fern and potting soil.

He felt torn between wanting Jennifer to walk back out the front door and never return—walk away as she had nine years ago—and wanting her to stay. Wanting to be around her again.

She'd slept with his brother. She carried his brother's child. What would make her become involved with Drew again? What the hell did she see in him? And why did he, Ross, feel even the least bit of interest in someone capable of such bad judgment?

"It's been a long time," she ventured. She stood

awkwardly in a corner, watching him at his task. "How are you?"

He shrugged. "Not bad. You?"

"Okay," she said. "Fine."

"And pregnant." He didn't look up as he said it.

"Yes."

After a brief silence, Ross switched on the vac to suck up the last of the dirt. When he was finished, Frank slipped out from under the sofa and trotted across the room to sniff at the visitor's toe. Jennifer knelt to let the dog smell her hand. Frank darted her tongue out, licked once and scooted backward as fast as her three feet could take her. She disappeared down the hall.

"Congratulations," he said, as Jennifer rose. Meaning her pregnancy.

"Thank you."

The conversation stopped again. Ross gathered his cleaning supplies and stood up.

They both knew where this was headed. He didn't want to ask the question but forced himself.

"Do I know the father?"

Jennifer faced him squarely. She opened her mouth but couldn't seem to find the words. Finally she nodded.

CHAPTER TWO

Nine years earlier

This is what it's like to be the new girl in school: first and foremost, you pretend not to notice people staring. You don't look at anyone because then they might see how lonely and uncomfortable you feel. Instead you pretend to have something important on your mind—much more important than anything that could possibly be going on around you. Alternatively, you bury your nose in a book. Books are very helpful when you don't want to look like an anxious wallflower.

I know because I've been the new girl *a lot*. It's only my junior year and this is the fourth high school I've attended. I love my mom, but when it comes to staying in one place, she sucks. You can't imagine how many different towns we've lived in.

By the time I meet Drew I've totally given up on making new friends. He doesn't seem to understand that, though.

He sits in the noisy cafeteria with his group, in the designated corner. A sign might as well hang above them: Beautiful People Only. As I walk by, something whizzes past me and lands in the soup on my tray, splattering overcooked vegetable bits all over my favorite sweater, the grayish blue one Mom and I found at a garage sale in Seattle. I hear snickers.

One of them isn't laughing, though. His gaze is sympathetic, and before I can make myself scarce he's beside me, taking the tray and offering me a napkin.

"You've got to forgive my friend Brian. He thinks throwing French fries around is amusing. Typical jock, right?"

I accept the napkin and dab at my shirt, not meeting his eyes. Wishing I didn't have to turn bright red like a complete moron.

"Your name's Jennifer, right? We sit next to each other in Spanish. I'm Drew Griffin."

I hazard a glance at him. He's pretty tall so I have to tilt my head up. It's like raising my face to the sun. His eyes are bright blue. His smile is warm and encouraging and ever so slightly goofy, as if he has no idea half the school is madly in love with him. I, on the other hand, figured it out right away, when I heard the girl with the locker next to mine gossiping with a friend.

"Look," Drew says, "I'm sorry about this. Let me buy you a new lunch."

And so he adopts me. At first I'm suspicious because my self-confidence isn't exactly soaring and I can't imagine why he would pay me so much attention. But I'm also pretty starstruck so it's hard to resist. Soon I forget all about my aversion to cliques and popular kids.

When I spend time around Brian, Kurt, Molly and Heather—and, wonder of wonders, they accept me, too—I feel as if I finally belong somewhere.

It's all so seductive—going to parties, constantly getting phone calls, hanging out with kids who have their own Saabs and BMWs and more spending money in their pockets than my mom earns in a week. Molly and Heather share their clothes and makeup with me, and I'm amazed when they figure out a new style for my hair—layered and blow-dried with a ton of gel—that makes me look about ten years older and a million times more sophisticated. Drew takes me out all the time and before long we're an item. He's drawn me out of my shell, helped me to become a new person—one who's self-assured and carefree and fun.

But then school gets out for the summer and Drew's older brother, Ross, comes home from college. And life gets a lot more complicated.

The present

THE CONFIRMATION that Drew was the baby's father made Ross feel as if he had a bad case of acid reflux. He realized he'd hoped Jennifer would say no. That somehow he'd been wrong.

Damn it, Drew. Not right now. So many people would be affected by this. Lucy. And their mother had barely left the hospital. She was recovering fairly well, but she needed to keep her life as stress-free as possible until her health was back to normal. She wasn't the kind of person who would greet the news of Jennifer's baby—and Drew's paternity—with equanimity.

Ross stifled the curse that formed on his lips. "I'll be right back," he said.

He stashed the broom and handheld vac back in the hall closet. In the kitchen he put the trash can under the sink, washed his hands and poured two glasses of water from the filter pitcher in the fridge. He hated that this wasn't easy, that he actually felt something for her after all this time. That some crazy part of him was actually happy to see her again despite the circumstances. Their past should just be a dim memory. He shouldn't care anymore. All he should care about was protecting the innocent bystanders.

When he returned, Jennifer stood by the bay window, looking out at the view of downtown Portland. The curtains were at the cleaners', due back next week. Without them the windows seemed raw, the curtain rods and cords a stark frame for the view.

He offered one of the glasses of water and she thanked him for it.

An unfamiliar white station wagon sat across the street from his house, crammed with stuff. He saw a lamp, cardboard boxes, a cactus plant and what appeared to be a bunched-up comforter. California license plate.

She sipped the water. "It's a lovely view," she said into the silence, her gaze on the city. "I like your house."

"Thank you."

"Do you live here alone?"

"Yes." Did she care? Did he want her to care? Ross glanced at her profile and felt the same pull of attraction he had as a college kid. This was the woman who, as a teenager, had felt sympathy for a rain-drenched flower seller. Who'd read Arthur Koestler and Noam Chomsky and had intelligent things to say about them. Who'd been willing to help out his aunt Lenora, a total stranger, when she'd broken her ankle.

And the last time he'd seen Jennifer they'd kissed. Kissed each other while she was still dating his brother.

He tried to push away the thought and the accompanying twinge of conscience. Drew didn't deserve his loyalty anymore—not after what had happened with Lucy and not if he'd slept with Jennifer during the past year. But the guilt still lingered.

"No family of your own?" she asked.

"No family of my own." He'd tried that route and it hadn't worked out.

"Drew said you're an E.R. doctor. Northwest?" The hospital.

He nodded.

Another moment passed. She stared out the window again, as if absorbed by the view of the city, then said, "I need to get in touch with him."

Ross thought that sounded like a singularly bad idea. "Does he know about the baby?"

"If he knew, I wouldn't be having so much trouble reaching him."

An opinion Ross didn't share. "He never told me he'd seen you again. I guess he didn't give you his phone number." When the two of you got together. When you conceived this child.

Her eyelashes flickered. "He gave me a phone number. It just wasn't his."

Nice. In that case he should have had the guts to give no phone number at all. But not Drew. He wanted to look good even when he was being a jerk.

Ross considered her belly, judging her to be about six months along. He remembered a business trip Drew had taken to San Francisco last December. The timing worked. And the timing made Drew's actions unconscionable.

Ross felt a strong desire to strangle his brother.

"I couldn't find him in the phone book," she said. "But he does live in Portland...?"

"More or less." Drew lived across the Columbia River in Vancouver, Washington. Which amounted to the same thing if you were driving all the way here from San Francisco. But even if she'd thought to check for Drew there, she wouldn't have found a number. His brother preferred not to be listed, claiming he didn't want his law clients calling him at home in hysterics.

To come all the way here without confirmation Drew lived in the area, Ross thought, had been a gamble. But maybe Jennifer was more desperate than she wanted to admit.

He observed her car more closely. Flakes of rust had gathered around the wheel wells. The rear door on the passenger side had a dent in it. Under its heavy load the car sagged onto its aging shocks. A car that belonged to someone who couldn't afford much maintenance, it fit with the bleach-stained shirt and the cheap shoes.

The accumulating evidence of her financial difficulties surprised him, though. When he'd known her, Jennifer had been bright and motivated. He'd expected her to do better. Much better.

"You drove here from California?"

She nodded.

"And you plan to stay for a while."

"Yes."

"Your mother—where is she?" Surely her mother would be able to help her at a time like this.

"She died last November."

"Oh. I'm sorry to hear that." He'd met the woman once, briefly, on the street outside his parents' house when she'd come by to pick Jennifer up. She'd seemed nice, if a bit tired. He remembered she'd worn a hairnet and some kind of uniform.

"Breast cancer," Jennifer volunteered.

"How long was she sick?"

"Seven years, on and off."

He knew what this meant. Knew the financial, physical and emotional toll an extended illness took, though he only witnessed the crisis points in the E.R. Jennifer's circumstances made more sense now.

"That must have been rough," he said.

She shrugged, and despite her attempt at nonchalance he saw that it had been excruciating.

"And now this." Her pregnancy. Her child by a man who would never acknowledge his paternity.

"Now this," she echoed.

He watched her. "When's the baby due?"

"September fourteenth."

She had less than three months to go. Not an easy time to travel. Not an easy time to pack your life into your run-down station wagon and move to a different state.

"Why now?" he asked. Why hadn't she contacted him sooner—as soon as she'd realized she was pregnant and couldn't reach Drew?

She understood his meaning. "I had my reasons," she said. "I needed time. I needed to come to terms with my situation."

Ross didn't press for a detailed explanation since she obviously didn't care to share more. Perhaps she'd considered an abortion but hadn't been able to go through with it. Perhaps she'd known about Lucy, though he wouldn't be surprised if she didn't. Perhaps she'd wanted to raise the child on her own, without Drew's involvement, and had finally had to accept that she couldn't swing it financially.

And she clearly couldn't. She clearly needed assistance.

Understandable. He knew how hard it was to be a single mother with no child support, especially if you already had to deal with the expenses associated with a long-term illness. At the free clinic where he volunteered each week he saw plenty of mothers who were forced to live on the edge of poverty—and not because they were stupid or lazy, but because keeping a single-parent household going was damn hard if you hadn't started out wealthy and weren't among the top twenty percent of income earners.

Ross didn't want to think about Jennifer living below the poverty level, especially with a new baby. And he could prevent it from happening. He could also prevent anyone else from getting hurt by this.

Not that he was concerned about Drew. Had Drew been the only one affected, Ross might have just jotted down his brother's information and sent her on her way. But that wasn't the case.

Ross walked closer to the window. Studied the front yard. The leaves of the climbing rose were getting specks on them, he saw, and made a mental note to bring it to his gardener's attention.

He crossed his arms, unable to make himself turn around and look her in the eyes. "How much do you need?"

"Excuse me?"

He knew the question was an ugly one, but he asked it again. "How much do you need, Jennifer? To raise your baby. And to do it somewhere far away from here."

JENNIFER STARED at Ross's broad, intimidating back. He'd told her where she stood—firmly outside the circle of people for whom he cared, people he considered his own. Just as her father had when she was thirteen. Now, as then, she was nothing more than a problem—a problem to be solved by throwing money at it.

Jennifer raised her glass to her lips and felt herself shaking. She finished the water, then walked out of the room with all the composure she could muster, which wasn't much. She couldn't be around him, couldn't handle it, despite the weeks she'd had to prepare herself.

Stumbling blindly down the hallway, knowing it was rude, she tried to numb herself from caring. From feeling anything.

At the far end of the hall she pushed through a half-open door into an airy kitchen overlooking the backyard. The counters were indigo tile, the sink white porcelain below a six-paned window. A work island took up the center of the kitchen and a separate breakfast bar divided the cooking area from the dining room.

She focused on her hands as she rinsed her glass and put it in the dishwasher. Pretending she was calm. Under control, the way she'd wanted to be. But her eyes stung with tears and her throat felt tight.

The past couple of months had been so stressful. Last winter when she'd realized Drew had left her a fake phone number she'd decided he wouldn't want to know about the baby, convinced herself she could go it alone. But then her profit-driven landlord had found a way to eject her from her rent-controlled apartment. To get a new one at the same price she would have had to settle for a hovel not much better than a refrigerator box in a back alley. Looking for a roommate, she'd quickly ascertained that few of the candidates—and none of those who weren't creepy—wanted to live with a newborn.

Some friends had put her up temporarily. But she'd seen how easily her life could slip, felt the vulnerability of a pregnant woman alone with few resources. She was deeply in debt, struggling to pay off her mother's medical bills. What if she lost her job? What if she couldn't afford good child care? What if something unforeseen happened, like her mother's cancer? The cancer had taken over their lives. Had forced Jennifer to quit college and steadily drained their finances. There had been countless treatments and periods of remission, periods of hope, renewed fear and then hope again. And when Andrea Burns had died after battling her illness so valiantly, she'd left Jennifer without any family. Even her father, she'd learned, had died in a car accident a few years earlier.

She'd awakened on her friends' couch one morning and known she couldn't let history repeat itself.

Her baby deserved a chance to develop a real relationship with his or her father, however imperfect that father might be. Her baby deserved, too, the additional security and emotional support a second parent would provide. A bigger safety net, which she alone couldn't give.

Ross entered the kitchen, interrupting her thoughts. Jennifer didn't turn around. Gripping the counter with both hands, she felt the edges of the wooden trim bite into her skin.

She stood there a long time, silent, wishing with a foolish part of herself for him to apologize, to take back his words, to welcome her and the baby into the Griffin fold.

But of course he didn't.

Finally she faced him, surprised to find him closer than she'd expected, standing between her and the tiled island. She crossed her arms, feeling her belly protrude below them. "I didn't come to your house to be bought off."

"I know that."

"So don't insult me."

He said nothing, just reached up and brushed the pad of his thumb across a spot of dampness under her eye. Then, as if he couldn't resist—and already regretted his lack of will—he settled his hand on her shoulder and drew her to him.

Jennifer felt herself step into his arms. She tried to stand stiffly in his embrace, to resist the urge to relax, to keep the gesture from affecting her. But she was alone in a new city, with all her friends back in San Francisco. And this was Ross Griffin. Still compelling, still irresistible, despite the words he'd spoken in his living room. She felt her body soften against his, felt herself lean in to him. It was the wrong thing to do—just as it had been nine years ago—but she couldn't stop herself.

Her belly made the hug awkward, but she soaked up the comfort he seemed to offer, savoring the connection to another human being.

No, not just another human being, of course. The connection to Ross. Even though he'd hurt her with his attempt to buy her off, she couldn't help her pleasure at being near him again. Or the irrational relief she'd felt when he told her he lived alone, without a wife.

Inside her, the baby moved. A fluttering kick followed by what felt like a full-body stretch. A limb pressed outward, against Ross's stomach.

He went still. "The baby."

She nodded.

He released her shoulders and placed both palms, fingers down, on the heavy curve of her stomach. Her secondhand maternity jeans had a low waistband, so only the thin layer of her pink cotton shirt separated his skin from hers. The baby kept moving.

Jennifer closed her eyes. She loved these active periods, loved feeling the unmistakable presence of a new person growing inside her.

Ross's hands were warm and broad. With a slight upward pressure he supported her belly's weight. The contact felt intimate and much better than it should have.

Eventually the baby quieted. She opened her eyes to find Ross watching her.

Abruptly the spell broke. She stepped back, unable to look into his eyes. Regretting her susceptibility to him.

She remembered the last time they'd touched. The way he'd kissed her and the price she'd had to pay. So long ago, but still she could remember it—a distinct moment ringing like a tuning fork in her memory.

"I'm trying to help you," he said.

"Then tell me his phone number. That's all I want."

As if he was the one who needed to get distance between them now, Ross went to the French doors opening onto the back porch. Holding each of the curved handles, he stared out into the yard. "Drew won't help you."

"You don't know that."

"I do. He won't. I can."

She shook her head, though he couldn't see her.

"Damn it, Jennifer," he said, sounding more tired than angry. "Take the money and run. Make a life for yourself. Leave Drew behind."

Why did it matter so much to him? Who was he trying to protect? And didn't he care, just a little, that he would miss the chance to know his niece or nephew?

"I can't do that," she said.

"You'll have to. One way or another, you'll have to."

She studied him, searching for the meaning behind his words, the thing he didn't say. The reason he was so sure Drew would never accept his responsibilities.

And then she knew the problem. Knew with a sick kind of certainty, an unexpected clarity.

She looked away from him, out the window over the sink. A line of trees at the back of the property blocked the afternoon sun, but still the yard seemed warm and inviting. Flowers bloomed in a bed running the length of the fence that marked the right-hand lot line. Daisies and daylilies and snapdragons. Herbs grew in a raised bed in the middle of the lawn, basil, oregano, mint, and others she couldn't identify.

One of the daylilies was taller than the rest. Taller by almost a foot. Absently she wondered why it had grown that way, what trick of genetics or cultivation had made it rise over its neighbors.

"He's married, isn't he?"

CHAPTER THREE

ROSS TURNED AWAY from the French doors. She felt his gaze and slowly moved her head until their eyes met. He didn't say anything, but the truth was evident in his expression.

Of course Drew was married. She shouldn't have expected anything else from him. And she supposed there were worse things for her child, growing up, to face. Drew could be dead. Or in prison.

But she'd hoped against hope he might actually *want* to be involved in his child's upbringing. Now that seemed highly improbable. Like her father when she'd run away to find him, Drew had another life, another family. Though her father, at least, had had the decency not to be married to another woman when he'd slept with her mother.

"How long has he had a wife?" she asked.

"A couple of years." Ross pulled out one of the spindle-back chairs at the kitchen table and sat down. He leaned forward, forearms on knees, hands clasped. "I'm sorry."

"It's hardly your fault," she said, her anger at Drew spilling into her voice.

Ross ignored her tone. "Have a seat," he said,

pulling out another chair and positioning a third in front of it. "Put your feet up."

She was too agitated to sit. "I've been in the car all day."

"Suit yourself." He watched her for a moment. "My offer still stands."

Idly she wondered exactly what his offer was. How much money was he willing to pay for her to go away? Of course, even if it was, to him, a pittance, it would surely allow her to take care of herself and the baby for a few years until she could finish paying off her mother's medical bills. Start saving again.

She leaned against the counter, hugging herself. "You want me to leave town," she said. "Leave before contacting Drew. Never tell him, so he can maintain his marriage without having to pay a price for what he did."

Her words sounded confrontational, but she felt herself wavering, wondering if she should do as Ross suggested—take what he offered and disappear. She could drive the coastal route back to California, stop at cute tourist towns, pretend she'd only gone on a sight-seeing vacation. She might even be able to talk Benita Alvarez into giving her back her old job at the office supply warehouse.

"Yes," Ross said. "That's what I want."

She had to admire his honesty. But suddenly her moment of weakness had passed, replaced by anger and indignation. Jennifer recalled her conversation with Drew at the tiny bistro—eight tables in all and the cheapest appetizer cost more than she made in an hour—when she'd asked him directly whether he was involved with anyone. He'd sat there across the linen-draped table and lied to her as easily as he breathed. No hesitation. No awkwardness. The perfect hint of self-deprecating charm in his answer. No clue that he was married. Committed.

"I thought we were two unattached adults," she said, the words coming out hard.

"I believe you."

"He's put me in a really crappy position."

"Jennifer."

"So I'm not particularly in a mood to disappear. He lied to me, right to my face, and if I slink off, that means he gets away with it. And I don't really want to hear how it's going to be tough for his wife. She'll just have to face reality."

"Jennifer," he said again, trying to slow her down.

She looked right at him. Waited to hear what he would say. Realized she wouldn't like it, not a bit.

"His wife is pregnant."

The news made her feel as if she were on an elevator that had stopped too quickly. As if her big belly had continued moving and was now ten feet below the rest of her body.

"Oh." Somehow a pregnancy seemed even worse than if Drew and his wife had already had a child. She knew firsthand what a fragile and emotional time this was. Your whole life was filled with a sense of possibility and joy, but also fear.

Fear that something would go wrong. Fear that you would lose your unborn baby. Fear that your husband would desert you or have a trashy affair with another woman, some tramp he'd known in high school.

Shame washed through her.

But she hadn't known.

Jennifer walked over and took the chair Ross had offered her a few minutes earlier, then sat with her hands clasped under her stomach. On the table was a single small flower in a narrow stem vase. She didn't know the variety. White petals, each with a flare of blue moving out from the yellow center.

She stared at it and tried to keep her voice from wobbling. "How pregnant?"

"Six months."

Six months? *Six?*

She told herself to keep it together, despite the awful coincidence. Told herself she could be better than this screwed-up situation.

Buck up, honey. Time to be strong.

"She's due the week before you," Ross said.

"Was the baby an accident?" she asked. "Or had they been planning to have one?" Not that Ross necessarily would have known.

But apparently he did. "Lucy has wanted kids for a long time." His tone was grim.

Jennifer looked up, met his gaze. Now she understood why he thought Drew would never support or acknowledge his child—and she wished she didn't. To harbor the illusion Drew was just a garden-variety sleaze would have been nice. Now she had to deal with the fact that he was despicable. He'd slept with her while he and his wife had been trying to conceive a child. He'd fathered two babies in one week.

"Does Lucy—" she tried the name on her tongue, not really liking the sound of it "—know the kind of man he is?"

And while she waited for Ross to reply, she had to ask herself the same question. *Did you?* The answer was painful. Because some part of her had known. Known not to trust him. Known he was capable of something like this. Yet she'd allowed him into her bed.

She took little consolation from the fact that it never would have happened if he hadn't caught her at a vulnerable moment right before the holidays, a time that had made her feel raw and alone, with her closest friends out of town and the recent loss of her mother weighing more heavily than usual. She'd needed something familiar. Drew had been a person from her past. Somehow that had comforted her, even though their shared history was a source of ambivalence.

But she shouldn't have been such obliging prey. She shouldn't have been so easily taken in by him.

A married man. Whose wife was already pregnant.

The craziest piece of it all, though, was that she still couldn't regret sleeping with him. It had given her the precious baby inside her.

"I don't know if she does," Ross said at last. "But I do know she loves him."

"Will she still?" *Will she still love him when she has proof of his infidelity? Will she still love a husband who impregnated another woman?*

Ross didn't answer. His jaw was tight. A vein pulsed at his temple.

It was a pointless question. No one could predict how someone else might react to such circumstances. But she sensed this woman's feelings would matter to Ross. His sister-in-law was one of the people he cared about, whose well-being and happiness he wanted to preserve. It was very noble of him.

"Don't think this makes me less interested in confronting him." She placed a hand flat on the tabletop. "You want me to go away. But I hope you understand that if Drew is going to try to reject his child, he has to look me in the eyes as he does it."

Ross watched her. He seemed to read something inside her, to assess her resolve. Finally he stood. "Okay," he said. "Okay. I'll arrange a meeting."

ROSS CLOSED HIMSELF in his study to make the call. He sat for a long moment behind his dark mahogany desk, figuring out how to handle the conversation.

Jennifer was so sure of her need to see Drew. So sure it was the best thing for her and the baby. He didn't agree, but perhaps he was wrong about his brother and the way Drew would conduct himself. Perhaps Drew would seize the chance to do the right thing, to become the man he always should have been.

Not likely. And who knew what the right thing was in this case? He didn't see any resolution that didn't result in someone getting hurt.

It was just past six, so he punched in Drew's number at the law firm on the chance he would still be at work. Voice mail answered after five rings, and Ross hung up.

He dialed Drew at home in Vancouver. Lucy picked up, as he'd anticipated, but still he heard her familiar soft voice and had to force himself to sound normal. He hated to know more about her life than she did.

"Hey, Luce."

"Oh, hi," she said.

"The baby doing well?"

She gave a small laugh. "As far as I can tell."

He thought of how it had felt to cup Jennifer's stomach, to feel her child move inside her. Incredible. And not an experience he would ever share with Lucy. They had certain lines they were careful not to cross now.

"Is Drew there?"

"His car just pulled into the drive. I'll go get him."

Ross picked up a pencil on his desk and tapped it against a yellow legal pad. Gazed distractedly around the study. Like the living room, it was missing its drapes.

Drew came on the line a minute later.

Ross did the small-talk thing, something he and his brother were good at, and then got down to business. "I need you to come over," he said, keeping his tone casual.

"Now?"

"Yeah. That would be good."

"Hey, I just got home."

Ross didn't feel too worried about his brother's convenience. "I know. When can you make it?"

"Not right now. Lucy's got plans."

"Later tonight, then."

"Maybe. What's this about?"

"Nine o'clock?"

Drew covered the mouthpiece. Ross heard a murmur of conversation.

Drew came back on. "I can be there at nine. What's so important?"

"Just something I want to get handled. In person."

"A mystery, huh? Okay, big bro. See you in a few."

Ross hung up. He closed his eyes and massaged his temples, momentarily giving in to the frustration that rose inside him. He would have liked not to deal with this. He would have liked... What? For Jennifer not to have come to him? For her to have struggled on her own, raised his niece or nephew in a lonely little apartment somewhere? Or for her and Drew not to have conceived the baby—for them not to have slept together in the first place?

Well, yes, definitely that, he admitted to himself.

But it couldn't be changed. And feeling the baby move had elicited an aching tenderness in him—one that vied with the wish for her not to be pregnant with his brother's child.

Ross reached for the phone again. He needed to call someone from the free clinic who'd invited him to see an action flick with a group of friends that night. "Sorry to do this, Barbara, but I have to beg off."

The nurse practitioner made an indignant sound. "Again?"

"Something came up."

"Huh. That's pretty convincing."

"Seriously. Something did. Family stuff."

"It's not your mom, is it?"

"No, she's fine."

Barbara let a moment of silence go by. "Oh, I see. Jackie told you, right?"

"Told me what?"

She sighed. "That I invited my sister-in-law to come along."

"Barbara…" he said, trying to sound stern.

"I know, I know. But she's really cute. You'd like her. I know you would."

Judging from the two other women Barbara had set him up with, he probably would. They were both nice. Both attractive. But neither had done anything for him romantically.

Nevertheless, it was good to stay in circulation—something he'd found difficult after his divorce four years ago.

Ross sighed. "This isn't about your sister-in-law," he said. "Jackie didn't tell me anything. I'd come out if I could, but I can't."

"Okay, okay. I believe you." Her voice softened. "Good luck with whatever's going on."

When Ross walked back into the kitchen, he found Jennifer still sitting quietly at the table. Her feet were propped up on a chair now, clad only in white socks, her sneakers on the hardwood floor below.

"Nine o'clock," he told her.

"He'll see me?"

Ross selected an apple from the basket of fruit on

the counter, washed it and took a paring knife from the drawer by the sink. "He doesn't know it's you."

"Oh."

"I thought it would be best that way." He sliced the apple in half and then in half again before coring the quarters.

"Where are we meeting?"

"Here."

"Okay…" Briefly she closed her eyes.

Ross arranged the apple slices on a plate and set it on the table within her reach. "Help yourself," he said, taking a seat.

He ate and she ate, and while they chewed they didn't make eye contact. His gaze passed over the swell of her belly. She was six months pregnant with no family and not much money. He couldn't help but feel compassion. He saw the courage it must have taken to come here and the strength of purpose that kept her here despite what he'd told her about her baby's father.

Jennifer turned her head, looking around the dining area. He saw her gaze settle on a formal portrait of his mother and father, taken several years earlier, which hung on the wall.

"How are your parents?"

A standard social question. Basic politeness. He would have loved to give the standard polite answer—that they were well, thank you. "My dad's fine. Mom just had a double bypass."

She looked as surprised as he'd felt the day they'd discovered the blockage in his mother's arteries. "Did she have a heart attack?"

"Yeah. Right on the tennis court. Luckily the ambulance got to her quickly."

Katherine Griffin had always been trim and active, but her diet hadn't been the healthiest and she wasn't the most relaxed person. Still, Ross hadn't seen it coming. And should have. But he'd allowed his schedule to get too hectic this spring, and had only visited his parents once, briefly, during the month before Katherine's attack.

"How long ago?"

"Four weeks. She's been home about three."

Jennifer frowned. "And…is she going to be okay?"

Ross raised his shoulders in a helpless shrug. These things were hard to predict. "She came through the surgery well. Her heart sustained some damage, though. How much is hard to tell at this point."

She sat silently. Maybe thinking about his mother. Maybe about her own.

"I suppose stress isn't very good for her," she said finally.

"No." The cardiologist had felt stress was a major factor in Katherine's disease. During the recovery period, Ross wanted to keep her mind on pleasant topics. Drew's illegitimate baby didn't qualify. "You can see why this whole situation is complicated."

Jennifer reached for another slice of apple. He watched her eat it in three slow and deliberate bites. "I'm sorry about your mother. And I'm sorry the timing's so bad."

He nodded. After another pause he said, "I'm not

trying to stop you from talking to Drew, but tell me—if it's money you need, what's the difference whether you get it from me or from him?''

She glanced up at him, then away. ''You're not the father.''

Of course he wasn't. Naturally she wanted the father to take responsibility for his actions, but no matter which of them helped her, the result would be the same: financial security for her and her child.

''It's that important?'' he asked.

''A child should have a father. Not a stepfather. Not a series of stepfathers or a series of stand-ins who don't particularly want the role. Not an absentee benefactor, either.''

He opened his mouth to say that a benefactor was better than nothing. Her look stopped him. It said she hadn't forgotten Drew had another family. *I know he won't want me or his child, but I have to do this.*

Yet he didn't understand why she did. Was it masochism? Pure stubbornness? A self-destructive love for his brother despite everything he'd done?

Ross was glad, though, that it wasn't just about the money. Irrationally. Because it shouldn't make a difference to him. And he shouldn't care, either, that she would probably be disappointed.

He tried to imagine how Drew might be a father to her child, but couldn't. Drew paying visits every Saturday afternoon? Drew cherishing him or her, taking an active part in his or her life? That wasn't how the world worked and it wasn't how Drew worked. It certainly didn't seem like something Lucy would be able to accept.

Jennifer slipped her feet into her shoes. She pushed back from the table and stood. "Well, thank you for calling Drew."

"You're welcome."

"I'm going to go get settled and find something to eat. I'll be back a little before nine."

Ross walked her to the front hall. "Where are you staying?"

He'd wondered if she still had any friends here who might put her up, but she said, "A motel in Beaverton."

Upstairs he had two spare bedrooms. For her to waste money on a motel room when she could just stay here didn't seem right. True, he would probably be better off to keep his distance from her. She affected him more than she should, more than was right, and in the past that had only caused problems. But he didn't want to think of her completely alone in some cheap, depressing motel room after the conversation she was bound to have with Drew. If he, Ross, couldn't give her money, at least he could give her a pleasant place to stay the night. And maybe some support as she tried to decide what to do next.

He didn't open the front door. "Have you checked in?"

"No."

"So don't. Stay here, instead."

"Ross—"

"Save your money for the baby," he said. "You'll need it. And it's no trouble to have you here. I've got room upstairs and plenty of food for dinner."

CHAPTER FOUR

JENNIFER BROUGHT IN the bare minimum: her toiletries and a few clothes. She'd allowed Ross to talk her into staying at his house but knew she shouldn't get too comfortable. This was just for one night. It would save her fifty bucks, but tomorrow she would still have to find an apartment.

And Ross's offer of a place to sleep didn't mean she was now one of the people he cared about and protected. All it meant was that he was a gentleman, a considerate host, or perhaps that he felt he owed her a small favor due to their past acquaintanceship.

The room he'd given her was at the back of the house, directly over the kitchen, with windows that looked down into the garden. It had pale-peach walls. A cream-striped duvet covered the double bed and the spindled headboard wore the soft patina of age. Summer evening light slipped in the window and warmed the eastern side of the room.

Much better than an anonymous motel, she admitted.

Jennifer took a quick shower in the attached bathroom, which also connected to another guest room. She dried off with a butter-soft towel and dressed in fresh clothes, feeling a lot more human without the layer of dust and grit from her drive up from San Francisco. After running a comb through her still-damp hair, she joined Ross in the kitchen.

He stood at the island, snapping the ends off a pile of green beans. "Feeling refreshed?" he asked.

"Mmm-hmm." She walked over and took a seat. The dog, Frank, was curled up on a cushion by the back door. She wagged her stumpy tail at Jennifer and then put her head down on her paws.

"I overestimated the contents of my pantry," Ross said. "I need to run out to the store for some tomato sauce. Do you want to come along? You're welcome to stay here if you don't."

She slipped off her stool. "I'll come."

He was her child's uncle. To spend some time with him, to learn more about his life, wouldn't be so bad, right?

Ross wiped his hands on a tea towel and led her to the front door, where he grabbed his keys and let them both out. He glanced over as she descended the steps beside him, not offering to help but seeming alert to the possibility of her needing it. She wasn't so pregnant that her movements had become that difficult, but she knew the day would arrive.

He opened the passenger door of his Camry for her. As she settled herself in the seat and fastened her safety belt she studied his hospital ID card, which was clipped to the dash. The photo was a few years old. His dark hair was longer and he wore a haggard expression. He had deep bags under his eyes. It looked as if it had been taken in the middle of the night, partway through a grueling shift.

She watched him for a minute as he drove down the hill, leaving the residential area and entering the outskirts of downtown Portland. "Is being a doctor what you expected?"

Ross smiled a little ruefully, perhaps remembering things he'd said to her a long time ago. "I was an idealist, wasn't I?"

"Reality is different?"

"Reality is always different. Especially from what you imagine it'll be when you're barely out of your teens."

"So, what's it like?"

"Harder. Sometimes more boring. You wouldn't think so, but even emergencies can feel routine sometimes. And I can't say I like the business aspects of medicine."

"But helping people?"

"Oh, that's gratifying," he said. "Especially at the free clinic my friend Kyle runs."

"Where's that?"

"Old Town. We get lots of patients who are homeless. Also people with low incomes who can't afford any other kind of health care."

He talked about it in a matter-of-fact tone, and answered several more questions. She sensed he wouldn't want her to make a big deal about his volunteer service there, but she was, actually, impressed. Impressed he'd found a way to follow through on some of the ideals he'd professed nine years ago.

"How do you have time to do that?" she asked as they pulled into the little grocery store parking lot. "I thought doctors worked eighty-hour weeks."

''I worked that much as a resident. Now it only feels that way. I spend less than fifty hours a week at the hospital, though I have to do a bit more at home. Paperwork and keeping up on my reading.''

Ross explained how the shifts were set up at Northwest Hospital. He had day shifts for a few weeks and then a series of night shifts, with a break in between to adjust his internal clock. She'd caught him at the end of a night series, so he had a few days free.

They did their shopping and returned home. Ross picked up the meal preparations where he'd left off. Half an hour later he presented a meal of chicken, pasta and green beans.

As they ate they ranged over many subjects, but stayed away, as if by mutual consent, from anything that had to do with babies or sleazy brothers or family illnesses. In the security and ease of Ross's house, Jennifer allowed herself to imagine, briefly, what it would be like to have had a child the traditional way. The way she'd always fantasized about. To be married and live in a nice house. To plan to conceive a baby and enjoy the act of making it. To share in the expectations and fears of pregnancy, to raise a child together in a house like this one…

Dreams. Just dreams. As Ross had said, reality was always different. She shouldn't waste her time when her life was so unlike the fantasy, when she had a meeting with her baby's father in less than two hours—the father who was married to someone else and expecting another baby.

So she let herself enjoy the rest of the meal and

even Ross's company. But she didn't fool herself that the interlude was anything other than a temporary glimpse into another person's life.

Nine years earlier

I've heard all about Ross Griffin by the time he gets home from college. Drew calls him Mr. Perfect because he always gets a four-point, does tons of community service, was student body president in high school, excels at sports, speaks two foreign languages, gets his car's oil changed every three thousand miles without fail, and never, ever leaves dirty dishes in the kitchen sink. You can tell Drew kind of resents him for it, but you can tell he worships him, too. He tries to be like Ross. Like, he's into this weird band called The Others that nobody in high school's ever heard of, and three weeks ago when we went into Ross's room to check out his vintage skateboard I saw an old concert ticket sitting on his desk.

Molly and Heather think Ross is gorgeous. But I've seen pictures of him all over the Griffin house and I don't see what all the fuss is about. Sure, he could pass for that British actor, what's-his-name, but so what? Drew's better looking. Plus he's laid-back and fun, while Ross is probably an uptight prig.

We're sitting on the deck, Brian and Heather and Drew and I, when Ross gets home from a shopping trip with Mr. and Mrs. Griffin. He flew back from Cambridge a couple of days ago, but I haven't run into him yet.

They come out onto the deck to say hello and I try to stand up because I've been sitting on Drew's lap, which seems a little trashy in front of his family, especially when I see his mom's gaze go to his arms around my waist. But Drew tightens his grasp, so I'm stuck there, embarrassed, when I meet his big brother.

Ross greets Brian and Heather and then turns his attention to me. "Jennifer, right? Nice to meet you." He actually offers me his hand.

I don't know if college kids go around shaking each other's hands when they meet, but I'm not used to that, at least not from anyone under thirty. Which is probably why I get such a funny, off-balance feeling inside, as if I just miscalculated where the ground was when I stepped off a ladder.

His hand is big and warm, his grip firm. He doesn't hold mine any longer than necessary or seem particularly stirred by the experience of meeting me.

"How are you?" I say, trying to look as comfortable as I can while I sit on his brother's lap.

We all chat for a moment. I ask a few polite questions about his trip back from college and he asks where I lived before Portland, and then Mrs. Griffin reminds Drew to keep the screen door closed so insects don't get into the house—he'd left it open this afternoon—and she and her husband go back inside.

Ross sits down on one of the dark-metal deck chairs his mom special-ordered from Europe last month. Drew and Brian start to talk about their new game systems and nobody's talking to me anymore, so I just stare at Mr. Perfect, curious to see if he's as arrogant as I had expected.

"So, how was your semester?" Heather asks him.

From her voice and expression it's obvious she's got a crush on the guy. I hope he's too self-absorbed to notice, because otherwise I'm going to feel embarrassed for her.

Heather gushes at him and he answers all her questions about Cambridge and Harvard and what his dorm was like. He's perfectly nice about it, but I start to get the feeling he thinks she's a ditz. That's not really fair. Heather may not be a super-brain, but she's not stupid. Plus, she's nice.

Finally I open my mouth to get into the conversation, just because I'm feeling left out. "What's your major?"

Heather answers before he can. "He's going to be a doctor," she says, as though he's already asked her to marry him or something.

Ross frowns, and I'm not really sure why. He's hard to figure out. I can't tell if he's annoyed with Heather and me or just distracted.

A couple of minutes later he catches Drew's attention. "Sorry to break this up, but we should be ready to go in about ten minutes."

Drew gives him a blank stare.

"Grandma," Ross prompts.

"Oh, man. I totally forgot."

I give Drew a "huh?" look over my shoulder—I'm still sitting on his lap—and he says, "We have to go visit my grandma. Mom promised her we'd both come by this afternoon. I completely forgot about it."

Ross says, "Can you be ready?" His gaze takes in Drew's swimming trunks and faded Martha's Vineyard T-shirt with the black dog on it. *He's* already dressed appropriately, of course, in gray pants and a crisp white shirt.

Drew grimaces. "I've got to run Jenny home."

His brother doesn't seem to like this, and now I feel as if he's annoyed directly at me. I'm going to make him late for his visit to his grandmother.

"I could ride the bus," I say, scooting off Drew when he lets go of me to check his watch. I stand up.

Drew looks relieved, but I'm a little bummed. It's less than ten minutes to my apartment by car, but a lot longer than that on the bus, especially since the stop is several blocks away. But I don't want him to get in trouble.

Ross shakes his head, sighing. "Drive her home," he tells Drew. "It's not that big a deal. I'll just call Grandma and let her know we'll be late."

"Thanks," I say. But I don't feel he's being

all that nice and I can tell he really is annoyed with me. "I'm ready to go right now."

Drew grabs his keys and we take off, walking out to the cars with Brian and Heather, and I'm happy to see the last of his brother for a while.

The present

DREW HAD A BAD FEELING as he drove from his home in Vancouver across the Columbia River, down I-5, across the Willamette and up to Ross's house—a feeling this wasn't going to be a social call.

He pulled into the driveway and parked behind a battered station wagon with California plates and a San Francisco neighborhood parking permit. It took him a second, then he remembered seeing it at Jennifer Burns's apartment and wondering how anyone could drive such a hunk of junk.

Glancing in the windows, he saw what appeared to be all her worldly possessions. Jesus. Was she moving here or simply stopping by on her way somewhere else?

She'd better not be the reason for this little visit. He'd expected her to figure out their night together was a one-time thing. Not that he would object to a repeat, but that started to smack of complications. And he didn't like complications.

He knocked on the door, realizing that if this *was* about her, it would hardly be about starting up a relationship. Ross wasn't exactly the type to act as a broker for his brother's extramarital affairs. Hell, if he even realized there *were* affairs he'd go ballistic.

Ross opened the door, his features tense, his eyes cool. Drew realized instantly that he knew about San Francisco.

Shit, Drew thought. Just what he needed today—to be called on the carpet by his saintly older brother.

Ross stepped back to let him enter. A small brown dog shot into the front hall on three legs. The crazed-looking Chihuahua spent more time moving in circles than going straight forward.

"Yours?" he asked. It would be just like his brother to take on a crippled dog.

"Kyle and Melissa's."

Drew didn't spend a lot of time socializing with Ross's friends. No time at all, in fact. But he'd heard Ross talk about these particular friends and their daughter. They seemed to have a perfect life. Drew wouldn't be surprised, though, if one of them walked into his law office someday seeking a divorce. Love was fun, but life was real. He didn't have a lot of illusions left about human nature, his included.

"So what's this all about?" he asked, pretending he didn't know.

"Jennifer Burns."

"Yeah? I saw her car. How is she?"

"She's in the study. Why don't you go see for yourself."

CHAPTER FIVE

JENNIFER WATCHED DREW saunter into the study with his cocky, self-assured stride, and wondered what she'd ever seen in him. As a teenager or as an adult.

He rescued you, she told herself. *And he charmed you. And he made you feel special when you couldn't do it for yourself.*

And look where it got you.

Ross stood in the doorway. He met her gaze and she read his expression.

I'll be fine, she tried to telegraph. *I can handle this.* And she could. She knew she could. Because she knew from Drew's demeanor exactly what would happen.

Ross stepped back and closed the door.

The study was simple, with a wall of medical books and a wide wooden desk. Jennifer sat behind it in Ross's large padded chair. His laptop computer rested, lid down, to her right. A single window looked out into the side yard. She liked the room's masculine feel—and the idea that Ross spent time in here gave her a kind of strength, though she didn't want to question that fact too deeply.

Drew sat down on one of the chairs across the

room. He leaned back and rested one ankle over a knee, smooth and relaxed, hands resting on his thighs.

She took a deep breath, reminding herself not to give up on him without giving him a chance.

"I'm sure this comes as a bit of a shock," she said.

He seemed unaware of her meaning, though he'd seen her full belly behind the desk. He flashed her a casual smile.

"How's it going? Must have been a long drive from California in that old car."

She stared at him. His appearance was the same as it had been last December. Lighter hair than Ross's, boyishly handsome face, great body, expensive blue suit. He did absolutely nothing for her.

"That's not what I'm here to talk about."

"Ah," he said. "Your pregnancy."

"Yes."

"You do look quite different from the last time we saw each other. But pregnancy suits you. What are you—five, five-and-a-half months along?"

He should know exactly how far along she was. But perhaps his math skills weren't up to par. "Twenty-seven weeks," she said.

"I always forget how it works. Is that twenty-seven weeks since your last period or twenty-seven weeks since you conceived the child?"

"This child was conceived on December twenty-second," she said, ignoring his question and his mention of her period, which was no doubt intended to embarrass her.

He betrayed no reaction. ''So you're trying to suggest it's mine.''

She'd expected the indirect denial but couldn't stop the shudder of pain it caused. ''I'm carrying your child.''

''Do you have any proof of your allegation?''

''There's a risk of early labor or injury to the baby with any of the sampling techniques.''

''So, that would be no.''

''No.''

''You're asking me to take you at your word.''

She forced herself to remain calm. He was acting like the lawyer he was, but she wouldn't let him intimidate her or provoke her into saying something she would regret. ''I'm not a liar,'' she said.

He raised an eyebrow. ''Are you implying that I am?''

''You're married.'' And Jennifer felt truly sorry for his wife. She would rather be in her current predicament, if the alternative included marriage to a man like Drew. If it included the awful disillusionment Lucy was sure to experience with the person she'd chosen as her life partner.

''Yes,'' he said.

''You told me you weren't.''

''Did I?''

''Yes.''

''Think carefully.'' Drew paused. ''You asked me if I was in a relationship. I said, 'Who would have me?' You didn't pursue it. You could have. I understood that you didn't really want to know.''

"You remember your exact words? Six months later?"

He shrugged. "Sure."

Jennifer realized why. Because he'd used those same words before or since. They worked. They'd worked on her because she hadn't wanted to believe he would take her to dinner if he was in a relationship. And they might work on other women who didn't care, as long as they didn't have to face facts head-on.

"It was a lie of omission," she said as evenly as she could.

"I'm not responsible for your assumptions."

"You weren't wearing your ring."

He glanced at the gold band on his finger, then waved away the issue. "Let's return to the matter at hand. And let me tell you how it will appear to an impartial observer.

"You've come to me with a claim you refuse to support, and you know your allegations could have a detrimental effect on my marriage. That smells of extortion. For all anyone knows, the child belongs to some other man, who won't acknowledge it, and you plan to hit me up for some quick cash and disappear before my paternity can be disproved. Now, I'm not saying that's what you're doing. But it could look that way."

Jennifer refused to back down. He could spin things any way he wanted. In the end, he was still the father. She cut to the chase. "When the baby turns out to be yours," she said, staying cool, "what are you going to do about it?"

"If that were to happen," he said, "which I very much doubt, then we would work something out."

"You'll be a father to your child?"

Drew looked at her as if she'd said something mildly idiotic. "Is that what you want?"

"Yes."

He gave an uncomfortable laugh and shifted around on his chair. "I would have thought Ross had told you. My wife is pregnant. Our child is due in a few months. I can hardly be a father to yours, can I?"

Thank goodness she *had* known about his other baby, she thought, or his careless announcement would have rattled her composure further. "So what do you plan to do?"

"Jennifer, this is all a surprise. I can't make any promises without time to consider. But if it's mine, we would come to some agreement."

Hadn't he just told her how he'd lied to her by relying on her assumptions? She wasn't about to assume the best in this case. "Please answer my question."

"For all I know, this is just a hoax."

"So your answer is nothing. You won't be accountable."

"Please don't put words in my mouth."

"Then, tell me yes or no. Will you be a father to your child?"

Drew brushed at the knee of his pants. "I want to be very clear about something, Jennifer. I don't like blackmail. Your unwillingness to take the simple step of backing up your allegation makes your case weak.

And I warn you that if you attempt to use your pregnancy against me by involving my family, you will pay a large price.'' He paused, checking his Rolex—the same one that had spent several hours on her bedside table six months ago. "It's late. I need to go home. And I urge you to think very carefully about your course of action from here on out."

He went to the door.

"So your answer is no," she said from her seat, in a voice that surprised her for its clarity.

He didn't turn around. "Good night, Jennifer."

ROSS HEARD THE SOUND of the study door and stepped from the living room into the front hall.

Drew appeared to be his usual confident self, but Ross thought he saw a little strain at the edges. Just a hint of tension around his eyes and a tight pull to his mouth.

"Well?" Ross asked.

"She's pregnant," Drew said. "She looks good pregnant."

Ross waited.

"It's not mine." Drew crossed his arms. "She tried to tell me it was. I'm sure she told you the same thing."

"She did."

"And you believed her."

Ross walked over to the front hall table. He picked up his silver letter opener—a wedding gift—and slit open a piece of junk mail from a wireless phone company.

The action was just the sort of thing Drew would

do. Reading his mail while Ross tried to discuss something important with him. He knew it was rude. He regretted it. But it was the only way he could keep from hitting his brother.

Ross had never been a violent person. Outside of some martial arts training in his early twenties, he didn't recall striking anyone in his life. His brother was the only person who ever made him feel this way, and he hated the power it gave Drew.

He scanned the contents of the envelope, not seeing it. Tossed the papers into the trash. "Yes, I believe her."

Drew didn't have anything to say to that. Ross expected him to make a fuss about family loyalty, about believing a virtual stranger over his own brother, but he was probably aware of how ridiculous that would sound.

Speaking of loyalty, he wondered what Drew knew about that summer, about what had happened between Jennifer and him. Because when you got down to it, his actions hadn't been any more honorable than his brother's. And he would have done a lot more than kiss her if she hadn't called it to a halt.

"What are you going to do?" he asked Drew.

"Nothing. It's not my baby."

He raised an eyebrow.

"Go to hell," Drew muttered.

Ross took it as an admission of the truth, though he was sure Drew didn't mean it that way. He felt his relationship with his brother shifting. Drew had failed the test. Things could never be the same. In the past he'd treated his brother with a kind of respect, had kept his hands out of Drew's business. He'd suspected things, of course, but he'd refrained from digging, hadn't wanted to know the truth.

And people who didn't want to know the truth often got slapped with it.

"Lucy," he said.

"What about her?"

"Think about it."

"I'm thinking," Drew said, in a tone that implied he saw absolutely nothing worth considering. "And I can't think why she would find out Jennifer is trying to blackmail me."

"Why wouldn't she?"

"They don't exactly move in the same circles."

Lucy was wealthy. Not a snob, but from a world different from Jennifer's. Under normal circumstances they would be unlikely to meet.

"I don't plan to cover for you," Ross said.

"Is that a threat?"

If you want to take it that way.

"Anyhow," Drew continued, "I don't see the problem. I looked up an old friend on a business trip. I took a girl I used to know in high school to dinner. Why would Lucy care?"

A lie. An outright lie. That was how Drew planned to play this. If confronted, he would deny everything but the fact that he'd seen her. He would claim they'd had an amicable dinner and nothing more. He would say she'd gotten herself in trouble and decided to blame it on him because she knew he had money. And how convenient that she chose to do it now, before a simple blood test could expose her lie—

because no conscientious doctor would perform amniocentesis just to prove the identity of the father.

"You'll have to face it eventually," Ross said.

But his brother had never been much good at facing things. And God knew he probably just hoped he wouldn't have to deal with this, either. That if he simply pushed it from his mind it would go away. That she would give up and leave town, or that someone else would step in to take care of things.

Someone like him.

Hell, he already had. He'd offered her money. A place to stay. And if Jennifer chose to keep his brother's actions secret, he would have to be grateful for their mother's sake, even though it meant he would be helping Drew and lying to Lucy in the process.

Lucy deserved to know the truth, but it wasn't Ross's place to tell her. She wouldn't trust his motives. She might not believe him. She might not want to know. Hell, maybe she had lovers on the side, too.

Hard to imagine. But maybe she would accept Drew's straying if she did find out, forgive him in order to keep what they had together. The outward success, the beautiful house, the social standing.

The family they'd started... Been able to start.

But Jennifer's baby complicated everything. A couple could survive a simple extramarital affair with therapy, time and hard work on the relationship. But a child was something else. An embodied reminder, forever, of the moment of infidelity. A human being requiring care and attention from Drew, if he had such to give.

Which he surely didn't.

It pissed Ross off that what was probably best for Jennifer and was definitely best for his mother—at least, right now—would also benefit Drew: for her to accept Ross's help and stay, with her baby, out of Drew's life. His brother would be getting off scot-free. But wasn't that what he always managed to do? Obtain what he wanted from people, whether they liked it or not?

Ross wondered when he'd gotten so sour. When he'd started to want Drew to be shown up for what he was, to pay for his actions.

Drew jangled his keys, ready to go.

"So that's it," Ross said.

His brother shrugged. "Seems so." He inclined his head toward the driveway. "Where's she headed, anyway?"

Ah, so he wasn't so unconcerned. Ross detected a trace of desperation in the question, a need to know that was more than the bland curiosity Drew tried to convey.

"Here."

"*Here,* here?"

That, at least, got Drew worried.

"Portland. She left San Francisco."

"Any chance she'll go back?"

"I don't think so. Not for a while."

"Huh," Drew said. "Interesting."

Ross got the strangest sense that along with whatever anxiety his brother felt, a part of him also relished this series of events, treated it as a game, a negotiation. A tricky situation he could wriggle out of with charm and intelligence. Like a rock climber attempting a perilous route, he loved the adrenaline rush.

And the hell of it was, he might escape cleanly.

ROSS WAITED until Drew pulled out of the driveway before he opened the door to his study. Jennifer was sitting very still behind his desk.

He watched her, waiting for her to speak. When she didn't, he broke the silence.

"You okay?"

"Yeah." She rose, pushing down on the arms of the chair.

He supposed he'd thought she would have tear tracks on her cheeks. She didn't. Her gaze was clear and direct, but her mouth was tight.

"You were right," she said.

He shrugged. "My brother's an ass."

"I should have known." She tucked a chunk of hair behind her right ear, leaving the other side to swing free. "I did know."

"He denied sleeping with you."

Her expression didn't change. "I figured he'd do that."

"He has things he's trying to protect." A lame excuse, which sounded lame on his lips.

"We all have things we're trying to protect."

"He doesn't realize it's too late."

"People never do." She walked toward the door. "I'm exhausted. This has been a long day. Thanks for giving me a bed—I think I'll go use it."

UPSTAIRS, JENNIFER SAT on the cream-striped duvet and stared at her reflection in the full-length mirror that stood in one corner. She saw herself as Drew must have. As a liability.

Badly cut hair, tired eyes, discount-store clothes. Swollen belly.

She was a man's worst nightmare. A pregnant lover. She was evidence, proof. She was a lapse in judgment.

Yet Drew had acted confident during their brief meeting downstairs. As if he'd already considered this eventuality and braced himself for it, talked himself through the steps to deal with it. What kind of man could do that?

Her image stared back at her, quiet and still. Her mother's statement returned to her, overheard so many years ago. *No one can resist a baby.* Andrea Burns had said the words to a friend, regretting she hadn't gone to visit Jennifer's father until Jennifer was well past infancy. *No one can resist a baby, not even a man like him.*

Jennifer had often wondered what a man like him—her father—was supposed to be. After she'd tried Drew's fake phone number in January, she'd suspected he was a similar type. Now she was convinced.

No one can resist a baby.

But a pregnant woman wasn't a baby. A pregnant woman was terrifying.

If she hadn't lost her apartment and been so far in debt, she might have waited. She might have been able to show up in Drew's life with an adorable baby who would smile and coo and gurgle, and would trap his heart. Proving her mother's theory.

Except, it wouldn't have worked. He would already have had a baby to whom he would have given whatever fatherly love he had to give.

She imagined the scene as it might have played out. Sitting on a chair in Ross's study, a baby on her lap. Drew walking in. Saying to him, *This is your daughter,* or *This is your son.* And having him stand there with a blank, shielded look, telling her he didn't believe her, telling her she should have come to him sooner, within the first trimester.

That would have been worse than this, she told herself. It was better not to have false hopes. But much more depressing.

Jennifer roused herself, scooting off the bed. She reached for the lilac knit maternity tank and shorts she used as pajamas.

Enough self-pity and despair. She had tomorrow to think about. She had to figure out where to go from here.

Buck up, honey. Time to be strong.

ROSS LAY IN BED, listening to the quiet creaks of the house settling onto its foundation for the night. Light from the street outside filtered through the venetian blinds, providing enough illumination for him to see the outlines of familiar objects around the room. The photographs of family and friends on the dresser. The carriage clock he'd inherited from his grandmother, silent since he'd allowed it to run down a few weeks ago.

To have Jennifer in his home, sleeping down the hallway, felt strange. It made him aware of the house in a way he usually wasn't. Of how large it was for one person to live in. Of course, when he'd bought it he hadn't been alone, and he'd imagined there would someday be children to fill it.

Probably he should move, he thought. Get a condo in a downtown high-rise. Give in to the inevitability of it. Accept what life had offered him.

But he knew he wouldn't. What was really wrong, after all, with a big, empty house? Except that, sooner or later, it made you lonely. Made you enjoy having a houseguest more than you should, and look forward to seeing that houseguest in the morning with an unsettling amount of anticipation.

It was just one night, he reminded himself. One night and one morning, because anything more than that would be too complicated.

And Jennifer was once again off-limits.

But as his brother had demonstrated on more than one occasion, just because you shouldn't get involved with someone didn't mean you wouldn't.

CHAPTER SIX

Nine years earlier

It's not as if I want to be an uptight killjoy. I can't help disapproving of Drew and his lame-brained cohorts, though. Constantly partying, sleeping until noon, watching MTV. Lying around the pool. Not doing anything redeeming.

And that girlfriend of his. She's got to be the third blonde named Jennifer he's dated in the past year and a half. Just once, I'd like to see him bring home a brunette named Roberta. Or Phuong-Mai. Someone interesting for a change.

I know I'm not being fair. But sometimes he just pisses me the hell off. I can't count on him to do what he says he'll do, like helping me move some furniture for Aunt Lenora.

"We'll do it tomorrow," he tells me, his hand over the mouthpiece of the phone, as he slouches on the kitchen chair, sockless in his dock shoes, taking a few seconds out of his busy life to shirk a commitment.

He's just made plans to go to his friend Kurt's house for a spur-of-the-moment party.

They're trying to figure out who can buy the beer. I guess he knows better than to ask me.

"Lenora's not getting back until then, anyway," he adds.

Our aunt broke her ankle a couple of days ago on a midnight hike, part of some New Age retreat in the mountains. Drew and I had plans to move her bed to the ground floor of her house so she won't have to drag herself up and down the stairs for the next few weeks.

"I can't do it tomorrow," I tell my brother. "I'm working."

And I'm not going to jeopardize my internship, which was damn hard to get, by scheduling it for my lunch break—since there's no way he'd show up on time.

Drew shrugs. "Hey, you're the one who offered to do this, not me. I said I'd help if I could. I never promised anything."

"Jesus," I say as Drew goes back to his phone call. Outside it's raining but not windy. For a moment I watch the drops patter down onto the flat surface of the pool.

I glance over at Jennifer. She's ignoring the whole exchange. For the past half hour she's sat at the kitchen table while Drew's been on the phone ordering clothes from the new J. Crew catalog and bullshitting with his friends. A copy of *Smithsonian Magazine* is open on the table, and I can see from the pictures that she's reading the article about insects in the Amazonian forest. I'm surprised she knows how to read—then feel like a jerk for even having the thought.

Oh, what the hell. I decide to struggle with the mattress by myself. "See you later," I tell them, and head for the front hall.

I'm reaching for my Gore-Tex pullover when Jennifer joins me.

"If you need help," she says, kind of off-hand, "I could do it. As long as it doesn't take too long."

I look at her. "You're not going to the party?"

She shakes her head. "I have to start work in a couple of hours. I'd need a ride home afterward, though. Otherwise, I have to go catch a bus right now."

"Where's home?" I ask her.

She tells me the address and cross street. It's not far, geographically, from where Lenora lives, but a different neighborhood. Not a great one, though certainly not the worst. "Where's work?"

"The Beauty Barn. Over by Lloyd Center."

"I'll give you a ride," I say. "I'd appreciate the help."

Jennifer goes to the kitchen to say goodbye to Drew. Then she's back. She's only wearing a T-shirt and jeans and she doesn't seem to have any rain protection.

"No umbrella?"

She shakes her head. "It was sunny when I came over. Anyway, this is Oregon, right?"

Oregonians pride themselves on not using umbrellas. Nevertheless, I get a large one from the hall closet and hold it over both of us as we dash to the car.

"The Beauty Barn, huh?" I say as we drive away from Council Crest. Water sluices along the gutters on both sides of the road and the wipers thwack back and forth at full speed.

"We sell discount cosmetics," she says. "It's probably not your kind of store."

At the bottom of the hill we hit a knot of afternoon traffic in front of the intersection by the freeway, and come to a complete halt. An old Cutlass is stalled in the right-hand lane and everyone has to shift to get around it. The light turns green, but only a handful of people make it through. We're still several cars back when the light turns red again.

I see Jennifer reach into her bag and come up with her wallet. She pulls out a five.

"I'll be right back," she says, then she opens the car door and steps out into the rain before I can reply.

As she crosses in front of me to the median and jogs toward the intersection, I spot a ragged-looking black man with a bucket of flowers to sell. He's drenched and his flowers are, too. Before Jennifer reaches him, he goes up to a couple of cars, but no one wants to open windows in the rain. I watch her buy a mixed bouquet and say something that leaves the guy laughing. Just before the light changes, she gets back to the car and buckles up.

The flowers are yellow and purple and blue with a clump of ferns as a background. Water drops cling to the petals.

"I thought these might be nice for your aunt," she says.

Following close on the bumper of the car ahead, I slip through the light on the yellow. I glance over. It doesn't ring true that she would go out in the rain to buy flowers for a woman she's never met.

"That's really thoughtful of you," I say. And then I add, "That guy sure looked miserable."

She makes a sound of agreement. "I hope I wasn't his only customer."

I know she went out there just to give the guy some business. So he wouldn't waste his whole day standing in the rain, making no money. I don't know many people who would do that.

Damn. It would be a lot easier to see her as a silly teenage party girl like all of Drew's past girlfriends. I don't want to start thinking about her being kind and considerate. About how—come to think of it—she doesn't seem to have much money, but she'll give away five bucks just to help someone have a better day.

I consider the five bucks. Can she really afford to spend it like that? Probably not. I'm the one who should have thought to get something for my aunt. "I'll pay for the flowers," I say.

"It's okay," she says. "Don't worry about it."

"No, really. I'll pay for them."

She doesn't answer me, and now I realize I've been too pushy. Made her feel bad. It's got to be tough hanging around with Drew and all his wealthy friends.

At my aunt's house, we park in the driveway

and I come around the car with the umbrella. "You could have used this when you went to get the flowers," I say, indicating the umbrella.

"I didn't want to miss the light."

She gets out of the car, cradling the bouquet. Her light blue T-shirt is soaked. The fabric sticks to her skin.

I keep my eyes averted, trying to remind myself again that she's not that cute. Kind of average. Not that smart or she wouldn't be dating Drew. And she works at the Beauty Barn, for Christ's sake.

Finally I remind myself she's still in high school. That fixes everything.

Inside his aunt's place, Ross heads for the stairs without even looking back to see if I've shut the door. The house is narrow, packed tightly in among its neighbors, but it's wonderful. It's funky and bright and colorful. The furnishings are a crazy mix, from a heavy walnut armoire that could have come out of an English estate to an orange shag runner in the hallway that's pure 1970s tackiness. But somehow it all works.

"If you're cold," he says over his shoulder, "I'm sure you could find something in the hall closet. And I can promise Lenora won't mind if you borrow it."

My shirt feels clammy against my skin and I regret my rash decision to buy the flowers. Not that Ross would notice if I were to walk around naked instead of in a wet T-shirt. But I still feel exposed.

His aunt's hall closet is crammed with jackets and coats and overflow clothes, but they're not exactly my style. I pick out the best thing I can find—a black long-sleeve western-style shirt with gold studs on the collar—and put it on over my T-shirt. It's too big, but I roll up the sleeves and it works okay as a jacket.

The bed is a queen-size and it's heavier than any bed I've ever tried to move. "Jeez," I say as we slide it down the hallway. "What's in this thing?"

At the top of the stairs we have to wrestle it around a corner, and then we both stand below it and tip it to go downward. We're side by side holding it up, keeping it from going too quickly, and it's good there are two of us.

We leave the mattress propped against a wall and go back up for the box spring, which is mercifully light. After that we grab the simple bed frame, and then move some furniture around in the ground-floor den so there's space for us to set it up. All together it doesn't take more than twenty minutes, and when we're through I ask if Lenora is going to need to have some clothes downstairs as well.

Ross says he doesn't want to get involved in trying to pick out clothes for his aunt. "I never understand what she wears. And anyway, clothes are easy. She can get a friend to bring some down. She's got a lot of friends."

"Just no one else who would want to move a mattress that heavy, right?"

He looks at me then, more directly than he has all day. "Thanks for helping out."

The way he says it is just so plain and simple and straightforward that it actually makes me embarrassed. I haven't blushed in months, it seems like—ever since I learned how to act like the cool kids—but now I feel my neck getting hot.

I can't figure out what the deal is with Ross. I didn't like it when he was all disapproving and aloof, but now that he seems to think I'm okay, I find I don't like that, either. He's making a big deal about the fact that I helped him out, but it really wasn't one. I would have been sitting on a bus, probably soaked to the skin, if I hadn't come with him.

He says, "What time do you have to be at work?"

I check my watch. "In an hour. I'd better get going. My work clothes are at home. Can you still give me a lift?"

"Of course."

We stick the flowers in a vase from the kitchen and then place them on the art deco table in the front hall. They're nothing special, really, but I think Lenora will like them. She doesn't seem like the kind of person to put her nose in the air about cheap flowers.

Ross doesn't ask me to tell him where I live again. He just drives there. When he pulls up to the curb and cuts the engine, I've already taken off his aunt's black shirt and draped it over the back of the seat. I start to get out, but he tells me to wait.

"Go change. I'll drive you to work."

I don't know what to say, mostly because

I'm suddenly afraid he'll want to come up while I get ready and I don't want him to see our tiny apartment. I haven't even let Drew see it. We're on the third floor, and the unit is drab and lightless. There's only one bedroom, which my mom made me take. She sleeps on the living room couch. The place is clean, but it's still embarrassing.

But my worry is for nothing. Ross hands me the umbrella. He doesn't make any move to get out.

Ten minutes later I'm back in the car, dressed in the plain white oxford shirt the Beauty Barn requires. At work I also have to wear a red apron with a barn on it and a button with my name, but they make us leave those in our lockers. The button boasts a picture of a cow. It looks like something out of Dr. Seuss, except it's wearing too much eyeliner and eyeshadow, like one of those televangelist ladies.

We cross the river, and get to the area where the Beauty Barn is located about half an hour before my shift. I figure he's just going to drop me off, and I don't mind because he saved me a lot of time on the bus.

But he says, "You haven't eaten."

I point to my bag. "I packed some snacks." Just an apple and some cheese and crackers. I didn't have time to make more.

"There's a good deli a few blocks away. I'll buy you a sandwich." He's already got the car moving.

"You don't have to do this," I say, though I can tell it's useless.

A few blocks turns out to be six, but we're there in just a couple of minutes. Ross suggests a tomato-basil-mozzarella sandwich he thinks I might like and orders some kind of meat-lovers combo for himself.

The sandwich is incredible. It's on a crusty baguette with olive oil and balsamic vinegar, and the basil tastes as if they just picked the leaves off the plant. Ross probably eats food this good every day. I don't, and I savor it.

"Was your mom home?" he asks, as I polish off the first half.

I shake my head. "She doesn't get off work for another few hours."

"And when does your shift end?"

"Late," I say. "My mom's going to pick me up."

He nods. "Good. I'd hate to think of you waiting for a bus in the middle of the night."

"Wouldn't be the first time," I say. And when his expression gets all concerned, I say, "Look, when you don't live in a big mansion in Council Crest, you just do what you have to do. It's that simple."

I pick up my sandwich and take a big bite. Too big. I'm stuck chewing an unwieldy mouthful, while Ross just kind of watches me.

"I can't figure you out," he says after a moment.

I'm still chewing, so there's nothing I can say.

He goes on. "You're a nice kid. What are you doing with my brother and his self-absorbed gang?"

The question pretty much hits home. Sometimes I don't really like Drew's friends, even Heather. All they want to do is party. Partying can be fun, I guess, but it gets boring. But I don't want to tell Mr. Perfect he's right to question my choices.

"I like hanging out with them," I say. "They're fun."

He must pick up the note of defensiveness in my voice. "Don't sell yourself short," he tells me. "Don't pretend you're someone you're not."

I feel as if Ross is lecturing me, and I don't like it. He's insulting my friends and making me feel like a hypocrite. Now that I hang out with the beautiful people, I'm just as shallow as I used to think they were.

The problem is, it feels good to be part of the group. It's addictive. And I don't want to do anything more to push myself to the edge.

"I can be whoever I want to be," I proclaim.

"Then, be someone interesting. The ditzy party-girl act doesn't cut it. You're better than that."

I am not and have never been a ditz. Just because I don't sit around trying to engage Brian and Heather and Molly in deep existential debates doesn't mean I'm not smart. But look where smart used to get me. Alone, hiding in a book.

"Why should I sit at home reading *Darkness at Noon* and thinking about how much the world sucks, when I could be having a good time?"

He seems to recognize the book, which I probably should have expected, since no one else I know has heard of it.

"You read that for school?"

"No, I just read it because it looked interesting."

"Uh-huh." He nods. "What did you think of it?"

"Well, it's got to be one of the most depressing books I've ever read, but I also thought—" I cut myself off. I don't want to get drawn into a discussion of the book, because that would only prove his point. But I have to admit I'm curious to hear what he thinks of it.

"I read that book before the Berlin Wall came down," he says. "I'm guessing you didn't. And I bet it's a different experience to read the book when totalitarian governments seem like they've failed, instead of when they still seem threatening."

I want to jump in and berate him for his assumptions. I mean, just because I'm younger than he is doesn't mean I can't understand things, or that I wouldn't do my homework to figure out how the book must have read when Koestler wrote it. But I don't want to get caught up in an argument with him about it.

Then I realize he's sitting there fighting a grin. So he was just baiting me and he knows it worked. I wrap up the remains of my sandwich.

"I've got to get to work," I tell him, standing up.

He sits there on his chair, leaning back. "You're a brainy one, aren't you?" he finally says. I don't answer, so he gets to his feet. "I know it now, so you don't have to pretend around me anymore. I won't think less of you because of it. Now, let's get you to the Beauty Barn."

CHAPTER SEVEN

WHEN JENNIFER WENT DOWNSTAIRS in the morning, Ross was sitting at his desk in his study. He was typing something into his laptop but stopped as soon as he caught sight of her in the doorway. His brown eyes assessed her with an unnerving thoroughness, as if he were making a diagnosis.

"How did you sleep?" he asked.

She saw from his expression that there was no point lying. "So-so." She'd had a restless night, and the baby, too, had been more active than usual. "I had a lot of things on my mind."

"Eat some breakfast. That always helps. Bagels, toast, eggs, cereal. Whatever you want. Just hunt around. I'll join you after I finish this e-mail."

Jennifer headed for the kitchen. The door was shut, and as she approached she heard Frank throwing her little body against it. Ross had mentioned he kept her in the kitchen after meals due to her sensitive stomach. Jennifer tried to block the dog's exit as she opened the door, but Frank scampered past with an excited yip.

"Frank!" she said. "Come back!"

The dog's toenails clicked as she made a skidding turn into the living room.

Jennifer started to go after her, but Ross came out of his office. He smiled. "Sneaky mutt."

"It's hard bending down to stop her and opening the door at the same time," she explained.

"She gets past me, too. I'll catch her."

Jennifer went into the kitchen, and Ross brought Frank in a moment later, shutting the door behind himself.

"Your e-mail?" she asked.

He walked to the cooking area. "It can wait. You want me to make you something?"

"I can do it."

With Ross watching, she cooked a quick meal of toast and eggs, choosing the eggs to keep up her protein intake. She ate at the table, while he nursed a cup of coffee with Frank on his lap.

Afterward he said, "Have you decided what you're going to do?"

Jennifer shrugged. "Find a place to live. Get settled." And wait to see if Drew would wake up to his responsibilities.

Ross was silent. As if he were wondering, after last night, why she didn't go back to San Francisco. Get on with her life and come back in a few years when Drew might have grown up a little, might be ready to accept the child he'd helped to conceive.

Her mother had tried that. It hadn't worked. And she knew her mother had regretted letting her father set the terms from the start, had regretted letting him shut her out of his life for what turned out to be forever.

"Drew's the father," she said.

"And if he continues to dispute it?"

"In three months he won't be able to."

He gave a small nod, acknowledging the truth of her statement. But they both knew proof of paternity wouldn't necessarily get her what she wanted.

Jennifer rose and took her plate to the sink, where she ran hot water and rinsed it off. Holding onto the counter, she bent down to put the plate and fork in the dishwasher. She straightened and squirted more dish soap onto the sponge.

"I know this isn't an easy situation," she said, reaching for the frying pan. She washed it, her movements brisk. "There's no magic answer. Don't think I didn't spend half the night trying to figure one out. But the facts aren't going to change. I'm going to have his baby. If he doesn't like that, tough. He shouldn't have slept with me. I'm not trying to break up his marriage. For damn sure I don't want him in my life any more than necessary. But my child needs a father, and I'm willing to deal with Drew being that father for my child's sake."

"So what, exactly, do you want?"

She rinsed the pan and put it in the drying rack. Squeezed out the sponge, wiped the countertop. Put the butter dish back in the fridge. "I want financial support for our child and I want Drew to act like a father."

"How does a father act?"

"I'm not asking for something out of *Leave It to Beaver*. I know he won't be a round-the-clock parent. I don't expect him to spend tons of time with our child. But I want this baby to have a dad—a dad who loves him or her even if the circumstances are complicated. One who will be there if our child needs to go to someone for help.''

''Is that what you told him last night?'' Ross asked from his seat at the table.

''He didn't give me a chance. Anyway, that's the absolute minimum I'll accept. I'm hoping, for the baby's sake, that he'll go further than that.''

''What if he doesn't cooperate at all?''

''Do you think that will happen?''

''I don't know,'' he admitted. ''But it wouldn't surprise me.''

''Well, I don't know what I'll do if he does that.''

''Would you tell Lucy?''

She shook her head. ''This is between Drew and me. I don't plan to involve the rest of the family. As much as I might enjoy it, busting the guy to his wife isn't going to get my child any closer to having a loving father.'' She walked back to the table and sat down, holding his gaze. ''And I should add that if your mother's not doing well, I certainly don't want to drag her into it.''

He seemed relieved to hear this.

''On the other hand, I'm still not going away.''

''No, I understand that.'' Ross paused. ''Do you have any leads on a place to live?''

''I was planning to check the classifieds this morning. Do you get the paper?''

''Uh-huh, let me grab it for you.''

He brought her the newspaper from the front porch and went back into his study to finish his e-mail.

Jennifer looked through the apartment rental section. Her price range was almost at the bottom of what was available, and not many cheap units were on the market. Some listings included street addresses and some showed only the general neighborhood. She circled the options and then went to the door of Ross's study with the newspaper in her hand.

"Do you mind if I tie up the phone for a few minutes?"

"No problem," he said. "Can I see what you've found?"

She walked over and handed him the folded section. He scanned the lines of type. The look he gave her when he was finished wasn't hard to read.

"Those are what I can afford," she said.

"Marginal neighborhoods…"

"I know."

"Do you want me to come with you?"

"It's okay. Thanks, though. I'll probably leave in half an hour, after I make my calls."

He nodded. "I'll be out for a while around two to go see my mother, but other than that I'll be home. There's a spare house key on the dish on the front hall table."

Jennifer made her calls and then drove downtown, a matter of a few blocks down the hill and across the freeway. At Front Street she turned left along the Willamette, then crossed the Burnside Bridge.

The first apartment on her list was located in a neighborhood that looked good from a distance but deteriorated sharply once she got within two blocks. The building, a converted house, had dark-gray asbestos shingles falling off in patches. The porch sagged and part of the railing was missing. One of the three front doors had been smashed in and the opening sealed with a black plastic garbage bag and silver tape. It was about what she would have been able to afford in San Francisco.

She didn't even stop the car. No doubt the interior would be worse. Without a baby, she might have considered it; a can of pepper spray could get a person a long way toward feeling safe. But this apartment was no place to raise a child—not if she could avoid it.

The next units on her list weren't much better. She drove past another one without stopping, but got out at the third and fourth, only to leave after a few minutes inside each.

And on the morning went. She stopped for lunch and then realized she was tired and needed to go back to Ross's house to rest.

Ross met her in the front hall. "How did it go?"

"Depressing."

He motioned toward the living room. "Let's sit down for a minute."

"Don't you have to leave to meet your mom?"

"Not for fifteen minutes."

Jennifer took a seat on one of the overstuffed chairs. Frank trotted into the living room and gave her ankle a welcoming lick, then dashed over to Ross. She rubbed her nose against his pant leg. He bent down and scooped her up, cradling her in one hand while her three legs whipped the air in delight.

"So what's up?" she asked.

"Drew called." Ross sat down on the sofa, near her chair.

"Oh? What did he have to say for himself?"

"He made an offer."

Frank wriggled away from Ross and pounced on a chew toy under the coffee table, growling in play.

"What kind of an offer?" Jennifer could tell from Ross's expression that she wouldn't like it, but had to ask.

He sighed. "Three-fifty a month for three years."

"If?"

"If the baby is really his."

"Of course. What else?"

"If you leave town."

Jennifer nodded, expecting it. "And?"

"And if you and the kid never contact him again."

She looked down at Frank, who'd brought her the chew toy. Bracing a hand on one knee, she leaned forward and picked it up. Tossed it across the living room and watched while the dog, barking, went after it.

She couldn't speak. There was nothing she could say.

"I told him to go screw himself."

Jennifer laughed despite herself. Uncomfortable, painful laughter. The image was absurd, as was the obvious pleasure Ross had taken in telling his brother off.

"I'm sorry I got you involved," she said.

"It's okay."

"I only wanted his phone number."

Ross nodded.

"A brother shouldn't have to say what you did."

He shrugged. "This particular brother probably should have said it a long time ago."

"Does he really believe I would walk away for that amount?"

Perhaps Drew thought she was desperate enough to accept anything. But she did have fairly good credit still, and some charge cards that weren't maxed out. She'd struggled hard to keep up with her bills.

"I'm sure it's just an opening bid," Ross said. "I could probably talk him into more money."

"You don't have to broker this. That isn't why I came to you."

"If I can help..."

"But you can't. Because this isn't just about the money." Frank brought her the chew toy again. She stretched down to collect it for another throw. "I appreciate your support, Ross. Truly. But this is a problem you can't fix. It's up to Drew now."

ROSS COLLECTED HIS MOTHER at home and took her to an appointment with her hairdresser. She still didn't have her doctor's approval to drive, and since her surgery Ross had tried to make sure someone besides his father was helping out. Sharing the load.

Katherine had been going to the same hairdresser in John's Landing for the past twenty-nine years, a tiny, sharp-tongued woman named Doreen. Ross sat by the door of the salon browsing a copy of the *New England Journal of Medicine* he'd brought, while his mother's hair was trimmed and styled and blow-dried.

In the end she looked—in his estimation—just about the same as when they'd arrived. But he knew she enjoyed the pampering, and returning to her normal life and taking pleasure in it were good for her recovery.

Back in the car, he drove a mile down the road to a small public park along the river. "It's a nice afternoon. Are you up for a walk?"

"I suppose you'll make me do it whether I want to or not?"

He smiled at her. "That's the problem with having a doctor for a son." He came around the car and helped her out. "Now, if you weren't feeling well I'd give you a break. But since I haven't heard any complaints…"

The air was still, the water's surface calm and glassy. They walked along a path that stretched a couple of hundred yards along the shore to the end of the park. Across the river the bank was covered in trees, with an occasional house visible. Birds chattered in the shrubs dotting the expanse of grass.

"I just received a wonderful catalog from my friend Joan," she told him. "All sorts of old-fashioned wooden toys and the most adorable baby clothes. You'll laugh, but I've already bought more toys than I should have. It's a good thing Drew and Lucy have a big house."

Hearing her talk enthusiastically about her grandchild pained him, just as having to keep from her the secret of her other grandchild—and the way its father planned to treat it—pained him. He wondered what would happen if or when she learned the truth. Would it make her love Lucy's baby more or less?

If. Who was he kidding? Eventually his mother would find out about Jennifer and her child. It might be months from now or it might be years, but he couldn't delude himself that it would never happen. The best he could hope for was to delay it until his mother was fully recovered from her heart attack.

"Sounds as if you're fulfilling your grandmotherly duties," he said.

"Anything to keep busy." She sighed. "I do feel very confined. So I suppose I should be a good sport and thank you for bringing me out here. It *is* beautiful."

At the park boundary they turned around, their pace slow and measured. They talked a few minutes longer about the course of her recovery, and then the conversation shifted to a Caribbean vacation his father planned to take her on in November, to celebrate the six-month point after surgery.

When they reached the car, he made her check her pulse.

"Next time we'll walk faster," he said, after she told him her heart rate. "You need to get that a little higher."

After taking her home, he stopped at a small store that sold organic clothes and baby items. He bought a soft white bear and had it wrapped up, then headed back to his place and Jennifer.

ROSS GAVE HER THE PRESENT right away, though he felt unexpectedly self-conscious.

''Every child needs a teddy bear,'' he said as she opened the box.

They were upstairs in the guest room, Jennifer sitting cross-legged on the bed. He stood, leaning one hip against the dresser, separated from her by a few feet of open floor. Glancing at her small, neat collection of belongings on the bedside table, he wondered where she planned to spend the night and if he ought to invite her to stay another at his place.

''I'm sure you'll get baby gifts from people in San Francisco,'' he said, ''but I wanted you to have something right now.''

''Thank you, Ross.'' She met his gaze, and he could tell his gift pleased her.

The bear had a nice round belly, like hers, and an expression that bordered on impishness because of how the mouth had been sewn. Ross had been about to buy the bear next to it, when he'd seen this one. He supposed people who ascribed human qualities to stuffed animals would say this particular bear had a good sense of humor. And that was something they all needed right now.

''I'm glad you like it,'' he said.

''I do. Some people at my old job actually threw me an early shower, but I didn't receive any stuffed animals for the baby. And everything's in boxes, of course, so it's nice to have something that isn't packed.''

He asked about her employment in San Francisco, and she described the office supply warehouse where she'd worked as a file clerk. It didn't sound terrible, but it was nothing like the career he'd envisioned for her when they'd been kids.

Ross remembered how smart she'd been, how she'd debated with him about any subject that came up. Of course, when she was with his brother she'd been different. Intellectual curiosity was not one of Drew's traits, and his influence had discouraged it in Jennifer, as well. Such a bright and thoughtful young woman wasting her life with Drew and his vapid friends had made Ross angry.

But perhaps he'd just been angry because he'd wanted her for himself.

"I'm hoping to find a job here as soon as possible," Jennifer told him.

"What kind do you have in mind?"

She put the bear carefully on top of her belongings. "Retail, temping, something like that."

"You could find better."

She pointed toward her stomach. "It needs to be short-term."

Meaning, she needed an employer who would look past the fact that she would be gone in a few months. "I'll keep an ear out for you."

"I'm not qualified for a lot of other jobs, anyway. I only have a high school diploma."

He'd guessed as much. Life—her mother's extended illness—had gotten in the way of a higher education. "What about after the baby's born?"

"I'm not sure."

"You could try something freelance. Work from home so you can be with the baby more."

"Like what?"

"I've seen books about teaching yourself to design Web pages. You could try that."

"It's hard to get established in that kind of field. You need connections."

"Maybe I could help with that." He paused. "Do you want to go to college?"

She shrugged. "I went for a year. U.C. Berkeley. Before my mother got sick. I just never made it back."

"You could now. You're only twenty-six," he reminded her.

She gave a half smile. "Sometimes I feel older than that." She reached out and touched the bear, tracing the contour of its smile. After another moment she said, "I may have found a place to live. It's a little more expensive than I'd hoped, but it sounds decent."

"You haven't seen it?"

"No. I called the manager. The apartment's in a complex, and he said it's furnished. If I like it I can move in tonight. But they won't take an out-of-state check. I've got most of the cash I'd need. Could I write you a check for the remaining two hundred? I'm good for it, of course."

He never would have thought otherwise. "No problem. Where is the place?"

She told him the address and nearest cross street. "That's an okay area, right? I mean, I'm sure it's nothing like this, but I don't remember it being awful."

Ross wasn't so sure. The place was on a major one-way artery heading south, not far from the river on the east side of town and on the edge of a light industrial area that recently had seen hard times, with more than its share of empty buildings and broken streetlights.

"Let's go check it out," he said.

The area turned out to be much as he'd expected. The apartment complex itself had once been a motel, with a faded, dreary facade straight out of the 1960s. The parking lot held an assortment of cars more beat-up than Jennifer's. Rush-hour traffic streamed by. The noise and exhaust pressed on him as he got out of the car.

"I called earlier," Jennifer said to the man in the rental office, who was barely visible behind a cloud of cigarette smoke.

The manager rose from his chair but didn't lower the volume of the radio talk show blasting out of a clock radio on the desk. He slapped a rental agreement down on the counter. "First, last, and a four-hundred-dollar deposit. Sign here."

"I'd like to see the unit first," Jennifer said.

The man shrugged and handed her a key from a rack on the wall. "Number 206. Knock yourself out."

"Quite the salesman," Ross murmured as they climbed the steps to the second level.

The units all opened onto an exterior hallway above the parking lot. Halfway down they came to number 206. Jennifer opened the dented blue metal door, to reveal a cheaply remodeled motel room, airless and hot. Grimy drapes blocked all daylight from passing through the plate-glass windows. A twin bed covered in a brown bedspread had been pushed against one wall. The single chair was upholstered in a drab plaid and was now threadbare, even in inexplicable places. Next to the bathroom, a tiny cooking area had been roughed-in with unfinished lumber. It included a half-size fridge and a two-burner compact stove.

Ross imagined Jennifer trying to live here for the next few months—trying to raise a baby here, if it came to that.

"Forget it," he said. "Let's go home."

"Ross…" Jennifer looked around the room, working to conceal her distaste.

"No," Ross said. "You're not living here."

"It's what I can afford. I've lived in worse places. I grew up without a lot of money, remember?"

"You're expecting a baby."

"This place is better than anything I saw this morning. I don't have a choice."

"Yes, you do. You can stay with me."

CHAPTER EIGHT

HE SAID IT CALMLY, decisively. As if it were the only rational choice. As if putting up an argument would be silly.

You can stay with me.

Jennifer glanced again at the simple kitchenette and the worn furnishings. A new bedspread would help, and a slipcover for the chair. Posters on the walls. Maybe another lamp.

Okay, so it would always look like a motel room. But she could park her car in the lot instead of on the street. And the apartment would be hers, dumpy as it was. Probably it would be safe, too, though the plate-glass window next to the front door was a little troubling.

Ross put his hands on her shoulders, warm and strong. He gently turned her toward the door.

"Let's go home," he said.

She allowed him to guide her onto the balcony. *Home.* It had a different sound than it had had just a few seconds earlier. For a moment she let herself think about staying with Ross for a while.

Oh, she wanted to say yes. Wanted badly to say yes. And not just because his house would be a pleasant place to live, but because the thought of being with him, of sharing meals, relaxing together, having conversations, was so seductive.

But it was probably a bad idea. She would get used to it. Come to expect it. Miss it when it was over.

And it *would* have to end. Even if Drew never came to his senses, Ross had his own life. He wouldn't want to be saddled with her and the baby indefinitely. And even if he did, she wouldn't take him up on it. Because her child's best interests were her first priority. And Ross was the uncle, not the father. Once the baby began to get older, living with Ross would be too confusing. Especially when she, the mother, still had feelings for him. Inappropriate feelings. You didn't go from brother to brother. It wasn't the example she wanted to set for her child.

They walked to the stairs and descended them. She gave Ross the apartment key when he asked for it, and watched as he walked over to the manager's office. He disappeared inside and reappeared only moments later.

They got into the car. "What a dump," he muttered as he pulled out of the parking lot and joined the traffic heading back toward the river.

Jennifer thought about going from his house tonight to the motel where she'd originally planned to stay. About trying to search for an apartment with the pressure of a growing motel bill. She doubted she would be able to find anything better than the place they'd just left—at least, not quickly enough. But if she had a few weeks, or even a month, maybe something would turn up. Or Drew would change his mind and would help her to provide a safe and comfortable environment for their child.

She wavered. "It would just be short-term..." she began, not yet accepting his offer.

"Of course."

"Until I can find a place." If she made new friends here, got to know people... That was how she and her mother had landed a rent-controlled apartment in San Francisco. They certainly hadn't gotten it through the classifieds. But it required time. "I don't know how long that would be. I'd do my best to make it happen, though. Less than a month, probably."

"Even if it took longer," he said, "it would be okay."

Jennifer glanced over at him.

He stared ahead, focused on the traffic.

She said, "If it took more than three months—which I can't imagine it would—you'd be living with a baby."

He spared her a glance. "I think I can probably handle that."

"I've heard they yell a lot," she said cautiously. "Babies."

The hint of a grin. "Yeah, that's the rumor."

Jennifer looked out the window, studying the buildings they passed, the cars parked along the curb. She wanted to hold on to this little unexpected moment between them, to the gentle humor and odd sense of peace. Because she suspected what she would say next would remind him that having her in his house was impossible.

"What about your family?" she asked. "What about your mother? What if she found out I was staying with you?"

He shrugged. "She'll definitely find out. I'll tell her the next time I see her."

"What would you tell her?"

"The truth. Part of it. That you moved back to Portland recently and I invited you to stay with me until you found a good apartment."

"And my pregnancy? Would you tell her about it?"

"Probably. I don't want it to be a surprise if you run into each other."

She folded her hands on her belly. "And if she wants to know about the father?"

"I'm not in the habit of answering to my parents. I don't plan to do so in this case."

"Even if they think the baby's yours?"

"They know me better than that."

Jennifer didn't speak for a moment. For it to be his baby they'd have to have made love, and the thought brought a slow heat to her face. She looked at his hands on the steering wheel—sexy and strong, doctor's hands—and had to turn away quickly, before she started to imagine them on her body.

She cleared her throat. "They could realize the truth," she said.

"I'm willing to risk it. Neither of them has any judgment when it comes to Drew. I doubt it will cross their minds he could be the father."

"And if it does?"

"I'll lie. If that's okay with you."

"You'd say the baby wasn't his?"

"Yes."

"I hope that doesn't have to happen."

"Me, too."

They pulled into the driveway a short while later. Ross cut the ignition and nodded toward her car, parked directly ahead of his. "So are we going to do this? Should we get the rest of your stuff?"

Hoping it wasn't a big mistake, Jennifer nodded.

AFTER SHE BACKED HER CAR UP to his detached garage, Ross helped her first to unload the things she wouldn't need, making sure to carry the heavy items himself. The rest they took into the house. It wasn't a lot—just the cactus plant, a maroon soft-sided suitcase, a box of books and miscellaneous items, and a small black plastic crate that held a dozen or so hanging file folders.

Upstairs in her room, while Jennifer hung a few items in the closet, he cleared out the drawers of the dresser, a large cherry piece he'd bought with Lucy at an estate sale. The top two drawers were already empty. The bottom two held sweaters and other out-of-season clothing, which he stacked outside in the hallway.

Ross leaned against the door frame to watch her unpack. The sight pleased him, probably more than it should. Despite their complicated situation, though, he wanted her to stay. Couldn't let her walk back out of his life. And definitely couldn't let her live in a squalid little room like the one they'd looked at that afternoon.

She set the cactus in the window and arranged a few books next to the teddy bear on the nightstand. One about natural childbirth, he saw, and another on baby care. A novel he'd seen reviewed recently. A collection of Tom Tomorrow cartoons. A volume of poetry by Mary Oliver. He liked the fact that she still read.

"I'm going to want to pay you rent," she said, putting the crate of files on the small desk that sat in a corner.

He shook his head. "Not necessary."

"Ross, don't be ridiculous. I'm not comfortable freeloading. I'll pay you what I was going to pay for the apartment we saw today."

For some reason his mind went to the afternoon nine years ago when she'd bought those flowers for Lenora. He'd wanted to reimburse her and she hadn't let him. That same stubbornness would make this a hard sell, but still he tried. "You're a guest in my home. One who happens to be carrying my niece or nephew. I'd be insulted if you gave me money."

Rolling her eyes, she grabbed an armful of toiletries and disappeared with them into the adjoining bathroom. "You'll just have to get over it," she said around the corner. "Opening your house to me is a big enough favor. You don't need to turn it into charity."

"It's not—"

She stuck her head through the doorway and gave him a look.

"Okay," he said. "Pay me rent. But don't even think about giving me first, last and deposit." He would put the money into an account for her and the baby.

"Deal." She emerged from the bathroom and started to transfer the last of her clothes from the suitcase.

Ross hoped she would relent a little by the time her child was born. Even if she'd found a decent apartment by then—a possibility he considered remote—he planned to help her out financially. Since he doubted Drew would come up with an offer she could accept. Maybe in a few months, when she'd had more time to come to terms with things, she would be more open to the idea of his help.

Speaking of Drew.

"I have to call my brother. I'll tell him you're staying here."

Jennifer nodded. "How do you think he'll react?"

"I think he'll be pissed. But he is already, so it won't change anything."

ONCE AGAIN he shut himself in the study. Jennifer didn't need to overhear the things he might have to say.

He dialed Drew at the office. "She's not going to go for your offer," he said. "And she's staying with me for a while. Just thought you should know."

"Hang on—"

Ross heard the sound of the phone clattering to the desk, and a moment later a door slamming. Then Drew came back on the line.

"What the hell are you thinking?"

He let his brother's anger roll right off him. "Until you figure out what you're going to do…"

"You're going to ride to her rescue on that white horse of yours," Drew finished, his tone mocking.

In his study, Ross pushed back his chair and stood. He planted a hand on his desk, leaning over. He spoke quietly, with control. "Your offer sucked, Drew. I'm embarrassed to be related to someone who would treat his child as badly as you plan to treat yours. Or do you still want to claim the baby isn't yours?"

"If she has proof, we can talk. Otherwise, get off my ass."

Ross shook his head, unable to fathom his brother's attitude. "You really don't know her at all, do you? You dated her for how many months? And yet you have no understanding of the kind of person she is."

Granted, that had been nine years ago. But she hadn't changed so very much.

"No one's that much of a saint. No one's perfect. Hell, *you're* not even perfect."

Ross ignored the remark. Drew had said something similar in the weeks after Ross's divorce. *Guess you're not perfect, after all.* An offhand comment, thoughtless. Or so he'd imagined, until subsequent events taught him how much Drew wanted to convince the world he was better than his older brother.

"Do you even want to solve this?" Ross asked. "Because there's probably some way you could. And it might be awkward and you might come off looking like a sack of shit for a while, but two kids' lives are at stake here.''

"Hey, easy for you to say from the outside. You don't have someone trying to blackmail you.''

Ross hung up. Continuing the conversation wasn't worth it.

JENNIFER SPENT the next couple of days job-hunting. She'd decided she needed employment more urgently than an apartment, now that she'd moved in with Ross. She signed up with a temp agency, which was how she'd gotten her job at the office supply warehouse. The agency had an excess of employees for the summer, however, and told her it might be a while before they needed her. A copy shop offered to hire her on the spot—but when she realized she felt light-headed and considered the nonstop exposure to toner fumes, she regretfully declined. She was no longer in the critical first trimester, but she wasn't willing to take any chances with the baby's health.

Ross insisted on setting up a basic prenatal appointment to get her blood and urine checked. Everything tested fine. She'd put on a decent amount of weight in the past month and the obstetrician was pleased with her overall health.

She called her friends in San Francisco to give them Ross's address and phone number. Her last paycheck had arrived in the mail, and they promised to forward it to her.

Ross had resumed his day shifts at the hospital. One evening after work he took her with him to return Frank to her owners, who were back from a trip to the East Coast, and to stay for dinner.

Kyle and Melissa lived in a light-blue bungalow on a street of small houses and a couple of genteel old apartment buildings. Ross parked by the curb and retrieved Frank's carrier from the back seat. The moment she saw her familiar front yard she nearly died of excitement, and her frantic barking brought Kyle, Melissa and their two-year-old daughter, Emily, to the door.

Ross set the crate in the front hall and unlatched the gate. "You're home, you crazy mutt," he said.

Frank danced out of the crate and leaped joyfully at Emily. Her little tail wagged madly and her pink tongue darted out. Emily squealed with happiness and ran around stomping her feet while Frank circled her.

Ross made the introductions, and then the adults sat down in the living room. Kyle and Melissa were warm and welcoming, and Jennifer liked them immediately. Melissa worked with Ross in the E.R. at Northwest and also volunteered at Kyle's free clinic downtown. Ross had told her on the way over that he'd become good friends with both of them during the past couple of years.

Kyle excused himself to go back to the kitchen. Emily and Frank finished their reunion and trotted into the room together. Then Emily went to a bookshelf by the window and painstakingly selected a picture book, which she brought over to Ross.

He scooped her onto the couch beside him and

looked at the book. "Ah, *Round Is a Mooncake*. My favorite!"

The toddler giggled at his enthusiasm. Ross opened the book and began to read the pages, which described various shapes encountered by a Chinese-American girl. His audience leaned against his side, obviously completely at ease with him and enjoying the story time immensely.

Jennifer couldn't take her eyes off the two of them. She'd never seen Ross interact with a child and hadn't expected him to be quite such a natural at it. He was comfortable and loving and able to meet Emily on her level.

He glanced up and met her gaze over Emily's head. Smiled. Just a simple smile with a simple message. *Aren't kids just amazing? Can you imagine anything more wonderful than reading to a child?*

The look hit her in the gut and she had to force herself not to betray her emotions. Painful emotions. Why couldn't it have been Ross who'd come to San Francisco and called her up last December? Why couldn't Ross have been the father of her baby? Her child deserved a father like the one he would be. Someone who would take her or him to the zoo, to go fly kites, to the fair. Who would teach her or him about the world and always be available for a talk or a hug. To think her child was unlikely to experience anything close to that made her feel hollow.

"Can I fix either of you anything to drink?" Melissa asked. "Soda water, juice? We have all kinds of things a pregnant woman can enjoy."

She and Ross both requested soda water, and Melissa left the room, promising to return right away.

Jennifer tried not to watch as Ross continued to read to Emily, and was relieved when Melissa came back with the drinks, bringing Kyle.

Emily slipped off the couch to choose more books, while the men discussed the next fund-raising campaign at the clinic.

Melissa took a seat on the chair next to Jennifer's. "So, how is it you know Ross?" she asked.

"I met him when I was in high school."

"You grew up in Portland?"

"I lived here for a while. We moved around a lot." They'd only settled down when they'd reached San Francisco, partly because her mother had gotten sick soon afterward.

"Where?" Melissa asked, seeming genuinely interested.

"All over. Seattle, eastern Oregon, Idaho. Even an island in the San Juans for a few months."

"Oh, Kyle took us there for our last anniversary. It's beautiful." She shared a loving smile with her husband, then returned her gaze to Jennifer. "So, how long were you in Portland?"

"Less than a year. In 1993."

"Wouldn't Ross have been out of high school by then? He's got to be older than that."

"Thanks," said Ross from the couch. "Make a guy feel like a dried-up prune."

Melissa grinned and indicated herself and her husband. "You're younger than both of us, so don't start."

They exchanged some more banter and then moved to the table for dinner.

After the meal the men disappeared into the kitchen to clean up, and Jennifer, Melissa and Emily went back to the living room. The toddler had been staring at Jennifer's stomach more and more as the evening progressed, and as they sat down she asked to touch it.

"Baby in there?"

Jennifer nodded, and when the baby chose that moment to move she guided Emily's hand to the spot.

"Kicking! Kicking!"

From that moment Emily returned constantly to feel for more kicks, in between playing with some wooden trucks on the floor.

"I hope you don't mind," Melissa said.

"Not at all."

Melissa tipped her chin toward Jennifer's belly. "Are you doing this alone?"

"Yeah."

"That must be hard."

Especially, she thought, *when I get a glimpse of exactly what I'm missing.* "It's not what I would have chosen."

"Is the father in the picture at all?" Melissa asked, concerned.

"He doesn't want to be."

Melissa gave her a look that expressed her opinion of the father.

"Yeah," Jennifer said, surprised by how easy it felt to talk with someone she'd met only an hour ago.

But Melissa was so sympathetic. And the fact that Ross knew and trusted her went a long way toward making Jennifer feel comfortable. ''Of course, he has his reasons.''

''Good ones?''

''How's a pregnant wife? One he somehow forgot to tell me about.''

''Oh,'' Melissa said. ''I'm so sorry.''

They discussed it for a few more minutes, though Jennifer decided she wasn't ready to mention the identity of the father—and Melissa didn't ask. Then they segued into a conversation about pregnancy and parenthood.

''How much do you know about baby care?'' Melissa asked.

''I've been doing some reading.''

''Not a lot of experience, I guess.''

''No,'' she admitted. None of her close friends in San Francisco had had children and of course she didn't have any nieces or nephews.

''I didn't have much experience, either,'' Melissa confided. ''But you'll pick it up quickly. Do you want advice?''

''I'd love advice.''

''Then, let me show you my diapering system.''

They walked back to Emily's bedroom, where a changing station was set up on a low dresser. Emily pulled a shape-sorting puzzle from a nightstand shelf and scrambled onto her bed to work with it.

''We decided to use cloth diapers,'' Melissa explained, ''because we were worried about throwing away all those disposables and having them clog the landfills. Not that I'm trying to pressure you," she added with a grin. She sat on the side of the bed and stroked Emily's hair for a moment, watching her do the puzzle. "I also researched the absorbent chemicals in a lot of disposables. No one's tested the gel substances for long-term safety, so I decided I wasn't comfortable having my daughter be a guinea pig."

"I've read that some people are concerned."

"I'm ranting, aren't I," Melissa said, standing again. "Do you want me to cool it?"

Jennifer shook her head. She would need to make some decisions about these things within a couple of months. "Do you use a service?"

"We tried that. It was fine, but I didn't love the style of diapers they used. Then a friend told me about a kind you buy and wash at home, and I tried using them at night." She pulled one out. It was shaped like a disposable diaper and had adjustable snap closures. "Now I use them exclusively. They fit a wide size range," she said, "and I never get blowouts. We've saved hundreds of dollars. And they're *so* much easier to deal with than people think. You use them with covers like these."

Some of the covers were made out of wool, and others were made from a lightweight polyester fabric treated with waterproof coating. All of them were much higher quality and more appealing than the basic plastic pants Jennifer had seen in secondhand stores.

Melissa offered to lend her Emily's outgrown diapers and covers. Then, because Emily needed a change, she demonstrated how the system worked.

Watching, Jennifer was overcome with the joyful thought that she would be doing this for her own child soon. Something about taking care of a baby moved her deeply.

"Your daughter is wonderful," she told Melissa.

"She's a dream." Melissa picked Emily up from the changing table and set her back on her feet. "I remember how hard, and how amazing, it is to be pregnant. If you need anything, or even just want to talk, you should call me."

"I will. Thanks," she said.

In the kitchen they joined the men, who'd made quick work of the cleanup.

Kyle said to her, "Ross tells me you're looking for work."

"I am." She knelt so Emily could pat her belly again.

"We've got a part-time opening at the clinic," Kyle continued, turning the dial on the dishwasher to start the cycle. The machine whirred to life. "One of our receptionists decided to move to New York. It's just eighteen hours a week, and no benefits, unfortunately." He described the position, which seemed to consist mainly of answering the phone, greeting and scheduling clients, and filing. "You'd really be doing me a favor if you took it."

"I could only commit to a couple of months," she warned him, standing back up. "I don't know what'll happen after the baby's born."

He nodded. "Ross said you wanted something temporary. We'll find someone else if you don't want to keep it. I would just be relieved not to have to search for someone right now. The next month is busy.''

The arrangement sounded ideal for both of them. ''When do you want me to start?''

Kyle got a pained look on his face. ''I know it's short notice, but how about the day after tomorrow?''

Jennifer looked at Ross, though she didn't know why. She didn't need his permission to take a job. ''Sure,'' she said. ''I can do that.''

In the car on the way home, Ross mentioned the clinic didn't have a Web page. ''A while ago Kyle told me he wanted to have one,'' Ross said, ''but I doubt he's done anything yet. Maybe you should ask him about it in a few days.''

''Why do they need a Web page?''

''Mostly for donors. But he also wants potential patients to be able to look up the phone number or read about our services to see if we can help them. I have no idea if he'd be able to pay you to design it, but even if he can't, you could use it as an example of your work, to get other jobs.''

''Good point,'' she said. To establish herself in a competitive job such as Web design would be difficult, but if she developed a strong portfolio of work for the clinic and perhaps for some other nonprofits she might be able to pull it off.

This evening had made her feel much more settled in Portland. She had a job, the possibility of another and a new friend in Melissa.

As Ross pulled onto their street he said, ''I think I'm actually going to miss that dog. Even though she's a pint-sized pain in the butt.''

"Oh, yeah?"

"I'd gotten used to her."

So had she, Jennifer realized. And she'd gotten used to living in Ross's house, to sharing his life, as well—too used to it. Just as she'd predicted.

She should be careful. More careful, frankly, than she wanted to be.

CHAPTER NINE

Nine years earlier

One Saturday night my parents are out and I happen to be in the kitchen the same time as Drew and Jennifer. I haven't seen her much since the day she helped me move Lenora's bed. I'm busy getting a jump on the reading for a philosophy class I'm taking in the fall, but I've also been avoiding her. She's just a kid. Seventeen. But I keep thinking about her and how she's so different from my first impression of her. I'm drawn to her, but I don't want to be.

For some reason Drew's in a particularly good mood tonight, and he's joking around with the two of us. When he acts this way he's a lot of fun to be around and it's easy to see why people like him so much. He and Jennifer are planning to go out to a party in Hillsboro. He invites me along.

"I don't think so," I say. The prospect of hanging out with a bunch of inebriated high school kids doesn't do much for me.

Drew takes my no with a smile. "Hey, come on, big bro. Stop being Mr. Perfect. Live a little. Come down from your ivory tower for a night.''

Jennifer doesn't say anything, but it doesn't surprise me that she wouldn't care either way.

Drew continues. ''You remember Kenny's older sister? Marissa? The really cute one? She was the year ahead of you at school. She's having some friends over, too, so it's not like you'll be the oldest old fogey.''

I remember Marissa. My freshman year I thought she was the hottest girl in the sophomore class, but I don't recall noticing her much after that, even though we were both on the tennis team. I guess my tastes changed. Still, I'm modestly curious to see what's happened to her since high school. And it seems Drew does actually want me to come along. A small sacrifice, I suppose. I mean, he's my brother, so I wouldn't mind having a better relationship with him. We're going to have to live with each other for a long time.

I drive. Jennifer insists Drew take the front seat, since he's taller and needs leg room. We arrive just before ten, and it's clear the party has been going on for a while. I guess there are about eighty people here, and judging by the number of red plastic cups left lying around, they've gone most of the way through the kegs. Great.

The younger generation is out by the pool, while the supposedly more mature folks are inside. I go over and say hello to Marissa. She remembers me, and we talk for a minute before she steers me to the bar and introduces me to some of her friends.

Half an hour later I'm dancing with some stridently attractive woman named Angelique. What the hell, I'm thinking, and my thinking isn't much different when she leads me to the stairs. At the top she pauses and leans in to me. She kisses me, reckless and tasting like damp ashes. The thought that she smokes distracts me, and reality inserts itself. She's drunk, and I'm not interested.

So I back away. I try to soften the blow, but the ensuing conversation takes the last bit of enjoyment out of the evening. Feeling like an asshole, I head outside. The front, not the back. As we arrived I saw a bench, and I'm fairly sure I won't have to deal with a crowd of teenagers there.

But the bench is occupied. Jennifer and a girl I don't recognize sit there, talking. Jennifer looks up as I approach. She greets me and introduces her friend, Amy somebody.

We talk for a while, the three of us, and then Amy takes her empty cup and goes inside.

"So, where's Drew?" I ask Jennifer.

"Somewhere out back."

"And you're not?" She'd tried to tell me the last time how much she enjoyed the social scene, but I was right not to believe her. I just can't see her by the pool with all those drunk teenagers.

She shakes her head. "I'm not in the mood tonight."

I look out at the road beyond the white rail

fence marking the end of the lawn. Streetlights illuminate the asphalt. There's no sidewalk, but the house is tucked away in a development, so there won't be much traffic except for people leaving the party. "You want to take a walk?"

"Sure," she says, as if it's mostly to keep her circulation going that she's interested in doing so.

But of course the only reason *I* want to go for a walk is so I don't have to stay at this lame party. It's not about Jennifer or wanting to spend time with her.

At first we don't talk much as we walk the curving streets, all of them far too wide for the amount of traffic they will ever carry.

Then we pass a house with a whole herd of fake deer stapled into the front lawn. There have to be at least a dozen of the damn things. Fawns and their mothers, adolescent males, even a buck with a magnificent rack. It's hard to be sure in the darkness, but I could swear there's a bullet hole in the stag's head that's been patched with putty.

"Oh, Lord," I say.

Jennifer laughs. "I've seen worse."

"Worse? How is that possible? Where?"

She tells me about this town in Idaho she once lived in. Apparently somebody there put a whole menagerie in the front yard. Flamingos, parrots, tigers, a five-foot-tall elephant, half a dozen rubber fish nailed to a sheet of blue-painted plywood, and even a little baby Jesus left over from someone's garish Christmas nativity scene.

After that we never really stop talking. The conversation twists as much as the streets in the development. One moment we're discussing her mom's job cleaning for a manic-depressive jewelry designer in Idaho and the next we've moved on to some unreadable Turkish novel that got a great review in the *New York Times*.

This is much more my idea of how to spend an evening than the party scene. I'm almost disappointed when we go back to the house and find that Drew is ready to go.

THE DAY AFTER THEY HAD DINNER at Melissa and Kyle's house, Jennifer bought a book on Web page design and, back home, sat in the living room to look through it. Ross had the day off and was working in his study.

It was a warm summer afternoon and she'd opened one of the windows. She hadn't gotten very far in her reading when a car turned in to the driveway. She heard the engine shut off and the sound of the parking brake as it engaged.

Walking to the window, Jennifer saw a shiny white Mercedes behind Ross's car. The passenger door opened, and Katherine Griffin, looking frail and a lot older than her years, put a foot onto the pavement. Jennifer had expected Katherine to look weak, but not quite this bad.

A dark-haired pregnant woman emerged gracefully from the driver's side. In her early thirties, she was tall and wore an expensive suit tailored to flatter her burgeoning shape. Jennifer felt a little skip of anxiety, knowing it had to be Lucy.

She watched as the woman gave Katherine a hand out of the car and then went to the trunk to withdraw three large white bags. Realizing she should alert Ross, Jennifer waddled down the hall to the study and poked her head in.

"Ross," she said. "Your mother's here."

He looked up.

"With Lucy, I think."

He got to his feet. Sighed. "I've asked Mom to call first. She never does."

Jennifer was glad he'd told his parents earlier in the week about her presence in his house. He'd been right not to keep it a secret.

"I suppose she couldn't resist coming by to check you out." He crossed the study. "Though I'm sure she'll have some ostensible reason for dropping in."

"Oh. *Now* I feel comfortable."

The doorbell rang.

"Don't worry," he said, giving her shoulder a squeeze. "You'll be fine."

Jennifer hung back in the front hall while Ross opened the door.

"Hello, Ross," his mother said. "We brought your curtains. Lucy and I were at the cleaners', anyway, so I asked if they'd come back yet. We thought we'd save you the trip."

She held out her cheek for a kiss, which Ross gave her, then turned to Jennifer. Mrs. Griffin assessed her figure, as if to confirm that she was indeed pregnant.

"Hello, Jennifer. How are you?"

In the past Jennifer had called her Mrs. Griffin. Now she decided they should be on a more equal footing. "I'm fine, thank you, Katherine. Ross told me about your operation. I'm sorry you haven't been well." Okay, so maybe her words still came off a little formal. To be completely at ease with the unknowing grandmother of your illegitimate baby was hard.

"I'm surviving," Katherine said.

Ross went to Lucy, who stood in the doorway, and took the three bags from her. "Lucy, Jennifer. Jennifer, Lucy. Lucy is my brother's wife," he added, as if she didn't know.

The woman smiled and extended a manicured hand. "I think we're just about as pregnant as each other. When are you due?"

"September fourteenth."

"I'm due on the eighth," she said. "We'll have to compare notes." And her smile was so charming that Jennifer had the sinking feeling she would end up liking Drew's wife.

Ross stowed the bags in the closet. "Would you like tea?" he asked his mother.

"That would be lovely."

He took her arm and led her to the living room ahead of Lucy and Jennifer. "If you had called first," he said, the reprimand good-humored, "we could have put the kettle on."

"I'll go start things rolling," Jennifer offered, eager to avoid being alone in the living room with Katherine and Lucy. Consenting to being inspected was all very well, but she didn't want this meeting to be any more awkward than it had to be.

"Good idea," Ross said, and she knew he understood her motivation.

In the kitchen Jennifer filled the kettle with cold water, set it on the stove and turned on the burner.

A minute later she heard footsteps in the hallway, and Lucy entered the kitchen.

"Need a hand? Ross is quizzing his mother about her rehabilitation," Lucy added by way of explanation for her presence.

"Sure. What kind of tea does Katherine like?" She scanned the boxes on Ross's shelves. "Earl Grey, Irish Breakfast, Orange Pekoe…? Or does she want something herbal?"

"Is there a tin behind those boxes?"

Jennifer lifted the Earl Grey out of the way, revealing a metal tea tin. "Pure Assam?" she asked.

"That's the one. Katherine's favorite." Lucy walked to the farthest set of cabinets and pulled down a teapot and cups. "I'd love some peppermint. How about you?"

"Sure, that sounds fine."

Lucy peered into the cabinet. "I know he's got a second teapot somewhere. Oh, here it is."

Apparently this wasn't the first time Lucy had come to tea at Ross's house, and for some reason it made Jennifer feel…what, jealous? Not really. Not quite. Excluded, maybe. As if she were just a temporary visitor in Ross's life.

To distract herself, she opened the box of peppermint tea and put two bags into the smaller of the teapots. She measured the black leaves into the other one, then found a tray in a drawer under the island and set the teapots and cups on it, along with a matching sugar bowl and empty creamer.

"Do you know if Ross and his mother take milk in their tea?"

"They both take it black. And I don't need anything, either."

Jennifer removed the sugar and creamer from the tray, then tried to figure out what else she could do until the water boiled. Rejoin Ross and his mother? Stay here and try to avoid awkward topics with Lucy?

Lucy leaned against the counter. "Katherine mentioned you dated Drew in high school," she said, half statement and half question.

So, here it was. Jennifer didn't know if Lucy was the type to be sensitive about a former girlfriend. She didn't appear upset. But in any case, Jennifer didn't want Lucy to spend much time thinking about the connection between Drew and her. As she'd told Ross, she didn't want to go through Lucy to try to reach Drew.

"Just for a few months," she said, going for an offhand tone. "That's when I met Ross. He came home from college for the summer and we got to be friends."

Someday, she thought, Lucy would learn everything about her and Drew. Jennifer wondered how she would react. Would she look back on this conversation and be angry that Jennifer had concealed from her what was going on? But it couldn't be helped.

"And you just moved back here?" Lucy asked.

"A week ago. I've had a little trouble finding a good place to live."

"So why come back to Portland? Moving when you're pregnant doesn't seem like the easiest thing. Of course, moving with an infant wouldn't be a cakewalk, either," she added with a smile.

"No, it wouldn't," Jennifer said, preferring to steer the conversation elsewhere rather than to answer Lucy's question. "I've tried to imagine what life will be like with a newborn, how I'll get anything done, but I bet reality will still surprise me."

"No kidding," Lucy said. "It's probably like being pregnant. You can imagine it, but until you experience it you don't really have a clue. I don't know how your pregnancy has been. Mine's been pretty smooth—supposedly. But I can't believe how uncomfortable I've been. All the aches and pains and then those odd twinges, which the doctor assures me are perfectly normal but which scare me nonetheless." Her voice softened. "And at the same time I was completely unprepared for how absolutely amazing it is to have a human being grow inside me."

Jennifer had a moment of guilt. Lucy must feel the same kind of overpowering love for her baby that she did. The same joy about her pregnancy. What had happened between herself and Drew would adversely affect Lucy's experience of all that. Drew's infidelity and his second baby would change his wife's life forever, and being in the same room with her made the consequences strike home in a visceral way.

"It is amazing," Jennifer finally agreed, deciding that, paradoxically, pregnancy and the bodily changes it involved, was probably one of the safest subjects they could discuss. "Sometimes it just blows me away."

Nevertheless, she was relieved when the water boiled and they could return to the living room.

BY THE TIME his mother and Lucy left, Ross was ready for a break. His mother had filled the conversation with talk about babies and child rearing, displaying her excitement about Lucy's baby without any awareness of how it affected Jennifer.

"I'm really sorry about that," Ross said, closing the front door after they'd watched Lucy and his mother drive away. "Are you okay?"

Jennifer sighed. "I've had better afternoons. But it could have been worse, I suppose."

That was true. "Do you think you'll want to come to the picnic?"

His mother had invited Jennifer to the Griffins' annual Fourth of July picnic the following week, an event that was somewhere between a real picnic and what most people would call an outdoor formal dinner. Jennifer had attended nine years ago with Drew and his teenage friends. Ross remembered spending most of the party that year trying to deflect the attentions of one of Drew's gang, Heather, who'd seemed less silly than Molly but not as interesting as Jennifer.

"I don't know if I should," she said. "I mean, until things are more settled."

He could understand why she would feel uncertain. On the other hand, to attend might be a good strategic move. "It could show Drew you're serious about sticking around. It could wake him up."

"I'll consider it."

"Well, let me know." Ross opened the hall closet, where he'd stashed the three bags of clean curtains. "I'd like to get these up," he said. "Can you lend a hand?"

She said yes, and he went to the basement for a stepladder. He set it up in the living room and she put out a hand to steady it as he climbed up. Then she held a clean curtain in her arms while he reattached it to the tracks over the bay window.

"I keep thinking about Lucy," Jennifer said. "She's nice. A lot nicer than I expected, since she's married to Drew. Will she take it hard when she finds out he cheated on her?"

Ross clipped in a few pins before replying. "Yes, she probably will."

He figured the infidelity would surprise her; it would also upset her deeply. For some reason Lucy didn't see through Drew's facade. As far as he could tell, they'd been genuinely happy together. Or at least, *she'd* been happy with *him*. Drew's lifestyle and interests—the ski trips, the constant socializing, the vacations to exotic spots around the globe—had suited her. And somehow Drew had managed to make her feel loved, though Ross was dumbfounded about how he'd done it.

Jennifer let him have another couple of feet of curtain. "Will she stay married to him?"

"I don't know." Ross kept hanging the fabric. He found he didn't really want to discuss his sister-in-law any more.

They worked in silence for a minute. Ross finished the first side of the bay window and then repositioned the ladder to work on the other side. Jennifer got out another curtain and held it up for him.

She said, "The more I think about it, the more likely it seems I'm not the only person he's cheated with."

Ross paused a fraction of a second, then clipped in the first hanger, remembering something he'd learned shortly after that summer nine years ago. He *didn't* know of any instances of infidelity during

Drew's marriage to Lucy, on the other hand, but he'd bet there were some. "Probably not."

After threading a few more hooks, he ran out of slack in the fabric. He glanced over his shoulder. Jennifer gripped the fabric with both hands. Ross gave it a tug. She looked up at him, realized she'd broken their rhythm and then released some fabric.

He attached more clips. "What was that about?"

"I guess I wouldn't be surprised if he cheated on me, too," she mused, as if she'd read his mind. "Back in high school."

Ross turned again and watched her. "He did," he said, his tone gentle but matter-of-fact. It wasn't the kind of thing he'd ever wanted to have to tell her, but since she'd brought up the subject herself, he couldn't avoid it.

Jennifer stared up at him, her expression showing that the confirmation affected her more than she'd anticipated.

"I'm sorry," he said.

She turned her gaze away, then back. "Did you...know at the time?"

"No." If he had he almost certainly would have told her, family loyalty be damned. But his motives wouldn't have been pure. "I didn't find out about it until the following winter break."

Although the knowledge had eased the gnawing guilt he'd felt for kissing Jennifer, the guilt hadn't vanished. Amazing, really—especially considering Drew's behavior over the years—that Ross still felt angry at himself for that one inappropriate moment.

"So, who was it?" she asked.

Ross stood on the ladder, still observing her. He

called up an image of the bouncy teenager Drew had been doing on the side. "Molly."

She'd been just Drew's type. Silly and willing.

Neither of which described Jennifer. Christ, it was hard to understand what his brother had even seen in her. She'd always been more Ross's type than Drew's. But perhaps that was the whole issue, the reason he'd chosen her. And she *had* been cute. No way around that. Drew had probably viewed Jennifer as a shy outsider, desperate for acceptance, who would reward his attentions with sex.

Only, she hadn't, not nine years ago. And Drew had obviously grown tired of the game, tired of the chase. When an opportunity had presented itself, he'd opted for an easy score.

"I guess I don't exactly have the moral high ground in this instance," Jennifer said.

Their kiss. Ross had wondered if they would ever acknowledge it. He watched her, knowing she was remembering it, wishing she would look up at him, make eye contact. Share the moment.

But she didn't.

"You have it more than I do," he said at last. Because he'd been the older one—the one who should have known better. He'd kissed his brother's girlfriend, and it didn't matter that Drew had been cheating on her, possibly at that very moment. Ross hadn't known about that when he'd kissed her.

But it had been more mutual than just him kissing her. It had been damn mutual. And the idea of his brother ever touching her again had made his gut twist, had propelled him into a hasty effort to break them up.

Even if he couldn't summon the nerve, the reck-lessness, to become involved with her himself.

Ross glanced down at her belly. At the curve of his brother's child. He thought of the grace and cour-age with which she handled her circumstances. "Drew didn't deserve you," he said, his voice com-ing out more intense than he'd planned. "He never deserved you."

"No," she said. "He didn't, did he."

She looked right at him then, finally, her gaze clear. And he felt a jolt of need, the sensation stronger, more profound, than anything he'd felt that whole painful summer of longing for the forbidden.

Ross held her gaze as long as he could stand to torture himself, wanting something they could never have together—not even if she wanted it just as much as he did. At last he turned away, knowing he'd let his feelings show too much.

Attaching the final few hooks to the curtain rod, he finished the bay window. He stepped down off the ladder, careful not to get too close. "Come on," he said. "We've got a few more windows."

CHAPTER TEN

DREW GOT HOME a little after nine from a business dinner with one of the senior partners in the firm. As had frequently happened since Jennifer Burns had shown up in Portland, he'd had to struggle to pay attention.

He knew he was taking a risk with his approach to her. His offer last week had been pretty modest, but it was about what he could afford. His finances were a lot tighter than anyone would ever guess. He might be able to pull off five hundred a month. It would be a stretch. Maybe worth it to have Jennifer disappear from his life, though. If that was even possible now. His damn brother, taking her in…

He found Lucy in the nursery, sketching mural designs for the walls on a wide sheet of drawing paper. He gave her a kiss and they chatted about her plans for the room. She went back to her sketching.

"I met an old friend of yours today."

He got a tight feeling in his stomach but tried to act normal. "Really?"

"Jennifer Burns."

Shit. What did Lucy know? He opted for the least disclosure possible. "Jennifer? No kidding."

"At Ross's house. Your mom and I went by to drop off his curtains."

Drew gave this a mystified, what's-up-with-the-curtains-but-don't-bother-to-explain look. "Jennifer Burns. Wow. No kidding. I assume she told you we dated in high school?"

"Your mom did. She seems like a nice person. I liked her. She's pregnant, you know."

Drew assessed her expression. She *looked* as if she didn't have a clue, but he couldn't figure out if she was just faking it, trying to draw him into a lie. "Pregnant?"

"Yeah. About as much as I am."

He raised his eyebrows. "Huh. She live in Portland?"

"Just moved here. She's staying with Ross for a while."

"What about the baby's father?" He was either digging a grave for himself of gigantic proportions, or not. Hard to tell which.

Lucy didn't even blink. "She didn't want to talk about it. I got the feeling he wasn't in the picture."

Drew watched his wife. She didn't know anything; he was almost sure of it. Maybe this meant Jennifer was acting the way he'd hoped she would. Maybe this would work out, after all. An expensive mistake, getting her pregnant—if, indeed, he was the father— but not a fatal one.

IN THE MORNING Jennifer went to work at her new job. The free clinic was in an old section of Portland, north of Burnside Street and not far from a huge new-and-used bookstore she'd frequented as a teen-ager. The area was undergoing a slow gentrification, but it also contained many single-room occupancy hotels, and many people still lived on the streets there.

The clinic occupied a small storefront. She arrived fifteen minutes early for her shift and the clinic wasn't yet open, so Kyle had to unlock the door for her. He gave her a quick tour of the back of the facility and then oriented her to her desk, which sat in the front, with a view of the sidewalk outside. He showed her how the phone system worked and how to handle the paperwork.

"Basically, if it needs doing, you do it," he said. "But don't let anyone push you around, and if you get tired, you tell one of us. You're here to help, not get yourself killed by stress."

Finally he introduced her to Barbara, the clinic's nurse practitioner, who told her to disregard everything Kyle had said. "Because this man is a *terrible* receptionist. The days he has to do it..." Barbara shook her head. "Phew. You don't want to be here."

Kyle socked Barbara in the arm, then got out of range before she could knock him down.

Jennifer thought she might like Barbara.

As Kyle retreated, Barbara said, "You get off at twelve-thirty, right?"

"Yeah." Today she would work only the morning shift.

"You got plans for lunch?"

Jennifer shook her head.

"All right. If you haven't quit by lunchtime, we'll

go celebrate. I'll take you around the corner to Buddy's.''

Jennifer sat herself down and the day began. Once the clinic opened, she felt as if she never got a break. Most of the clients were in pretty difficult situations and couldn't pay for their medical care, but almost everyone tried to contribute something, even if it was just a token amount. They wanted to hang on to a little pride, she thought. To show they weren't completely dependent on others. She knew the feeling.

The restaurant Barbara took her to, Buddy's Café, turned out to be a spot that served food to the homeless and low-income population of downtown Portland. A full plate of good food cost less than two dollars. Jennifer enjoyed the busy camaraderie of the café. She noticed one of the patients from the morning sitting at a table with a couple of friends. He still looked ill, but seemed in much better spirits than he had when he'd dragged himself into the clinic.

"I could eat here every day," she told Barbara.

"Hey," Barbara said. "I do. When I'm not eating at Thi's *Pho* Shop. Ever had Vietnamese beef noodle soup?"

Jennifer shook her head.

"Well, you better make sure to get Ross to take you sometime soon."

On the walk back to the clinic Barbara said, "I hear you've shacked up with him. Our Dr. Ross."

Jennifer knew better than to take Barbara seriously. "I'm staying with him for a few weeks, yes."

"That his baby in there?"

"No."

"Good. Because if it was, I'd have to give that man a piece of my mind. Hate to think he would be the type to get a girl pregnant and not marry her."

"He's not." Ross would never have done what Drew did. If he'd conceived a baby with someone— with her—she knew he wouldn't hesitate to do the right thing.

"All right, then." They got to the clinic's front door and Barbara reached for the handle. "He's taking good care of you?"

Jennifer dug her keys out of her purse. "Yes."

"You might want to consider returning the favor," Barbara said. "He doesn't get a lot of that." And then she disappeared into the clinic.

As Jennifer made dinner that night, Ross sat at the breakfast bar leafing through the newest issue of *Emergency Medicine*. Trying and failing to concentrate. The sight of her, perfectly at home in his kitchen, was difficult to ignore. And her body had become so wonderfully ripe. Her curves suited her, and the extra weight she carried gave her a presence she hadn't quite had as a slender teenager.

Not that he'd been pining away for her for the past nine years. But having her here, moving easily between stove and cupboard and sink, measuring brown rice and water, lighting the flame on the gas stove and pressing a brick of tofu between two plates, made him wonder if perhaps he should have been.

He considered the reaction he'd had to her the day before. The rawness of it. He couldn't pretend he wasn't interested in her. Despite the impossibility of their situation, he wanted her.

And the attraction wasn't just physical. Every time they talked about something she impressed him. After her prenatal visit, for example, they'd discussed her feelings about childbirth. As he'd guessed from her book on natural methods, she wanted to give birth with as little medical intervention as possible. What he hadn't realized was that she wanted to give birth at home, with a direct-entry midwife—a midwife without a nursing degree.

That attitude went against his medical training. He considered the hospital, with its equipment, resources and personnel, the safest place to have a baby. But Jennifer had done her homework thoroughly and laid out a cogent argument for the benefits of home birth. She also admitted her preference came partly from a wish not to spend more time in a hospital, having spent so much time there during her mother's illness—a bit of self-awareness he could appreciate.

By the end of the discussion he'd been mostly convinced home birth would be a safe alternative for the great majority of women. This was the kind of conversation he'd missed. Interesting and challenging. He liked talking with her, and always had.

Jennifer sliced the drained brick of tofu into cubes, drizzled some oil into the hot frying pan and put the tofu in. She gave the pan a shake. From the fridge she withdrew a plastic bag of organic swiss chard. She set a colander in the sink and began to wash the leaves.

"If he hadn't been married," Ross asked her, giving up on his magazine, "what would you have wanted?"

She turned to look at him. A chard stem in her hand dripped water onto the floor. "The same thing I want now."

A father for her child.

Jennifer glanced down at the dripping chard, moved it back over the sink and washed it. After pausing to stir the tofu, she rinsed the rest of the chard leaves and put them in a steamer.

"You wouldn't have wanted him to marry you?"

She grimaced at him over her shoulder. "Isn't it bad enough he's my baby's father?"

Ross looked down at the magazine, folding it closed, to cover his relief. Yesterday she'd agreed Drew hadn't deserved her. It hadn't changed her determination, though, to get Drew to behave like a father to their baby. Which bothered Ross. It seemed out of touch. But he was glad to know she had some sense left.

They ate at the dining room table and talked about other things. Jennifer splashed lemon juice and soy sauce on the greens and tofu. The simplicity of the meal allowed the natural flavors of the ingredients to come through. And it was healthy, which was good for her growing baby.

It was still light outside when they finished dinner. Ross offered to clean, and she took him up on it. After pouring herself a fresh glass of water, she let herself out onto the back porch. He heard the *creak* of the hanging rocker as she sat and began to swing.

Through the window over the sink, he saw her legs move slowly in and out of view.

As he washed out the frying pan, he thought about how good and how easy it felt to share a house with her. He'd shared houses before, with friends in medical school and when he was married. This was different.

Different because their relationship was platonic, though he'd once thought they had something between them, something real, something...sweet.

But of course they hadn't. You couldn't have anything sweet when the woman you thought you had it with was your brother's girlfriend. It wasn't sweet. It was tacky. Embarrassing.

Finished in the kitchen, he joined Jennifer on the porch. This time of year was the best in Portland. All winter it rained and the sky hung gray with clouds. But for ninety days in the summer the clouds pulled back and the sun shone down on green trees and grass. Ross had never lived anywhere that had more beautiful summers than Portland, and he could almost convince himself they were worth the dull, slushy winters.

The backyard was quiet, but it was the quiet of summer. Through the open windows of neighboring houses, drifts of music and conversation escaped. The clatter of dishes. Words too soft to be understood.

Ross crossed the porch, passing in front of Jennifer. He leaned against one of the columns at the top of the stairs. The garden spread out in front of him and he could see Jennifer out of the corner of his eye, moving slowly backward and forward. He knew she was looking at him, studying him, and he let her, not turning around.

The silence between them was as peaceful as the breeze, but at last he broke it—foolishly, perhaps, yet unable to stop himself. "Some people would say you should want to marry Drew no matter what. That you would grow to love him."

Her swinging paused for a moment, then started up again. "I've seen marriages," she told him. "And what I've seen hasn't always been pretty."

"But you haven't been married."

"No. My mother was married, though. Twice."

And that must be where her lousy impression of stepfathers had come from. "Not all marriages are bad," he said, though he wasn't really one to talk.

"Hers were." Jennifer was silent then for a long time.

He sensed she was remembering her mother, grieving for her and maybe grieving for whatever part of her childhood had been affected by the men her mother had chosen, by those bad marriages.

Ross respected her silence. He stood motionless, watching a bumblebee dance around a pale-pink climbing rose in the bed by the steps. The bee circled and buzzed and finally alighted on a petal. Ross watched it crawl to the center of the flower, watched its limbs at work, raking up pollen. And then, without a running start, without any signal of intention, it flew off, purposeful, heading home before darkness fell.

"People sometimes marry for the wrong reasons,"

she said at last. "For sex, or out of greed or desperation. Or from a sense of obligation. They don't usually know what they're getting into."

"Is that what happened to your mom?"

"Mmm-hmm. And to a friend a few years ago."

"Maybe it's not marriage. Maybe it's the fact that people sometimes make bad choices."

She rocked gently. "I certainly have."

In his peripheral vision he saw her hand move to her abdomen. He shifted his weight, leaning more heavily against the column. The wood pushed back against his shoulder, solid and strong.

"So have I," he said.

A silence; moments ticked by.

"If you're talking about what happened nine years ago—" she began, but he interrupted her.

"I'm talking about when I got married."

More silence. A different kind of silence, though. Of surprise, almost confusion.

"You were married?"

He turned, found her staring at him with near disbelief. "For a couple of years."

"When... When was that?"

"It ended four years ago."

She took a moment to digest this. Perhaps putting the dates together, figuring out it had been the final years of medical school, perhaps imagining the stresses that might have put on a marriage.

"So, what happened?" she asked at last.

He allowed himself a small and self-mocking smile. "Well, she left me."

"Ross, I'm sorry. You—you didn't have kids?"

"We couldn't. It was a while ago. We still try to be friends."

"She lives here? You have to see her?"

"Fairly often."

"Is it hard?" she asked. "When you see her?"

"Sometimes. She got married again." He hesitated, looking out over the lawn, knowing he had to tell her. "It's...complicated."

"Why?"

"Because she married my brother."

CHAPTER ELEVEN

JENNIFER WAS BARELY ABLE to process his words. She brought the swing to an abrupt halt, planting both feet on the ground. The seat twisted a little before it came to rest. "Lucy? You were married to Lucy?"

"Yes."

Lord. Oh Lord. That was so screwed up.

She looked at Ross's broad back. At his rigid posture, the tension in his jaw, visible even from her angle, as he stared across the yard. "Please tell me they weren't having an affair. Please tell me he didn't sleep with your wife when you were married."

"They didn't. Not as far as I know. It happened later."

"But still…"

"He moved in on her," Ross said, his voice tight. "Caught her at a vulnerable time during the months after the divorce came through. I'd never told her quite how much I disapproved of him, the things he was capable of. And he can be very charming."

"She was your ex-wife." And that should have been enough to put her firmly off-limits. Though Drew obviously wasn't good at staying within the limits of appropriate behavior.

"Yeah. He shouldn't have done it. But maybe he fell in love. Or maybe he just wanted to prove he could win her when I hadn't been able to keep her."

The latter sounded like the Drew she knew. *She deserted you, but she wants me.* It didn't explain, though, why Lucy would get involved with her former brother-in-law.

"Why would she do that to you?"

He sighed, still facing the yard. "Why does anyone do anything? I don't think she meant to hurt me. I think she honestly believed she would be happy with Drew. More than she was with me."

Jennifer wondered how any woman could have been unhappy with Ross, but didn't say it. Maybe Lucy simply had different needs in a partner, or was one of those women who always thought something better was around the corner and couldn't see a good thing when they had it. Maybe she couldn't deal with a husband who, apparently, couldn't conceive children. Maybe she didn't want to adopt or go to a sperm bank.

She recalled how Ross had behaved with Lucy the day before. He'd acted completely normal. As if his sister-in-law were only that, as if she'd never shared his life, shared his bed. Shared this house, too, as her familiarity with his kitchen revealed. How did he manage it? Jennifer doubted she could. But perhaps he felt it was important for the sake of his family to maintain the peace, to allow them all to pretend the situation wasn't as messed up as it was.

And it was definitely messed up. In her life now, as well as in theirs.

Jennifer felt sick. It wasn't enough she was carrying the illegitimate baby of a married man. Her child's half sibling belonged to Ross's ex-wife. Even more than before, Ross was a man with whom she couldn't become involved.

She wondered how they would all manage to deal with one another in the years to come. How she would raise her child to understand the intricate relationships among the various adults in his or her life.

Buck up, honey. Time to be strong.

"Thank you for telling me," she finally said. And she began to swing again, sitting on the hanging rocker on the back porch of Ross's house, the house he'd once shared with Lucy. "I might not have figured it out."

He shrugged, his back still to her as he leaned against the post. "You needed to know."

But she didn't believe his attempt at nonchalance.

THE GRIFFIN RESIDENCE took up a huge chunk of land in the Council Crest area, with a sweep of front lawn and a spacious backyard protected by trees on all sides. The house and the grounds were pristine, designed with a timeless taste. The multileveled deck, washed with warm afternoon sunshine, was larger than Ross's entire house.

Jennifer had decided to attend the Fourth of July picnic, and she and Ross arrived after it was in full swing. A giant grill smoked on the back lawn and people stood in groups, talking loudly and drinking gin-and-tonics. Music came from a jazz band. A catering crew worked the grill and kept the buffet stocked, and within five minutes three different waitresses had offered Jennifer and Ross appetizers.

In the end Jennifer hadn't been able to turn down the chance to see Lucy again. The chance to look more closely, to satisfy some of her curiosity. The news of Lucy's former marriage to Ross had made her an undeniable source of interest—more so, even, than her current marriage to Drew. Jennifer wanted to know who she was, this person who'd gotten Ross Griffin to the altar, only to decide, two years later, that she didn't want him.

She spotted Lucy the moment she and Ross walked onto the deck. The other woman sat in the sunshine surrounded by friends, tilting her head to the side as she listened attentively to what one of them was saying. Obviously it was a joke, because everyone in the group chuckled, Lucy included. Her teeth flashed white as she smiled. She ran a graceful hand through her glossy dark hair, brushing it away from her face, and as she did so she caught sight of them.

She waved in greeting, neither too welcoming nor too dismissive. It was, Jennifer thought, the absolutely perfect gesture for a woman to give the man who was both her ex-husband and her brother-in-law.

Jennifer couldn't wrest her gaze away. Lucy had the poise of an aristocrat and the beauty of a cover model. Her dress, a pale-peach silk, made her rounded stomach look attractive and womanly. The fabric's soft color brought out the healthy glow in her face. And her posture, her expressions, everything about her...

Ross's ex-wife.

She had a certain aura about her. In high school she would have been homecoming queen. The most popular girl in the class. The type of person who, intentionally or not, made every other girl feel awkward and insufficient.

If this intimidating woman was what Ross required in a wife, no wonder he hadn't remarried. Jennifer herself wouldn't stand a chance, even if she *weren't* carrying Drew's baby.

And Lucy was the type of person Katherine and Edward would be delighted to have in the family—perhaps enough so, even, that they were now willing to pretend there was nothing strange about her previous marriage to Ross.

"Come say hello to my mother," Ross said. He led her to the opposite end of the deck, by the pool, where Katherine Griffin held court on a wooden bench against the railing. She looked better than a week before, Jennifer noted, as if she'd made progress in her recovery. As if, too, this social event—and her place at the center of it—gave her great enjoyment.

While they greeted each other, Jennifer noticed Drew down by the pool. He faced away from her as he spoke with two other men—one of whom she thought might be his high school friend Brian. At some point they might have to interact, but she assumed Drew would treat her politely while they were around other people.

Leaving Katherine to her friends, she and Ross made their way over to Edward Griffin. He broke from his conversation long enough to say hello but didn't seem inclined to chat, so they moved on. Ross knew most of the guests, it seemed, and introduced her to many of them. After a short while they ran into his aunt Lenora.

When she saw them she waved them over. She wore a flowing purple caftan that swished around her with every movement. "Hello, Jennifer," she said in her warm and gravelly voice, leaning forward over Jennifer's belly to enfold her in a hug. "It's a pleasure to see you again. And congratulations on your pregnancy. You look wonderful, just wonderful. I've never forgotten how kind and helpful you were during the summer I broke my ankle. Moving my bed downstairs, running errands for me."

"It was no problem."

"Well," Lenora said, "I'm not sure I had a chance to thank you properly. I was a bit twirly that year, what with my husband walking out on me. Unhappy business, that. But well in the past, thank the Goddess. You must let me take you to dinner sometime…."

After a minute she turned to Ross, questioning him about work and then asking if he'd ever tried out a yoga class she'd attempted to sell him on—which he hadn't.

"You don't know what you're missing," Lenora chided, shaking her head in good-natured disappointment. "We've got to get you away from the gym. There's more to exercise than treadmills and weight machines."

Ross grinned. "Sorry to be so conventional."

"Humph. Keep it up and you'll end up with one of those overly pumped-up, vein-covered physiques like the Berengers' youngest son."

"Uh-oh. Wouldn't want that."

Jennifer didn't think Ross had anything to worry about. His tall frame had just the right amount of long, sinewy muscle. Athletic without being muscle-bound. But she kept her mouth shut. Tried to pretend she wasn't so aware of his body, his attractiveness.

Lenora switched gears again. "Well, enough of that. Tell me, Jennifer, where do you plan to have your baby? My best friend's daughter just gave birth in her hot tub, if you can believe it."

Ross waited until the two women were comfortably involved in a discussion of home birth, then touched Jennifer's elbow. "Come find me when she finishes with you."

He made the rounds of the party, talking with friends of the family. He couldn't keep from glancing back, though, glad Jennifer seemed to enjoy her conversation with Lenora but feeling more possessive than he'd anticipated.

After thirty minutes he dragged her away with the offer of a plate of food, but lost her again after lunch when one of Lenora's friends took her to meet a psychic astrologer, whose presence at his parents' party mystified Ross to begin with.

He socialized a little more but couldn't get too excited about it. At one point he stood at the railing pretending to admire the view, but actually keeping track of Jennifer from the corner of his eye.

"Lovely girl," his father said from behind him, indicating Jennifer.

Fishing, Ross supposed. He nodded. "And nice, too. She's had a hard time of it. Her mother died last fall."

"Didn't realize the two of you were so close. How does Drew feel about this?"

Ross gave his father a sideways look. "What does Drew have to do with it? He's married. He shouldn't be worried about what his ex-girlfriends do."

His father conceded the point. "How long is she staying with you?"

"Until she can find a place of her own. Possibly until after the baby is born."

Edward looked uncomfortable with the prospect. "People are going to talk."

Ross shrugged. Gossip didn't bother him much, and anyone whose opinion he valued would realize he would have married Jennifer already if the baby were his. Or would know the baby *couldn't* be his.

"Mom looks good today," he said, changing the subject.

"Better than she feels, I think. I imagine she'll be exhausted tonight."

"But otherwise fine?"

"She's exercising, sleeping, taking her meds and working on her diet. That's about all we can do."

Ross gazed across the crowd at Jennifer, who glanced up at that moment and gave a small wave. He smiled back at her, hoping his mother continued to recover speedily.

BY THE TIME the thin, wispy-haired astrologer began his impromptu reading of her horoscope, Jennifer

was relaxed and enjoying the party. Drew had disappeared some time ago and she'd lost track of both
Lucy and Ross. But then she spotted them standing
side by side on the other end of the deck.

Before Ross's revelation, the sight wouldn't have
affected her so strongly. Now she viewed them as
two people who'd once been a married couple. She
couldn't stem her reluctant fascination.

The astrologer continued to talk and Jennifer attempted to listen, but her gaze returned repeatedly
to Lucy and Ross. They stood a few feet apart, an
entirely appropriate distance, and seemed to be engaged in a casual, friendly, entirely appropriate
conversation. No doubt they'd done so countless
times in the past two years. In the large gathering
Ross was very good at concealing the negative
emotions he'd allowed Jennifer to glimpse the
other night.

The two of them looked good together, Jennifer
thought. Mr. and Mrs. Perfect. But they hadn't been,
of course, or else they wouldn't have gotten di-
vorced.

The reading ended and Jennifer thanked the astrologer, who was soon distracted by another person
who wanted his interpretation of her natal chart. Jennifer drifted away and wandered over to Lucy and
Ross, not really deciding consciously to do so but
compelled nonetheless.

They saw her coming and made space for her.
Ross touched her arm, his gesture welcoming. Lucy

noticed the contact, but if she had a reaction to it, Jennifer couldn't tell what it might be.

"I was just asking Ross how your job at the free clinic is going," Lucy said.

"Oh, it's fine. Enough to keep me busy but not enough to overwhelm."

"What were you doing before you moved to Portland?"

"I worked for an office supply company. Pretty boring stuff, but the benefits were great."

Lucy sipped from her glass. "Where was that?" she asked. "I forgot to ask the last time I saw you."

"California."

"Really? Where in California? I spent a lot of time in the Los Angeles area as a kid. My grandparents lived there after they retired. We used to go down for all my school vacations. Is that where you were, by any chance?"

"No, I was in San Francisco."

"Oh, that's such a beautiful city. I love it, though I haven't been back in years." She shook her head. "Drew went down on business last year. It was right before Christmas."

Jennifer felt an involuntary flush warm her skin at the mention of Drew's trip to San Francisco. She hoped it didn't show.

"I almost went with him," Lucy continued cheerfully. "But I didn't, and then he had to stay over an extra day. He had to work on a Saturday night, which I couldn't believe, but it was the only time they could talk to this one person they had to depose." She laughed. "I guess it was because it was almost

Christmas, but I got pretty steamed. I'd just gotten pregnant, though I didn't know it yet, and I wanted my husband to come home. He's lucky he brought back a beautiful Hermès scarf. Otherwise all those pregnancy hormones coursing through my body might have made me do something I would have regretted.''

Jennifer tried not to squirm. She felt guilty and wretched. Ross, she noticed out of the corner of her eye, managed to keep his face expressionless. Yet somehow she sensed his tension. She tried to think of something to say, but words failed her.

''Hormone surges,'' Lucy went on. ''The bane of pregnancy.'' She smiled at Jennifer, tilting her head, her lustrous dark hair swinging in the sunlight. ''That was right about the time you got pregnant, too, wasn't it? It would have to be if you're due—'' She broke off, her expression faltering.

Jennifer froze, panicking inside.

''If you're due the week after I am,'' Lucy finished, the smile back in place and the exact same pitch to her voice. ''At any rate, it was quite a week. How long did you say you lived in San Francisco?''

''Nine years,'' Jennifer said, hoping she'd imagined the moment of startled awareness she'd seen on Lucy's face. ''It's a beautiful city at Christmas,'' she added inanely. ''People really go all out with their decorations.''

LUCY REMAINED IN THE CONVERSATION as long as she could stand it, then excused herself and walked carefully inside the house. She felt incredibly fragile, like spun glass. As if the slightest misstep would send her shattering to the ground.

After abandoning her mineral water on the dining room table, she picked her way through the house to the staircase. She clung to the handrail as she climbed, then lost her composure and stumbled down the upstairs hallway to the farthest and most isolated of the guest baths. She pushed inside and leaned back against the door to close it, locking the knob at the same time.

San Francisco. December.

She stepped away from the door and stood in front of the mirror. The glass reflected the opulent surroundings. The marble vanity, the gold-plated fixtures, the exquisite decorator soaps, the plush monogrammed hand towels.

The pregnant woman.

''Get a grip,'' she said, her voice a harsh whisper. ''You're being paranoid. Your husband is *not* the father of that baby.''

Her stomach roiled. Still, it made an awful kind of sense.

There had been that infinitesimal awkwardness when she'd started to talk about California, about San Francisco. Another person might not have noticed it. After all, Ross's expression hadn't changed. But she'd been married to the man for two years, known him almost seven, and she could tell when something made him tense. She'd also seen that faint uncomfortable blush on Jennifer's face.

Lucy told herself to stay calm. To think things through. She was obviously jumping to conclusions.

Drew had given her no reason to distrust him. She must be having some kind of strange hormone surge, just as she'd joked about, one that was affecting her judgment.

Women got pregnant all the time. There were millions of men in San Francisco and any one of them could have conceived that child with Jennifer.

Except none of those men was Jennifer's high school boyfriend. And Drew had been in San Francisco exactly thirty-eight weeks before Jennifer's due date. And Jennifer had come to Portland, moved here in the middle of her pregnancy and was living with Drew's brother. What else would have brought her here except the father of her baby?

She stared at her reflection in the mirror, trying to breathe.

If there was a better explanation, she couldn't see it.

Her gaze dropped to the swell of her belly. The baby growing inside her. She cupped her hands under her stomach, feeling the weight of her child.

What was she going to do?

HALF AN HOUR had passed since Lucy had gone inside, and she still hadn't come out. The party was winding down. Ross had grown increasingly concerned. He remembered the way she'd hidden her growing dissatisfaction with their marriage until the day she'd informed him she wanted to separate. She could control her emotions, and the fact that she didn't seem to have figured things out didn't mean she hadn't.

He should have done something to interrupt the conversation as soon as the subject of Drew's visit to San Francisco had come up. But he'd been on his own mental track, thinking of his brother and Jennifer together last December. Wondering, jealously, what their night together had been like, whether Drew was worth the havoc he'd caused.

And Ross had missed the chance to intervene. But there must have been some way, something he could have said to prevent Lucy from figuring out the truth about Jennifer's baby.

"I need to go see if Lucy's okay," he said to Jennifer. "I'd better do it alone."

She nodded her understanding, and he made his way inside. The caterers had taken over the kitchen, and the rest of the house was empty. He climbed the stairs. The bathroom doors stood open, as did the doors of all the bedrooms except one—the one that had been Drew's.

He tapped on the door. A moment passed and then he heard Lucy's voice.

"Yes?" she said.

The door brushed the carpet as he opened it. Lucy sat on the single bed. She'd been crying and now held a balled-up tissue in her hand.

Ross pushed the door closed. He stood across the room from his ex-wife, keeping silent and still. She had her head down, her eyes focused on the tissue in her hands. She looked up, searching his face.

"I need to know," she said. "I need to know the truth."

"I won't lie to you," he said. He waited for her

to speak again. He wouldn't lie to her, but neither would he tell her a truth she hadn't yet asked to hear.

"Is he...?" She took a breath and tried again. "Jennifer's baby. Is Drew the father?"

CHAPTER TWELVE

LUCY DROVE FOR AN HOUR, north on the interstate, past Vancouver, before turning east onto rural roads. Here the traffic was light and the blurring in her eyes wasn't as dangerous as it had been on the freeway. She drove aimlessly, taking turn after turn as she wound through the countryside in the late-evening light. She wanted to lose herself.

Eventually she made it back to the house. Drew's car sat in the garage, the hood still warm when she checked it the way she'd seen people do in movies. He'd driven separately to his parents' place and had left the party early, saying he needed to squeeze in some work at the office. Had he really gone there? Or somewhere else? She realized she didn't really want to know. Not tonight.

She steeled herself before opening the front door, then walked in. Dropping her purse on the hall table, she looked around her house as a stranger might, seeing it as the shell of an existence.

It was beautiful, with splashes of color interrupting the white and black and gray that were the dominant themes she'd chosen. She loved it, and tonight it felt foreign and unwelcoming. Empty.

She found Drew in his study, staring at his computer screen.

He glanced up at her. "How was the rest of the picnic?"

Lucy took him in. Wondered whether he suspected everything was about to shake loose.

He seemed just like her husband, just like the man she'd been married to for the past two years. Nothing different. Nothing out of place to tip her off.

But Lucy couldn't see him the same way she used to, and she wondered if he would notice. She didn't answer his question about the picnic. She watched him for as long as she could stand to do it and then finally said, "I know."

He met her gaze. "You know what?"

"I know about Jennifer Burns's baby."

For a fraction of a second he actually appeared confused. And then he laughed, the laugh of an innocent person caught up in a crazy situation where, despite the facts, he looked bad.

"That it's supposedly mine? How did that subject come up?" he asked, appearing amused.

"It's not true?"

"Of course it's not truc."

He said it so smoothly, without defensiveness. He didn't redden, didn't fidget, didn't squirm on his expensive leather executive chair.

She wanted to believe him.

It would have been so easy to believe him. To tell herself their life together was what she'd always thought it was, that she'd made the right choice in marrying him.

"Why would she say it?" Lucy demanded.

"I don't know. I really don't."

"Have you seen her recently? Apart from today?" She realized as she said it that she hadn't seen them interact at all that afternoon. Which suddenly seemed odd. Of course, she hadn't been keeping track of either of them. Hadn't seen any need.

Drew sighed. "Yes. Ross dragged me to his house to talk with her. It was before you went over there. I'm sorry I played dumb the other week, but I really hoped to spare you the whole situation."

Lucy remembered the night Drew had gone over to Ross's house. She hadn't bothered to ask what the visit was about. At the time it hadn't seemed significant. Plus, she'd trusted Drew to tell her important things without her having to ask.

"And was that the first you knew about this?"

"Yes," he said.

Lucy walked over to the black leather sofa that lined one wall of the study, forcing him to swivel around if he didn't want her sitting behind his back. He did so. She sat down with her legs crossed on the seat, hands folded on her lap. Stared at him closely as she spoke.

"You saw her in San Francisco."

"She's someone I knew a long time ago," he said. And then he added, "We had dinner together when I was down there in December. It was no big deal."

"Drew, she was your high school girlfriend."

His mouth twisted. "Yeah. We hardly even kissed."

"I'm not really interested in what you did a decade ago. You slept with her in San Francisco, didn't you."

"No." He appeared to be holding on to his patience with an effort. "But she obviously slept with someone around that time. She thinks she can pin this on me because it looks bad for me. I took her to dinner, and so in everyone's eyes it's possible that I did this. She knew it would happen this way."

"She's due exactly thirty-eight weeks after you were there."

"So she says."

Lucy felt a moment of hope. True, they had only Jennifer's word about her date. She could be due any time during the month of September or even halfway into October. But then Lucy remembered Ross's certainty when she'd spoken with him. His absolute trust in Jennifer.

"She'll have the tests done after the baby is born."

Drew didn't take this seriously. "She won't be around by then. She'll have realized she can't get anything out of me and she'll leave before the tests prove the child isn't mine."

"You should have told me."

"I didn't want to worry you. I figured she would have left by now, given up. I guess I was wrong."

Lucy stood up from the sofa. She walked quietly down the hall to the master suite, where she went into the bathroom and locked the door behind her.

She stripped and got into the shower, and it wasn't

until she got under the water that she started to cry again.

THE PHONE RANG as Ross was getting ready for bed. He picked it up quickly so the sound wouldn't wake Jennifer, who'd gone to sleep half an hour earlier.

The line was silent, and then Drew spoke. "Someone," he said, "seems to have told my wife about Jennifer's allegation."

"Lucy made it home." Ross had been concerned about her emotional state, but not so much that he could forbid her to drive.

"Yes, big brother. She's home. Safe and sound. So, what did you tell her?"

"She figured it out for herself."

"She took a wild guess and you confirmed it."

Ross stepped over to his bedroom windows and closed the venetian blinds. "I told you I wouldn't cover for you." Though, seeing Lucy that afternoon, he had wished he'd been able to.

Drew made a frustrated sound. "Can I at least assume you had the tact to conduct this conversation in private? Not in front of a hundred people?"

Not in front of their parents, was what he meant. Ross wished his brother had the guts to say it. But he was scared, of course. He must be. Facing consequences he'd probably told himself he could avoid.

Ross wondered what Lucy had said to him, how she'd handled herself.

"Mom saw her leave," he said after a moment. "Looking upset. She asked questions."

"Oh good Lord. You didn't tell her, too?"

"No. I said she asked questions, not that I answered them." He'd attributed Lucy's grim demeanor to pregnancy–induced moodiness, and Katherine seemed to accept the explanation.

Drew made a relieved sound. "Good. Because if she heard it the wrong way, or believed it... I just wouldn't want to stress her out right now. Not while she's recovering."

"I worry about that, too," Ross said, glad to hear his brother express concern about their mother's health, though not entirely trusting his motives.

"Well, Mom's always been strong. We've got that on our side, at least."

Ross ignored the comment. "You've made a mess here. It's time to start cleaning it up. And it would be easier on all of us if you'd decide to be honest and take responsibility for what you've done." Even Katherine, when she found out, would probably be able to handle it better if Drew could act like an adult.

But he wasn't ready to hear it. "Christ. Spare me another of your lectures, big brother."

Ross thought about counting to ten but doubted it would help. He walked over to the nightstand. "Don't want to hear my opinion? Don't call me."

And he hung up the phone.

JENNIFER AWOKE the morning after the party feeling achy and unrested. She'd tossed and turned, and then, when she'd finally settled down, a painful leg cramp had jolted her from sleep.

Thinking of Lucy, she padded into the bathroom and splashed cold water onto her face. Though she'd known Drew's wife would probably find out sooner or later, the reality of it pained her. As it had pained Ross. The look on his face when he'd emerged from his parents' house yesterday... During the drive home they'd discussed it only briefly, but Jennifer could tell the conversation between him and his ex-wife had been difficult. She imagined what it must be like to confirm to your former spouse that her new one—your brother—had fathered someone else's baby.

For a moment yesterday it had been almost too much for her. She'd almost wished she could disappear and things could go back to the way they'd been. She'd wished Lucy and her child wouldn't have to pay such a price for something that wasn't their fault.

But it had been too late, of course. And even if it hadn't been, Jennifer had to be selfish on her own child's behalf.

Not a situation she enjoyed, but there it was.

Downstairs Jennifer found Ross had already left for a shift at the E.R. She fixed herself breakfast and settled at his desk to go through some exercises in her Web design book—something she tried to do every day now.

Developing some new skills and establishing herself in a more satisfying career would be nice. If possible after the baby was born—if she could swing it—she would take a few classes at the community college, too.

First she tried a few examples from the book. Then, since Ross had encouraged her to use his computer equipment, she connected to the Internet and looked around for a while, searching not for information but for designs she liked. She found a few, picked one of them and printed the page on Ross's color printer. Telling the Web browser to show her the underlying code of the page, she printed this, as well.

She put the two documents side by side. On the left was the attractive Web page. On the right were three sheets of small type that told the computer software how to draw it. As suggested in her design book, she tried to match one to the other.

After she'd spent an hour staring at the sheets, struggling to decipher them, her head was spinning. She got up to make a cup of raspberry leaf tea. No sooner had she poured the water than the doorbell rang. Leaving the tea to steep, she went to answer it.

Edward Griffin stood on the porch. He wore a navy-blue business suit and a grave expression.

"I'm sorry," she said. "Ross isn't here. He's at the hospital until this evening."

Edward cleared his throat. "I came to see you."

Jennifer thought he didn't look particularly pleased about it. Which possibly meant he knew what had happened yesterday—and knew about last December—though she couldn't imagine who would have told him.

She stepped back to let him in. He was a big man, imposing, with gray hair and intelligent eyes. Jennifer suspected he was used to getting his own way.

He entered the living room and waited for her to sit down before taking a chair. She sat toward the front of the couch, back straight, and attempted to handle this encounter with the same kind of poise a woman like Lucy would.

"Drew called me this morning," Edward began, "to explain your return to Portland. He informed me you're trying to blackmail him. That you falsely claim your baby is his."

She understood instantly what Drew had done. Damage control. Lucy must have confronted him last night. He'd called his father to give his side of the story before Lucy or anyone else could reveal what had happened. A preemptive strike. Drew would know, from his years of lawyering, the importance of spinning events in his favor before the other side got a chance. But his version of the story wouldn't hold up for more than a few months, she reminded herself.

"That's the position he's decided to take," she said.

"But you believe he's the father?" He said it simply, as if to confirm her position. Jennifer bristled, though, at the implication: that she'd slept with so many men in December that she was merely guessing the father was Drew.

"He *is* the father."

"Yes." Edward steepled his hands. He rested back in his chair, perfectly at ease. "So you say."

Jennifer kept her voice calm. "Please don't imply I'm lying simply because you don't like my answer."

He held up a hand. "I apologize." He let a moment pass. "But what if he isn't?"

"He is."

"But what if you changed your mind? What if you decided he isn't the father, after all? Went away and left my family in peace?" He paused. "My wife's not well. The thought that you were blackmailing her son would upset her deeply. She would be even more upset if she believed you were telling the truth."

"I could never make such a decision," Jennifer said. "Drew is the father of my baby."

Edward reached into the breast pocket of his suit jacket and withdrew a black leather checkbook. He rested it on his leg and began to write with a gold-barreled fountain pen. The scratch of the nib on the paper was the only sound in the room.

He stopped and held up the checkbook. "What amount should I put?" he asked. "Fifty thousand dollars?"

Fifty thousand dollars. Her head swam at the thought of receiving that amount of money. Money that might have helped to keep her mother alive. Money that, properly invested, would pay for her child's college education.

And then she thought of what she could possibly tell her son or daughter, how she could rationalize selling off a father for any amount of money.

She met Edward's gaze directly. "I'm carrying your grandchild."

He hesitated, as if for the first time making the connection; her baby would be his relation. As if he'd just realized what the child could mean to him. But it didn't last.

"A hundred thousand, then," he said, beginning to write.

"No."

"I can only go so high."

"Please don't offer me any more money. Your grandchild and I will live in a homeless shelter before I accept money from you on the terms you've proposed."

Edward capped his pen but didn't close the checkbook. "If my son made a mistake…" he began.

"He did."

"If he did, then we need to find a way to move beyond this. His happiness is at stake. Lucy's happiness. Their child's. And also my wife's."

Jennifer studied him, understanding his urge to protect his family, impossible though it was. "Let's say I go away. What happens when it turns out I'm telling the truth? Everyone in my family is dead. Do you want your grandchild to grow up without any relatives, without a father or grandparents?"

Edward's gaze dropped briefly to her stomach. His voice was gruff. "You've placed us in a difficult position."

"Your son did that," she said. "He did that when he told me he wasn't married. I'm truly sorry for the pain his actions have caused. But I have no intention of going away." She rose. "If you'll excuse me," she said, "I need to get back to my work."

AT HIS OFFICE DOWNTOWN Edward settled himself behind his expansive mahogany desk. The day's business needed his attention, but he wasn't ready to tackle it yet.

Sighing, he reached for his checkbook and tore out

the check he'd begun to write at Ross's house. The check made out to Jennifer Burns.

He had nothing against her personally. A nice enough young woman, as far as he could tell. But if she was trying to get the better of his son...

This morning when Drew had called, Edward had believed his calm, rationally presented explanation of Jennifer's blackmail scheme and understood his need to get her out of town immediately—even if that entailed secretly giving in. He'd also accepted Drew's claim that none of his investments were easily liquidated.

Edward had agreed to help. What father wouldn't?

But Jennifer's demeanor, her response to his attempt at intimidation, put his faith in his son into question. She certainly seemed to be telling the truth. And if Drew had indeed told her he wasn't married, then Edward wouldn't even have the comfort of condemning her as a knowing home-wrecker.

He didn't like to think Drew had lied to her. Lied to him, too, it would appear. He wanted to trust his son. Wanted to think the past occasions when he'd bailed Drew out of his scrapes had been legitimate, reasonable—because he'd at least been acting on accurate information. But perhaps he hadn't been. And perhaps Drew would have to extricate himself on his own this time.

Edward dropped the check into the shredder that sat beside his desk. The motor came on, the metal blades sliced the paper into ribbons and then it was silent again.

CHAPTER THIRTEEN

Nine years earlier

Sometimes I feel guilty. Sometimes I almost feel as if we're having an affair behind Drew's back. Nothing physical is going on, but whenever Ross is around I'd rather be with him than Drew. And I'd rather be alone with him so we can really talk.

He has this way of drawing me out, and I keep thinking about what he said the time we went to his aunt's house. About me not selling myself short. When I'm with him I don't feel as if I am. But he's in college. He doesn't have to deal with another year of high school. I do, and I don't want to go through it without friends, now that I've had a taste of what it's like to be accepted. The thing is, I'm not sure I'd still have friends if I stopped dating Drew.

The worst part of the whole situation is that even though nothing physical is going on, even though all we do is talk, I'm becoming more and more attracted to him. I guess getting to know him has just made him seem *interesting* to me. I could stare at his face for hours, and I worry that I do it too much, that he'll catch me looking at him one too many times and realize I've got a stupid crush on him and from then on he'll keep his distance.

Sometimes I wish he were boring and repulsive and life could go back to how it was before he came home for the summer. But that never lasts long. It feels too good to be near him.

The whole month of August is like this. Then one night at the end of the summer we all go to a carnival along the river. It's noisy and bright, with flashing lights, music, rides and all sorts of deep-fried things to eat. I'm with Drew and the gang. Ross is there, too, but he's with some of his friends. In two days he's going back East, but I try not to think about that.

I'm actually having a pretty good time with Drew. We're all running around and acting crazy. We ride the Ferris wheel and the dizzy cars. Just being teenagers.

But then Kurt comes back from getting a soda and says he's scored some pot. Everyone decides to go smoke it. This has been happening more and more in the past few weeks. It's awkward for me—I'm just not into it. And it's no fun to sit around watching other people get stoned.

I tell them I'll meet them in half an hour at the stage, where some local bands are performing. I plan just to wander around for a while, but then I run into Ross by the ring-toss game, and he's alone.

"Where is everyone?" he says.

"Getting high."

Ross rolls his eyes. "You'd think they could find something more interesting to do."

He buys me a turn at the ring-toss game. I win this incredibly tacky little stuffed elephant that's supposed to go on your key chain. We start walking together, and soon we're past the edge of the carnival and heading down along the river. The park is about twenty feet above the water level, with a wide paved walkway right against the railing. If you lean over the railing you see the river moving slowly below you. Now that we're away from the buzz and jangle of the carnival, the night is actually kind of peaceful. Little knots of people walk by. The sky is dark and there's no moon.

It's hard to explain what happens next. We're leaning against the railing watching the black water below and talking about, I don't know, Kafka or something, and I'm not paying too much attention because I'm having this huge crush event thinking how I wish it had been Ross up at the top of the Ferris wheel with me because I'd much rather...well, I'd just much rather it had been him—when all of a sudden the mood between us is different. I realize neither of us has actually said anything for a long time—at least a minute. I look up at him. He just stands there staring down into my eyes, and I can tell he's been watching me the whole time I've been spacing out in a haze of longing.

"What?" I say.

Ross doesn't answer. He leans in toward me. Kisses me. He cradles the back of my neck with a warm hand and draws me toward him to deepen the kiss. It's not as if I need the encouragement.

I seem to have slammed into a parallel universe and I'm pressed hard against him without a shred of concern for the fact that he's not my boyfriend—he's my boyfriend's brother. His kiss is everything I've imagined it would be. Achingly tender. Intense, sexy and sweet at the same time. And very grown-up.

Then I freak out. It's as if my brain switched off for a few seconds so I could get this tantalizing glimpse of a forbidden treat, and then, *wham,* it comes back on line to remind me exactly what the hell I'm doing.

I jump away from Ross and cover my mouth as if I could erase what just happened. I can't, though, and I'm certain in that moment I'll always remember exactly what happened and exactly how it felt. Right here by the river in front of everyone walking by. In front of Drew, even? I look around, whipping my head back and forth. I must appear wild. There's no sign of him, no sign of anyone familiar. Probably our public kiss has gone unnoticed. No one will know about it except us.

I say to him, "That didn't happen."

It's a moment before he replies. "Yes, it did."

I'm frantic. "We have to forget it. We have to pretend it never happened."

He gives me a hard look. "You shouldn't be with my brother."

This floors me. We made a mistake here, but

that doesn't mean I shouldn't be with Drew. In the back of my mind I'm aware there are good reasons I shouldn't be with Drew, but I rebel against it when Ross says so. "What are you talking about?"

Ross turns away. He starts walking. Walking farther away from the carnival, farther into the quiet and the darkness.

I go after him, and I have to repeat myself. "What are you talking about?"

"He's not right for you."

"What do you mean, not right for me?"

"Can you honestly tell me what you have with him is worth it?" Ross sounds angry now, but I can't tell if it's at me or himself. "You can't talk with him the way you can with me. He isn't interested. He never will be. What makes it worth settling for such an empty relationship?"

I don't know if he's saying this because a relationship between him and me *wouldn't* be empty, if he's trying to tell me there should *be* a relationship between us. Part of me hopes that's it, but the bigger part of me realizes the idea is silly. For one thing, I can't be sure he's seriously interested in me, even though he kissed me. Maybe it was just a weird moment and he didn't really mean to do it. For another thing, he's four years older than I am. That's a big difference. He's going to be a senior in college. He's going to start medical school a year from now.

And then there's the matter of my dating his

brother, which makes the whole thing seem un-cool. Inappropriate.

I don't answer his question. I don't have an answer because I don't want to think my rela-tionship with Drew is empty, but I haven't taken a hard look at what makes it worth it for me, except that I'll be alone again, without friends, if we break up.

"What are you suggesting I do, instead?" I ask.

"Jennifer…"

The way he says it makes it sound as if he does want to be with me. But I don't want to seem like a pathetic teenager with a crush—so I say the words before he has a chance. They're true, anyway. "I'm in high school, Ross. *High school.*"

There's a long silence, and I'm sure I mis-read him and he wasn't thinking that at all. The silence gets more and more uncomfortable.

"Yeah," he says at last. "Yeah, I know. It would never work."

He's got this dismissive tone in his voice. Mocking. But again, I can't tell if it's himself he's mocking or me.

Shit. This is a total nightmare. I remind my-self he's leaving for college in a couple of days, so at least we won't have to face each other. I wonder why I feel so hurt by his saying it would never work. Maybe it's because I wanted him to say it would, to contradict me about my being a high school girl. I want him to say that we actually do have something special. That what we have is worth waiting for. That being four years apart in age is a big deal right now, but in a few years it won't make any difference at all. I want him to tell me to break up with Drew so I can be with him—someday if not right now.

But isn't that just the stupidest adolescent fantasy? Like he's going to go back to college and pine after me? He goes to Harvard. There must be a thousand intelligent, fascinating women there. Women, not girls.

No, this is all too crazy.

"I'm going back. I told Drew I'd meet him." I turn and head the way we came. I don't look over my shoulder, and soon I know I'm alone.

At the stage Kurt and Heather are listening to whatever grunge band is playing. They say Drew left a while ago to take Molly home because she wasn't feeling well. It's a long time before he shows up. He says he got a flat and had to change the tire, and I'm too shaken to be annoyed he was gone so long. All I want to do is go home.

The next night is Ross's last night in Portland. His parents have planned a family dinner and they invited me, but there's no way I can go. I just can't face Ross again. Drew's annoyed that I don't want to go. He tells me he had to convince his mom to invite me because she didn't want any outsiders at first, and so now he's going to look bad for pushing it so much. I don't care. It was his choice to do that, so he can deal with it. I spend the night at home, alone.

The following day Drew breaks up with me.

He doesn't even do it in person. He calls me up just before I have to go to work. Without even bothering to be nice, he says it's over between us.

I really didn't expect this. I'm caught off guard and all I can say is "Why?"

"I need to move on with my life," he says. "Things with us were fine for a while, but we're growing apart. Everyone can see that. Even Ross has noticed it."

The mention of Ross sends a jolt through me. Did Ross tell him what happened the other night? Surely if he had, though, Drew would have said something about it. He doesn't sound angry with me, just bored.

"What did Ross say?" I ask.

"Look, I know you guys like to hang out. But he's watching out for my future."

"He told you to break up with me?" I can't quite believe what I'm hearing.

"Jennifer, it doesn't matter what he said. He just made me think about whether I really want to be with you. And he said if I didn't, I shouldn't drag things out. So I thought about it last night after talking with him and realized he was right. I mean, you're a sweet girl and I like you, but we're not really a good match. This way we can both find people we'd be better with."

I don't try to argue. I'm not in love with him and I know it. In fact, I admit to myself, I don't even know if I like him anymore.

Still, I'm pretty upset, especially about Ross's involvement in the whole thing.

After letting things lie low for a few days, I call Heather to see if she and Molly want to hang out. She's busy, but the next time I call we make a plan. We go to a movie and I can tell she's just doing it out of pity. I'm not one of the group anymore. I call a few more times, but the message is clear.

When we go back to school, everything returns to the way it used to be. I'm no longer welcome in the cool corner of the cafeteria. I'm on the outside again, and it's almost worse, because everyone knows I was cool for a while. It makes me see, again, how shallow that whole scene is.

So school is awful, and home is, too, because I keep tormenting myself with the thought that Ross will call. Or write. But he never does.

I miss him, but I'm also angry at him. Who did he think he was to push Drew into breaking up with me? That wasn't his decision to make and I'm the one who has to face the consequences, not him, since he disappeared and went back to college. He's probably never felt lonely in his whole life. He's certainly never had to be a loner the way I always end up being.

My mom doesn't know exactly what happened, but she knows something did and she's always coming up and hugging me. It must be something about my expression. I've basically been wallowing in self-pity.

At the beginning of October my mom decides she wants to move to San Francisco. I'm only too happy to go. Before this I always hated my mom's impulsive moves. This time I'm ready for a fresh start. Ready to do things differently.

And you know what? I do. Slowly but surely I make a few friends—real ones this time.

CHAPTER FOURTEEN

IN THE EVENING after Ross's father's visit—an episode she hadn't mentioned—the doorbell rang as they cleaned up from dinner. Ross went to answer it and Jennifer kept working on the pots and pans. Over the hum of the dishwasher she couldn't hear his conversation.

Ross came back into the kitchen, shutting the door behind himself. Jennifer turned to him with a quizzical look. They hadn't closed the kitchen door since Frank had gone back to Kyle and Melissa.

"Who was that?" she asked.

Ross walked closer. He leaned against the counter, one hand on the tile. "Are you up for a visitor?"

"A visitor?"

"Lucy."

Lucy was here? Jennifer felt her body tense up. Another impromptu visit from someone she didn't really want to see.

"She'd like to talk to you," Ross said. "To ask some questions."

Turning back to her soapy pot, she took a moment to rinse it. "Ross, I don't know…" God, what could she say to the woman?

"You don't have to see her if you don't want to."

She inhaled and exhaled. "Is she going to make a scene?"

"I doubt it. I've already told her you didn't know he was married. She understands you didn't set out to hurt her."

Jennifer rinsed her hands. Dried them on a towel. "I should just face her. After all, we'll have to deal with each other for a long time, won't we." She looked up, meeting Ross's eyes. "I'll do it. But I'd like you to be there, if you don't mind. For moral support." She attempted a smile. "And to make sure she doesn't try to kill me."

They went to the living room. Lucy stood by the bay window. As polished and put-together as ever, she wore a cream maternity suit, with gold post earrings that matched a simple gold necklace. Only by examining her could Jennifer see the hint of darkness beneath her eyes. If she hadn't known better, she would have thought Lucy's life was running smoothly.

"Thank you for seeing me," Lucy said. "I'm sorry to barge in. I was in town and…I suppose I just need to hear your side of the story. To hear you say it."

Jennifer watched her for another moment. "I'm sorry," she said at last. "I'm truly sorry. But this is definitely his baby."

Lucy closed her eyes. Accepting it. Believing it. "Ross told me it was a one-time thing."

"It was."

Lucy went to the chair by the window and sank onto it. She folded her hands protectively over her belly. "Will you tell me how it happened?"

"What do you want to know?"

"Did he ask you out or was it the other way around?"

Jennifer sat on the couch.

Ross sat beside her.

"He asked," she said.

At Lucy's urging, she described Drew's phone call. The usual pleasantries between two people who haven't seen each other in years. The playful fishing for whether she had a man in her life. *Anyone going to come after me if I ask you to have dinner with me?*

"Why did you accept?"

She met Lucy's gaze, avoiding Ross's. "Curiosity. To see what he'd become. To find out why he'd bothered to contact me. It wasn't obvious. He'd dumped me...pretty suddenly. I wondered if he would apologize."

"And did he?"

"Yes."

"How smooth of him. And after dinner?"

Ross leaned back against the cushions, but he was not relaxed, despite his posture.

Jennifer caught herself watching him out of the corner of her eye, wondering what he was thinking. With an effort she brought her gaze back to Lucy. "We stopped at a park and talked in his rental car for a while. Then he drove me home."

Lucy wrapped her arms more tightly around herself. "You invited him in?"

"Luce," Ross said. "You don't have to do this to yourself."

She shook her head. "No, I have to hear it."

"He asked."

"And then you had sex."

Jennifer winced. "Yes."

Lucy closed her eyes, pain evident on her face.

Jennifer stayed silent, thinking of that night, regretting everything but the child inside her. She'd known immediately that letting Drew into her bed had been a mistake. Something hadn't connected between them and the sex had been impersonal and unfulfilling. When she'd wakened in the morning, she hadn't been surprised to find he'd departed without a goodbye. She'd filed away the little white square of notepad paper on which he'd written his phone number, never planning to use it.

And then she'd missed her period. Taken a pregnancy test.

Even now, she remembered that moment with complete clarity. The sense that her life had changed irrevocably sometime in the past and she'd just then learned it. The knowledge that things would never be the same. But she'd been certain she would accept the challenge. Her mother might have been taken from her, but another life had been given. A new person. Someone she would love unreservedly and unconditionally, whose existence would help her go on with her life.

Ross got to his feet. "I think we've accomplished our purpose here. As you can see, Lucy, it's perfectly obvious she's telling the truth. Now it's up to Drew to figure out what he's going to do about the baby. And up to you what you want to do about your marriage."

Lucy was still for a moment, then rose. She went to the front door, where she turned. "I do believe you," she told Jennifer. "And I'm very sorry my husband did this to both of us."

Ross walked Lucy to her car briskly and silently. Surprised by the abruptness of it all, Jennifer stood in the open doorway, hand on the frame, as he said good-night and watched Lucy's white Mercedes disappear down the street.

Striding back to the house, Ross seemed tense and angry. He softened a bit as he approached her, though, stepped inside and closed the door with a gentle *click*.

"You okay?" he asked her.

"Fine, I guess."

"Could have been worse."

"Yeah," she said. "Yeah."

He headed for the hallway. "I've got some things to do before tomorrow. I'll be in my office."

He disappeared, leaving Jennifer in the entryway, feeling lonely and abandoned.

She had hated to have to talk about his brother in front of him. What had happened with Drew sounded so awful. As if she were just easy, or had been carrying a torch for him all these years. She wanted to set Ross straight, to explain the circumstances. Try to make it look a little better. She didn't want him to think badly of her.

Jennifer took a minute to work up her courage and then walked down the hall to his office. The door was closed. She knocked.

"Yes?"

She turned the knob and opened the door. Ross sat behind his desk, staring at the screen of his laptop.

"Ross," she said.

"What?"

"Thank you for being there. While Lucy was here.

Play the
LUCKY
Carnival Wheel
Game....
GET YOUR
3 GIFTS
FREE !
PLAY FOR
FREE !
NO PURCHASE
NECESSARY !

How To Play:

1. With a coin, carefully scratch off the 3 gold areas on your Lucky Carnival Wheel. By doing so you have qualified to receive everything revealed—2 FREE books and a surprise gift—ABSOLUTELY FREE!

2. Send back this card and you'll receive 2 brand-new Harlequin Superromance® novels. These books have a cover price of $5.25 each in the U.S. and $6.25 each in Canada, but they are yours ABSOLUTELY FREE.

3. There's no catch! You're under no obligation to buy anything. We charge nothing—ZERO—for your first shipment. And you don't have to make any minimum number of purchases—not even one!

4. The fact is thousands of readers enjoy receiving books by mail from the Harlequin Reader Service®. They enjoy the convenience of home delivery…they like getting the best new novels at discount prices, BEFORE they're available in stores… and they love their *Heart to Heart* subscriber newsletter featuring author news, horoscopes, recipes, book reviews and much more!

5. We hope that after receiving your free books you'll want to remain a subscriber. But the choice is yours—to continue or cancel, any time at all! So why not take us up on our invitation, with no risk of any kind. You'll be glad you did!

A surprise gift

FREE

We can't tell you what it is…but we're sure you'll like it! A

FREE GIFT!

just for playing **LUCKY CARNIVAL WHEEL!**

Visit us online at
www.eHarlequin.com

LUCKY Carnival Wheel

Find Out Instantly The Gifts You Get Absolutely FREE!

Scratch-off Game

Scratch off **ALL 3** Gold areas

YES! I have scratched off the 3 Gold Areas above.
Please send me the 2 FREE books and gift for which I qualify! I understand I am under no obligation to purchase any books, as explained on the back and on the opposite page.

336 HDL DNWU   135 HDL DNWK

FIRST NAME

LAST NAME

ADDRESS

APT.#

CITY

STATE/PROV.

ZIP/POSTAL CODE

Offer limited to one per household and not valid to current Harlequin Superromance® subscribers. All orders subject to approval.

(H-SR-08/02)

© 2002 HARLEQUIN ENTERPRISES LTD.
® and ™ are trademarks owned by Harlequin Enterprises Ltd.

The Harlequin Reader Service®—Here's how it works:

Accepting your 2 free books and gift places you under no obligation to buy anything. You may keep the books and gift and return the shipping statement marked "cancel." If you do not cancel, about a month later we'll send you 6 additional novels and bill you just $4.47 each in the U.S., or $4.99 each in Canada, plus 25¢ shipping & handling per book and applicable taxes if any.* That's the complete price and — compared to cover prices of $5.25 each in the U.S. and $6.25 each in Canada—it's quite a bargain! You may cancel at any time, but if you choose to continue, every month we'll send you 6 more books, which you may either purchase at the discount price or return to us and cancel your subscription.

*Terms and prices subject to change without notice. Sales tax applicable in N.Y. Canadian residents will be charged applicable provincial taxes and GST.

If offer card is missing write to: Harlequin Reader Service, 3010 Walden Ave., P.O. Box 1867, Buffalo, NY 14240-1867

BUSINESS REPLY MAIL
FIRST-CLASS MAIL   PERMIT NO. 717-003   BUFFALO, NY

POSTAGE WILL BE PAID BY ADDRESSEE

HARLEQUIN READER SERVICE
3010 WALDEN AVE
PO BOX 1867
BUFFALO NY 14240-9952

NO POSTAGE
NECESSARY
IF MAILED
IN THE
UNITED STATES

I'm sure it was awkward for you, having to hear about…''

He shrugged away her words. ''It was no big deal.''

''Ross, I need to explain.''

''You don't need to explain anything.''

''Yes, I do. Why I slept with him. Why I—''

Ross stopped her with a raised hand, the gesture so like his father's. ''Look, Jennifer. If it's all the same, I really don't want to hear the details about you having sex with my brother.''

Because he was jealous? Because he cared about it, about her, more than he wanted to admit?

''Why I made the biggest mistake of my life,'' she continued, ignoring his request for her to stop. ''Because I was missing my mom like crazy and it was going to be my first Christmas without her. And into my life walked this piece of my past, someone who'd known me before everything went downhill, before she'd gotten sick. And it was just so…comforting that I let myself do something I never should have done. It doesn't matter whether or not he was married—I shouldn't have slept with him no matter what.''

Because it was you I was thinking of. It was you I wanted to be with, you I wished had called me up out of the blue and swept me off my feet.

But she couldn't say that. Not when their lives were already so messed up. Not when she was carrying his brother's baby, and he'd been married to Lucy, and his father wanted to give her a hundred thousand dollars to disappear. And not when she'd never been entirely sure how he felt about her.

Maybe that was what it all came down to. Maybe she was just a coward.

Ross closed the laptop. In the quiet room she heard the soft click of the latch.

He watched her. "Have a seat," he suggested, indicating the chair on the other side of the desk.

She did so, perching.

Ross leaned forward, resting his hands on the lid of the computer. The single desk lamp washed his serious features with a warm light. "Thank you for telling me."

She relaxed into her chair. "I thought you didn't want to hear it."

"I didn't." He gave a rueful smile. "But I needed to. And I'm sorry if I was gruff with you."

Her gaze slid downward to the close-grained surface of his desktop. "It's okay."

"No, it's not. And now it's my turn to explain." He waited for her to raise her head, for her to give him her full attention. "It makes me nuts to think of the two of you together. I hate it that it does. But there it is. It drives me crazy. It does now and it did nine years ago."

Jennifer couldn't formulate a reply. She sat across the desk from him and didn't move.

Ross picked up a book lying next to his laptop. He rose and went to the bookcase to reshelve it. His arm dropped back down to his side but he didn't turn to face her. "That night," he said. "After we kissed by the river. I pushed him to break up with you. I shouldn't have done that behind your back. I shouldn't have tried to affect the course of your life. But I just couldn't stand the thought of him being with you when I couldn't."

His words filled her with a crazy kind of joy and a gentle, aching sadness, and she knew she'd been wanting to hear them, even though they would make it that much harder to live in his house and be near him.

"You never wrote," she said. "You could have written."

He returned to his chair, standing behind it. "You were in high school—"

Her own words back at her.

"And you'd dated my brother. It didn't feel right. It felt wrong."

She thought of what Drew had done to him by courting Lucy, by marrying her. So much worse. There were rules about relationships, rules about whom you should and shouldn't have them with. And some people didn't follow those rules. Some people didn't care who got hurt when they did whatever they wanted, slept with whomever they wanted.

"Ross," she said. "Your brother and Lucy…"

He read the compassion in her face and waved it away. "I'm sorry I was such a bear just now. I'll try to be nicer."

ROSS HAD THE NEXT DAY OFF from the hospital. He put in some volunteer hours at the free clinic and had lunch with Barbara and Kyle. In the afternoon, after running errands and working out at the gym, he came home, to find Jennifer in the laundry room washing baby clothes.

Melissa had dropped off several boxes of Emily's old things. Jennifer was sorting through snap-closing body suits and receiving blankets, with a pleasantly sappy expression.

He lounged against the side of the washing machine as it rumbled through its cycle. Picked up a tiny yellow baby sock. "Hard to believe Emily was ever small enough to fit into this."

Jennifer smiled.

He still regretted his testiness the night before. Wanted to make it up to her. "We'd better go buy you some baby furniture. You'll need somewhere to put all this stuff."

She opened her mouth as if to say no, but paused as he hopped up to sit on the washer. "What put you in such a good mood?" she asked.

"Go ahead." Ross grinned. "Tell me all the reasons we shouldn't."

She laughed. "Because the baby and I will only be here for a short while."

"Right. So? You can take it with you when you go. Next?"

"I'd prefer to get stuff at garage sales," she said. "Cheaply."

"The baby's due in barely two months. You don't have time. If you did, it'd probably be fun to hunt down everything. Too bad. Next?"

"I don't know. I can't really afford it."

"My gift to the baby. Next?"

She gave him a fake glare. "You're being very annoying."

"Guilty."

"No matter what I say, you'll still drag me out shopping."

"True."

"So I might as well give in."

"Yup." He swung down to his feet. "Let's go."

Jennifer gave a good-natured sigh. "I'll get my purse."

Twenty minutes later, Ross parked in the lot of the Baby Castle, a children's furniture store located in an old warehouse on the east side of the river.

No matter what else was going on, they still had a baby to prepare for. Soon Jennifer's pregnancy would make a trip like this more tiring and she wouldn't have as much energy to get everything in order.

He ushered her across the parking lot and into the building, a cavernous space containing every kind of furniture and accessory for babies and children. As they walked past beds shaped like race cars and spaceships, past dollhouses, child-size dressers and desks, he thought about his parents, who were still apparently in the dark about Jennifer's baby. He hoped they stayed that way as long as possible. He certainly didn't expect Drew to tell them the truth, and it was hard to see what Lucy would gain by it.

In the infant furniture area he steered Jennifer toward one of the larger changing tables, with drawers and cabinets to hold all of the stuff Melissa had lent her. The size of a regular bureau, it had two levels— one for diaper changes and a taller part for extra storage.

But Jennifer wasn't convinced. "It'll fit in your spare bedroom, sure, but what am I going to do when I move out on my own? I won't have the space."

"Your place won't be as tiny as what you apparently expect."

"You saw that apartment…"

"If that's the situation you end up in, I will, one,

eat my shoe, and two, sell this lovely piece in *my* garage sale.''

They moved on to cribs, where she was even more reluctant. She looked at the tags. ''These prices are crazy. Especially for something I don't even want.''

''I thought everyone wanted a crib. Basic baby furniture.''

She met his gaze. ''Actually, I want the baby to sleep next to me at night.''

In her eyes he saw the love she felt for her child and he knew he wanted her to feel that way about him, too. Wanted this to be their own son or daughter they were buying furniture for. But that wasn't possible.

He wouldn't be happy when she left. All her talk of taking the furniture with her, talk he'd started, kept reminding him she would be moving on with her life in a few weeks or months. She might not have any romantic interest left in Drew, but in the best-case scenario Drew would become her reluctant protector, providing for her and her child. Ross would be on the sidelines.

He didn't want her to move out of his house. He didn't want to have to make special arrangements to see her rather than just to stick his head out into the hall.

Jennifer stepped away from the crib area. ''In San Francisco I was planning for the baby and me to share a bed,'' she told him. ''It's called co-sleeping. I've done some reading on the subject and it's wonderful for the babies. Don't you think it makes sense?''

''I guess I never considered it.'' He and Drew had slept in cribs.

"For a baby to be able to sleep right next to its mother, to bask in her warmth and be able to turn to her for comfort whenever it wants? That seems so much better than having to spend all those hours alone in a separate room, or even in a crib in the same room."

Ross asked about safety, and they looked together at various designs for co-sleeper units, little sidecars for the bed, in which an infant could sleep and still be within reach of its mother, but not risk falling off the bed or getting tangled in the bedding.

He listened to all she had to say and then put his hands on her stomach.

"The baby's not moving right now," she said.

"I know. I'm just thinking what a lucky kid this is."

"Lucky?"

He looked down at her. "It has you. You're going to be an amazing mom."

She seemed to lean in to him at the compliment, allowing the weight of her belly to rest in his hands. But then a flicker of sadness crossed her face.

"Sometimes one parent isn't enough."

"Maybe," he said. "But I still think your baby is incredibly lucky to have you as a mother."

"Thank you," she said, voice soft. "I appreciate hearing that."

She hadn't pulled back. He still cradled her belly. It was bigger now than it had been a few weeks ago, he noted, and warm against his palms.

"She asleep?" he asked.

"Uh-huh. Or he. It's been half an hour or so since I felt movement." She smiled. "Sometimes I miss the wiggling when the baby's at rest."

He looked down at her face, so beautiful to him and so close. He wanted to kiss her but fought the urge.

Not here, he told himself. Not now. Maybe not ever.

He felt an all-too-familiar anger at his brother. For what he'd done to Jennifer. She didn't deserve for her baby's father to try to evade his responsibilities. She deserved happiness. Someone who could cherish her and her child and make a real family with her.

And he also felt angry at Drew for what he'd done to *him*. For putting him in this position, for throwing Jennifer back into his life in such an impossible way. Even if Ross had been able to circumvent his own conscience, there was Jennifer's, as well. And she didn't think a romantic involvement between them was any more acceptable than he did.

When he'd offered her money that first day, urging her to go away, he'd told himself he was only protecting her and the innocent bystanders. But that wasn't the whole story. He'd been protecting himself, too. He'd known that if she stayed, he would fall for her all over again. And he'd known that this time, not having her would be much more painful.

Gently he released Jennifer's stomach. He smiled down at her, trying to recapture his previous good mood. "Come on," he said. "Let's pick out what we're going to buy. And after that I'll take you out to a movie. You need to watch as many as you can while you still have the chance."

LUCY WALKED through the house one last time, confirming her decision to ask Drew to move out. She looked at the flowers she'd arranged on the piano, the paint colors she'd chosen, the view outside, which she'd sculpted with the help of the best landscaping firm in the Vancouver area. This was a house in which she'd wanted to raise a child, create a family. But that wouldn't happen now, at least not the way she'd envisioned.

She felt torn between wanting to keep the house for herself and wanting to move out and get a fresh start. But to move out meant she would be the one making the sacrifice. She shouldn't have to do that when this wasn't her fault.

Yes, she'd made the right decision.

And what choice did she have? She could let him stay in the house, in the marriage, in her bed, as if nothing had happened. But what kind of a life was that? He'd broken something in their relationship and she didn't think it could be fixed.

When Drew got home from work, she met him in the front hall and said a sentence so unoriginal that it almost caught on her tongue. "I think you should move out."

Drew blinked at her. She didn't say anything, waiting for him to respond and absolutely unperturbed by his surprise. He tried to form words, tried to gauge the situation to determine how to play it, how to lawyer his way out of it. She saw someone she didn't want to be married to, someone she couldn't respect, much less trust.

"Lucy," he said.

She let a shuttered expression be her answer.

"Lucy."

"You crossed a line."

He slipped out of his suit jacket and unknotted his

tie. "I should have told you about taking her to dinner. That was my mistake."

She couldn't believe he still wouldn't admit the truth. "I can't live with you right now."

"And in the future, when she goes away?"

"Doubtful."

Drew looked upset by her answer, but she had no other answer to give. Right now, she couldn't imagine when she might want to live with him again.

He'd helped to create the life inside her, and she knew breaking up their marriage would have huge consequences. Consequences that would shape her son or daughter's life. *My parents separated before I was born,* her child would have to say. And would she or he ever know Drew at all? Would he do a disappearing act? Would he be as bad a father as he was a husband?

She felt so ill-used. If she'd known her husband was about to sleep with another woman, about to conceive a second baby, she wouldn't have wanted to get pregnant. No matter how long she'd been waiting to do so.

"We'll need to figure out how we're going to handle things," she said, resting her palm on her belly.

"What are your thoughts?"

"I don't know yet. It's complex. You should think about what you want."

"But I probably shouldn't be too attached to getting it."

"No."

He didn't seem to have anything more to say to this.

She turned away. "Let me know where you'll be. How to reach you."

"I'll be at the Regency."

Lucy imagined the gossip when friends and associates found out he'd moved to a hotel. Felt another wave of anger at Drew for doing this to her, when all she wanted was to be private and take care of her pregnancy and make plans to be with her baby.

She reached for her car keys. "I'll be back in a few hours. Pack what you need."

"You'll be changing the locks?"

"Is that necessary?"

He stuck his hands in his pockets, pouting a little. "No."

"Good, because it didn't occur to me."

"Thank you."

She opened the front door. It was a beautiful day, the sun clear, the temperature perfect. "I'm not sure you should be thanking me."

"It *is* my house," he reminded her after a pause.

Lucy didn't answer at first, just stared him down with a look she doubted he'd ever seen on her face. She could afford lawyers, good ones. If he wanted to make this a battle, she would meet him head-on.

She hoped it would go another way.

CHAPTER FIFTEEN

WHEN THE MOVIE ENDED, Ross insisted on taking her to dinner. Jennifer went along willingly, enjoying this time spent with him. She'd needed a break from the stress of the past few days and suspected he did, too.

She still hadn't told him about his father's visit and had decided never to burden him with it. The event didn't reflect particularly well on Edward and she didn't want Ross to think badly of his father. Especially since she suspected Edward had believed her in the end—though she didn't know what effect, if any, that would have.

It was late by the time they got home. When they pulled into the driveway Jennifer saw a red BMW parked behind her station wagon.

"Is that Drew's?" she asked.

Ross sighed as he pulled up behind it. "Yes." After a pause he put the car into park, then shut off the ignition. He pulled the key out and looked over at her. "I guess he decided to pay us a visit."

The interior of the house was unlit. They walked around to the backyard and found Drew sitting on a lounger in the middle of the lawn. He wore his lawyer-at-leisure clothes: khaki pants, a white oxford shirt open at the neck, tasseled brown loafers.

Jennifer lagged a few paces behind Ross, waiting to see what direction this would take. If Drew had only come to talk to his brother, she didn't want to be involved. Of course, she didn't particularly want to be involved if he'd come to talk to *her,* either. She hadn't spoken with him since the first night she'd arrived, and that had been fine with her.

The backyard was dark and cool. Pleasant, had it not been for Drew. A slight breeze had picked up while they were out. It wafted the scents of lush summer growth and freshly cut grass to her nose. From a neighbor's yard came the familiar rhythmic sound of a sprinkler.

It was the kind of summer night when people had their windows open and the divisions between inside and outside, home and neighborhood, became less distinct than usual.

As if he were aware of how sound would carry on a night like this, Ross spoke softly. "Hello, Drew," he said, the words coming without any particular warmth.

Drew picked up a long-neck bottle of beer from the grass beside the lounger. He tipped it back and took a big swallow. Jennifer saw the outline of several empties on the other side of the lounger.

Drew dangled the bottle from his fingers. He smiled, but not with pleasure. "Rat bastard," he muttered.

Ross didn't appear to react to the insult. Jennifer

guessed he would respond in his own time, in his own way.

"Looks like you've been drinking," he said.

"Yup."

"Sounds like you're drunk."

"Getting there."

"My beer?"

Drew shrugged. "Your back door was unlocked. I got bored."

Jennifer cleared her throat. "Should I leave you guys to it?"

Ross glanced over his shoulder at her. "Maybe that would be a good idea."

She stepped up onto the porch and reached for the doorknob.

"Wait," Drew said.

She paused, half turning back to them.

Ross said, "If you want to talk with her, you can do it when you're not drunk."

"I'll do it whenever I damn well please," he said. "I'm the one she's blackmailing. I'm the victim here."

No one said anything, and eventually Drew seemed to realize that he sounded like a complete ass. But instead of apologizing, he took another swallow of beer, muttering "And screw you both" into it.

"Go home, Drew."

"Can't," he said. "She kicked me out."

Jennifer had thought this might happen, but it still sounded drastic and final when Drew said it. She hadn't come here to break up a marriage.

Ross said, "I'm sorry to hear that," though he didn't really sound as if he were.

"Go to hell," Drew snapped. "I'm not leaving here until everything is fixed. I want you—" he pointed at Jennifer "—out of my life. Permanently. Forever. For good. I don't want to hear any more crap about blood tests. And I'm going to give you a very generous amount of money to convince you to keep your problem yours, instead of trying to make it mine."

"Wouldn't that be giving in to blackmail?" Ross asked.

"I want my family back."

"How much are you prepared to pay her?"

"Twenty-five."

Ross looked at Jennifer. She shrugged. It wasn't an offer she would ever be interested in. Certainly not after turning down four times that much.

"Twenty-five and I never hear from you again and neither does Lucy or anyone else in my family. Then she'll know you were lying and everything will be better."

Ross waited a moment before speaking. He sat sideways on the top step of the porch and leaned his back against the post. He had his knees bent, one foot on the step below. "Twenty-five?"

"Yeah."

"Final offer?"

"Yeah."

Ross seemed amused by the whole interaction. "Pretty measly amount," he observed.

"She doesn't deserve more. She ruined my life."

"You're the only one who did that, Drew. All she did was tell the truth."

"Screw you both."

"They teach you how to negotiate like this at law school?"

Drew made a sound of disgust. "So you're rejecting my offer."

Jennifer wasn't sure if he directed the comment at her or at Ross, but she answered "Yes."

"Why?" he demanded. "Besides the fact that you want to ruin my life."

"The terms are unacceptable."

"Ah," he said knowingly. "I get it now. You don't want to have to part from your new best friend. You've got a cozy thing going here with Ross and you want to milk it for all it's worth, don't you." Drew turned his attention to Ross. "She's taking advantage of you and you're letting her."

"She's carrying my niece or nephew," Ross said in a quiet voice.

Drew didn't heed the warning. "She's a gold-digging whore. Kurt was right about her back in high school. She was after the big score, trying to hook me by holding out on the main course. Well, you're cute, honey. But you're not that cute. And it looks like you've loosened up on your precious moral code since then. I bet the lucky bastard who got you pregnant enjoyed it."

Jennifer tried not to rise to the bait, tried to let the insults wash over her. Drew wasn't worth it. What she felt, most of all, was a crushing sorrow that this man was her baby's father. And the growing realization that even if he'd wanted to be in his child's life, she wasn't sure she could allow him there.

Ross had gone very still. "You're drunker than you think."

Drew scoffed. "You just want me to shut up before I ruin things for you. Think you're going to be able to sample the merchandise if you ride to her rescue like a gallant knight?"

"Jennifer," Ross said, getting to his feet, "would you mind calling a cab for my brother?"

She hesitated. "You're not going to hit him."

"I'm tempted."

"Go on," Drew goaded. "Hit me."

"No."

"Scared?"

"No."

"Come on, hit me." Drew stood and stuck out his chin, making an easy target.

Ross deliberately looked away. "Everyone always gives you want you want, Drew. It's time you learned to deal with not getting it."

"Ah," he said. "Tough love."

"Call it what you want."

"I call it you're scared to hit me because Jennifer doesn't want you to. You think if you go against her wishes, you'll ruin your chances of sleeping with her. Well, I wouldn't be so worried about it. She's not that great in the sack. Not exactly a tigress. More like a cold fish."

Jennifer could see Ross's whole body tighten. She was gratified that an insult to her, no matter how meaningless, upset him so much. But she didn't want him to get drawn into Drew's game. She said his name. When he turned slightly she shook her head.

"It's okay," she said. "It really is. I was cold with him because I already regretted it. And anyway," she added with a small smile, "he's a premature ejaculator."

But she shouldn't have said it. Drew swung, his face ugly with anger. Ross deflected the blow with a relaxed but quick movement. Almost faster than Jennifer could watch, he grabbed Drew's fist and pulled it past him, leaning his shoulder into Drew's arm. Jennifer heard the crack of a bone breaking as Drew flipped to the ground, landing heavily on his back. He started to curse, filling the soft night air with his yell of pain and frustration.

"You broke my arm!"

Ross stood over him. "Sorry. I'm out of practice." He looked up at Jennifer. "I'm going to take my brother to the hospital. I'd make him drive himself, except he's a danger to other people on the road. I don't want him anywhere near the wheel of a car."

"I'll come with you."

AFTER ROSS SPLINTED the broken arm and secured it in a makeshift sling, they bundled a subdued Drew into the back of the Camry and buckled him in. Jennifer handed him an ice pack and sat in the front seat for the short drive to the hospital where Ross worked.

They parked in the lot by the emergency room and walked to the entrance. Drew kept his distance from them, and she was grateful he'd stopped talking after his arm broke.

Ross knew the people at the reception desk and the triage nurse who processed Drew into the system.

"You want to go back and fix him up yourself?" she asked.

"Nah. We're not in a hurry."

"Have a seat, then," she told them. "It could be a while. I guess you could always do some paperwork, huh?"

They walked over to the waiting area. Jennifer and Ross took seats next to each other and Drew sat alone across the aisle. A dozen other people occupied the room, but none was close to them.

No one spoke. After a few minutes Ross reached for a couple of battered magazines. He handed her one. She took it and leafed through it.

Eventually Ross put his down. He glanced at Drew, then at her. "As long as we're stuck here, I've got a ton of stuff to catch up on. You'll be okay out here?"

"Sure."

"Bet you wish you'd stayed home."

She shook her head. "It's fine."

Ross went off to the back of the E.R. Jennifer was actually glad to have the time alone with Drew, despite the awful things he'd said. They needed to talk.

Watching him for a moment, she wondered what he would be like if he hadn't enjoyed so many advantages all his life. Everything had been handed to him—his looks, his education, his opportunities and his wealth—sheltering him from anything difficult. If only he'd had a bad case of teenage acne, she thought. Or even a really big nose that kids made fun of all the time—some hardship that instilled just a bit of character in him. Would he have turned out differently? Developed some inner maturity and self-awareness?

And suddenly she pitied him.

She waited until he met her eyes. "You have a choice, you know," she told him.

"What choice?"

"You could just face it."

He looked away again. "Face what?"

"The truth. That I wouldn't be here if this wasn't your baby."

"Can we not talk about this? My arm is killing me."

His sullen tone annoyed her. "It's always something, isn't it."

He didn't answer.

She felt the baby move, and on an impulse she went to sit beside him. She took his uninjured hand and held it against the curve of her belly.

Inside her the baby stretched and wriggled. It kicked right into the spot where Drew's hand rested. He didn't respond at all. He must have felt Lucy's baby plenty of times, she realized, and this was nothing new to him.

She noted how different it was to have his hand on her than Ross's. With Ross she sensed the connection right away. With Drew she was trying to make one, and she detected an increasing resistance in his touch.

She was torn by the situation. By the contrast between her feelings for Ross and her need, for her child's sake, to make some kind of effort with Drew.

She realized this particular effort, however, had failed. She released Drew's hand. He cradled his broken arm with it, pretending that was the reason he'd wanted it back.

Pretending. That was the sum of his life. He was always pretending, trying to stay one step ahead of the truth.

She levered herself up and returned to her original chair. "Drew, do you love your wife?"

"Yeah."

"Really?"

"Yes, damn it."

"Then, maybe you should stop acting as if you don't."

"It's too late."

A nurse came out through the double doors leading to the back. She called a name. A feverish-looking young boy went in with his parents.

Their end of the waiting room was deserted now, the nearest person a middle-aged man who appeared to sleep sitting up.

"Did Lucy say that?" she asked.

"Not in so many words."

"Then, maybe it's not."

He shifted position on the plastic waiting room chair. The movement jostled his arm. He winced. "It's too damn late."

How much of this, she wondered, was about Drew's reaction to the idea of having a baby? Perhaps everything that had happened resulted from his unpreparedness for fatherhood.

"Did you want a child?"

He looked at her belly.

"With your wife?"

He shrugged.

"That's it? A shrug?"

"You weren't this much of a pain in the ass in San Francisco," he said.

"I wasn't so mad at you then. And I didn't know what a screwup you are."

He held up his uninjured arm. "Here, why don't you just break this one while you're at it?"

She smiled, despite herself. "Broken bones heal."

"And you want to do something to me that won't?"

"So you didn't really want children." It was a statement rather than a question.

"I don't know. I guess I was thinking of having them later—and I don't know why the hell I'm even telling you this."

"Because I'm asking." She paused. "Do you want a relationship with your child?"

"How about finding me some morphine."

"How about growing up."

He rose, cradling his arm, and crossed to a window. She followed. The window looked out on a cement courtyard where a few scraggly trees clung to life. Security lights provided minimal illumination without any attempt at beauty.

Drew said, "What exactly are you after, besides my enduring humiliation?"

"Respect. Acknowledgment. A father for my child."

"You want me to divorce Lucy and marry you? Is that it?"

"God forbid. Sleeping with you was stupid enough. Marrying you would be idiotic."

"Lucy did it."

Yes, and Jennifer still didn't understand why. But that was probably something she would never have access to. In any case, she wouldn't encourage Lucy to stay with him now. The only real choice Drew had to make was what kind of relationship he would have with his child. God knew he would probably choose to alienate Lucy completely, drive her away and engineer it so she didn't want him around his baby. Hard to see him making sure they could tolerate each other and do what was best for their child.

But maybe it would happen. And perhaps if he figured out how to be a father to Lucy's child, he might still manage to be a father to hers, as well.

She was no longer willing to count on it, though.

"You know what I think is going to happen?" she said. "I think you won't make an effort with Lucy because you want to pretend you're not responsible, that you're the victim. You'll tell yourself a big story about how you made one tiny mistake and then your wife kicked you out and you never got to have a relationship with your child. That'll be a great line for picking up loser women in bars, but you'll end up an old man, all alone, with a kid who wants nothing to do with you. So just choose. Live your life based on self-pity or else buck up. Deal with having been a total jerk to your wife. She doesn't have much reason to want to live with you anymore, but you have a child together so you're going to have to figure something out. And maybe, just maybe, you could be one of the few fathers who don't abandon their kids when their marriage goes south.''

Drew stared at her. Angry, embarrassed.

''Yeah,'' she said. ''And we haven't even gotten to your other child. Don't start with that B.S. about how I'm trying to extort money from you. Don't even start with it. I'm not going to hear it.''

Drew gripped his broken arm as if he wanted to pass out from the pain.

Again Jennifer felt compassion for him. ''Sit,'' she told him, pointing toward a nearby chair. She sat opposite. ''So,'' she said, ''how are you going to play this? Are you going to keep pretending I'm lying?''

''No,'' he said in a defeated voice.

''Good.''

She'd won an important point, but the man in front of her was drunk and half delirious with pain, and she took as much pleasure in the victory as if she'd just gotten the better of a five-year-old in an argument. Big deal.

Drew held her gaze. ''So, what do you want me to do?''

''Start telling the truth.''

''And besides that?''

She shook her head. Not with impatience but sadness. ''You're going to have to figure that out on your own.''

A few minutes later Ross returned from the back of the E.R. He walked over to their new seats and took one next to Jennifer, putting an arm around her shoulder. "Everything okay out here?"

Jennifer let herself lean in to him just a bit. She nodded. "We had a good talk."

"He behave himself?"

"Yup. I think you should break his arm more often."

Ross smiled, but without much humor. "The last time I was responsible for one of Drew's limbs breaking it wasn't nearly so productive."

Drew gave him a funny look that Jennifer didn't know how to interpret.

Ross changed the subject. "They say about five more minutes."

The three of them waited in silence until the nurse called Drew back.

Once they were alone she said, "I think I may have gotten through to him." But she didn't know how that made her feel.

"Well, good," he said. "Glad you got it all figured out."

She glanced at him, startled. Realized he felt threatened. When he picked up another magazine, she pretended not to notice.

"I want my child to have a father," she said, "but I don't want to have to lead him by the hand, teach him how to be a parent. I want it to come from inside him, to be real and heartfelt. Because I've realized my baby doesn't just need a dad but a dad she or he can trust."

She felt Ross's silent question. *And you think Drew will ever be that person?*

"I'll tell you what I want most of all. I want my child to have someone besides me who will love him or her totally and unconditionally. Someone who will stay in their life forever. That's all I really want."

She knew what it was like to be raised alone by a mother who had no one. She knew how isolated that could feel, how jealous you were of the other kids who had real families. And how when things went wrong, you had only one person to turn to, one person to rely on. And sometimes things went wrong with the parent and it was the child who had to take care of things, as Jennifer had done.

Ross was silent, the magazine closed on his lap. "You deserve that," he said at last, turning to face her, gaze intent. "You and the baby definitely deserve that."

From him? she wondered, knowing now, finally understanding—that she wanted the answer to be yes. Drew could never be as good for a child as Ross would.

She wanted to ask him straight out, *Will you be there for my baby in every way its father can't?* But that meant asking him to choose to be in her child's life—and in hers—for the rest of his.

And she wasn't ready to do that.

DREW CAME OUT OF THE BACK of the E.R. with his arm in a cast and a sling holding it against his body. He looked haggard and exhausted as he approached.

"Six weeks," he said. He held up a slip of paper. "I need to get this filled."

They walked out to the parking lot. Drew climbed into the back seat and fumbled with the seat belt. Jennifer quashed her instinct to help. She didn't think Drew would appreciate it at this point and she didn't want to be any closer to him than necessary.

Ross looked back. "You need a hand?"

"I've got it," Drew said, his voice tight. A moment later they heard the *click* of the mechanism as it latched.

Ross stopped by an all-night pharmacy to pick up Drew's bottle of painkillers, then drove to the downtown hotel where Drew was staying. He pulled up to the curb.

"You'll be okay?" he asked.

"Yeah. Peachy."

"Call me tomorrow. We'll figure out what to do about your car."

Drew looked as if he'd just remembered it. "Crap."

"Yeah, but I wouldn't have let you drive it home, anyway. You'd had too much to drink."

"Always so careful."

"It's the other people on the road I worry about."

"So I could drive off a cliff and you wouldn't care?"

"I didn't say that."

Drew walked away without another word.

CHAPTER SIXTEEN

Thirteen years earlier

It's not exactly running away, because I plan to come back. And I left a note for my mom so she knows exactly where I'm going—to see my father.

The bus ride from the middle of Idaho to Spokane, Washington, lasts forever. I'm on the local, so we stop at every little nowhere town. I sit up front right behind the driver and I keep my headphones on, but still I get all these creepy middle-aged men asking me where I'm headed and why I'm traveling alone.

I'm thirteen and my mother just gave me a crappy birthday present—we got in a fight and she started saying mean things about my dad. I've never met him, at least not that I can remember, but I'm sure it didn't happen the way she said. I'm sure she drove him away, that he wanted me but couldn't stand to live with my mom because she's such a bitch sometimes.

The bus gets in about two o'clock. I looked up his address in the phone book at the library back home, but I was too scared just to call him. I also looked at a map, so I know how to get to his house. It isn't that far from the bus station. I start walking, and within an hour I'm there.

It's a cute house on a street that's got trees all down it and shade everywhere. The front lawns are small but beautiful. It's like paradise. I'm thinking about how he'll welcome me, maybe take me to dinner. And then everything will be okay.

I see a car in the driveway and I get a major case of nerves. I walk around the block, almost shaking, but finally decide that since I took the bus all the way here, I have to follow through. After working up my courage for five minutes, I ring the doorbell.

A woman answers. It surprises me. I don't know why since I should have expected it. She says, "May I help you?"

"I'm looking for Sean Trumbull," I say, only I'm nervous and I swallow my words. She has to ask me to say it again.

"That's my husband, but he's not home now." And she looks at me and adds, "Do I know you?"

I shake my head.

"You look really familiar."

It's then I realize she doesn't know about me, doesn't know my father had another family, because if she knew he had a daughter she'd be able to figure out who I am.

I ask when my father's going to be home, only I don't say he's my father, and she tells me it'll be about an hour. Right then, a car pulls up on the street and two kids get out. They're about nine and eleven, I guess, and they come running across the lawn, so happy and well adjusted that I start to feel nauseated. They hug their mother and then the older one, a girl, turns to me.

"Who's this?"

Their mother says I'm someone who wants to talk to their father and then she invites me in for a snack. I haven't eaten since breakfast and I want to see the inside of my father's house, so I say yes.

I've read about families where the mom stays home and has cookies ready for the kids after school, but I've never experienced that myself, so it's kind of weird. The mom serves up milk and cookies and fruit—the girl actually eats fruit instead of a cookie—and then she excuses herself for a minute. The kids ask where I'm from and I tell them Idaho, and I don't realize my dad's wife has called him at work until a car pulls into the driveway ten minutes later.

I hear the car door slam and then my dad walks into the house. It's a moment before he and the woman come into the kitchen, but when he does I feel my pulse thud. My mom doesn't have any pictures of him, but I know right away it's really my dad. He looks just like me except his hair is blonder. And I think to myself, I'm seeing my father. This is my father, right here, and it's like a new beginning for the world, like time has just started again.

My father stares at me and says to his wife, "No, I don't have any idea who she is."

But I can see his eyes and I'm sure he's lying. He knows who I am and he's afraid. I feel like crying, but all I can say is the truth.

"My name is Jennifer," I tell him. "I'm your daughter."

His wife moans a little and the two kids are watching me with big round eyes like I just stepped off a spaceship. No one knows what to do.

My father points a finger at me. His voice is cold. "I don't know what kind of game you're playing, but I don't have a daughter except for Alice. I don't have a daughter named Jennifer and I don't have a daughter who's thirteen, so get out of my house and leave me alone."

I feel as if the whole world just vanished from under my feet. I wanted him to take me to dinner. I wanted him to ask me about school, about my interests. I wanted him to love me— and he just wants me to leave.

I get up from the table. Slowly, because I feel like I'll fall down if I try to move too quickly. Then I realize I didn't tell him I was thirteen and I didn't tell his wife, either.

I look at him, my father—this man who knows I'm thirteen, even though I only turned thirteen a few days ago—and I feel more lonely than I've ever felt in my life, which is saying a lot.

His wife has a funny expression on her face, as if she's figured it out, too, but my father hustles me out the door. The kids watch me go and so does the mother, but my father follows me out. Like he wants to make sure I leave.

On the step I say to him "But I'm your daughter," as if it will do any good.

He says, "I have a family now. I have children. You shouldn't have come here."

So this is how it is. The final truth. My mom was right. He just didn't want me. He's perfectly capable of being a good father, but he doesn't want to be a father to *me*. It hurts so much I think I'm going to die.

He opens his wallet and pulls out some bills. "Here," he says. "Go home. Don't come back."

I have to take the money because I don't have any of my own. Without it I can't buy a bus ticket back to Idaho. I'm so ashamed as I walk away, so hurt, that when I get to the end of the block, out of sight, I can't even move. I can't remember which way to go, or where I am, or where I should be, and it's not until a cop car pulls up and the woman behind the wheel rolls down her window and asks if I'm lost that I break down and start sobbing.

At the police station they call my mom, and when they put her on the line I can't even talk, but she knows I'm in Spokane and I'm at the police station and she says to me, softly, like she wants to love me enough for it all to go away, like she's rocking me on her knee when I was little, "Oh, honey. Oh, honey. Come home."

ROSS WENT DOWNSTAIRS at six-thirty. As he filled the kettle for his morning coffee he looked out the window above the sink and saw Jennifer kneeling over a bed of daylilies, pulling off dead flowers. She'd spent time working in the garden since her arrival, enough that his gardener had commented on the decreased workload. But she seemed to enjoy the activity.

Waiting for the water to heat, he simply watched her, assessing the change in her even in the past few weeks. Her pregnancy moved inexorably onward. Soon her baby would be born. He suspected that even if the baby came late it would be sooner than they were all prepared for.

When the water boiled he made a cup of tea for her and took it and his coffee out onto the back porch. The mugs steamed in the cool dawn air.

"Good morning," he said.

The porch was in shade, but the sun cast its rays across the garden and on Jennifer as she turned to smile a welcome. Such a difference from the way she'd looked at him that first day on his porch—cautious, nervous, restrained.

Straightening, she levered herself up with her hands on one knee, then walked across the lawn to the porch, her white sneakers wet where the dew had dampened them.

"Couldn't sleep any longer?" he asked as she climbed the steps.

"Nope."

She'd been up early on other mornings, as well, he knew. Her hips bothered her in the night, forcing her to switch from lying on one side to the other every hour or two and finally driving her out of bed.

Ross hadn't slept well, either, thinking about what

had happened with Drew. He'd never seen his brother get quite so ugly. It worried him.

He held out the mug of tea for her. "Raspberry leaf," he said.

Jennifer took the dark earthenware mug by the handle, her fingers touching his. She inhaled over the rising steam. "Thank you."

Ross sat on one of the outdoor chairs. He motioned with his coffee mug toward the other. "Join me."

She lowered herself onto the chair. The knees of her jeans were damp. She brushed away a blade of grass. "Was it really an accident?" she asked. "Breaking his arm?"

He sipped, debating his answer, not knowing what would please her but choosing, inevitably, the truth. "I should have been able to prevent it."

He hadn't set out to break Drew's arm. But at the moment when he could have backed down, thrown his brother differently, he hadn't.

Certainly he was out of practice. He hadn't studied martial arts in years. But he was honest enough to admit he'd wanted to hurt his brother—repay him for the things he'd said about Jennifer. For the way he'd chosen to treat her.

Not his proudest moment. But Drew *had* swung first.

"Does it bother you?" he asked.

She shook her head, the movement gentle. "He had it coming. But you didn't need to defend me," she added, as if she thought it was sweet that he had. "You really didn't."

"You can take care of yourself."

"Mmm-hmm."

He wondered what she would have done if she'd

been alone at the house when Drew came. She probably would have been able to talk him down, no matter how obnoxious he'd been. Send him home with his tail between his legs. All without violence.

"I did fine with him at the hospital," she reminded him.

Yes, she had, hadn't she. Again Ross wondered exactly what had happened between them in the waiting room.

He hadn't particularly wanted to leave her alone with Drew but had needed time away from his brother. Unable to concentrate on his work, he'd slipped out a side door and taken a walk.

"Ross," she said, "I can't imagine what last night was like for you. To have to deal with your brother like that."

He shrugged. "You had to deal with him, too."

Jennifer nodded. "But he's not my brother. I don't love him. I didn't grow up with him."

Her words struck close to home. He did love Drew. He just didn't really like him right now. And that was something else he felt guilty about.

Jennifer sipped her tea. Set it down on the little table between their chairs, watching him. "I'm sorry all this has made things hard between you two."

"It's not your fault."

She held his gaze. "I know. But I'm sorry."

He smiled, appreciating her concern. He wished things were different, too.

They lapsed into silence. The morning was peaceful and he wanted to stay there for a long time, to blow off going to work and just be with her. He knew he couldn't, though he did have a few more minutes.

After last night he thought Jennifer was starting to

let go of her need for Drew to act like a real father. Drew's behavior must have shown her that he could never be the loving, trustworthy person she was looking for.

Ross could, though. Or could have been if their situation were a normal one. But it wasn't, of course, and everything was so much messier than it had been nine years ago.

Compared with this, he realized, kissing his brother's high school girlfriend really hadn't been as big a deal as he'd thought. Hell, he probably should have just stolen her away from Drew back then, instead of wallowing in angst and guilt.

The thought ran through his brain. He liked it.

But of course they would have been too young for it to last. She'd been seventeen. Even if you got past the sheer embarrassment of being a college senior involved with a high school student, there remained the issue of the ways they would each change. No doubt she would have gone off to college and met other men, younger men, men she wouldn't just fall for because they were off-limits.

But if it had worked, if they'd stayed together, he might have been able to help when her mother got sick, taken up some of the slack so Jennifer could stay in college. So she could have gotten a good job and established herself and still been able to look after her mother. Their lives would be totally different.

And she wouldn't have been able to have children. Not with him. Which might have made that situation every bit as difficult as their current one. It had certainly caused problems in his marriage to Lucy.

He watched her sip her tea. Wondered where they

could go from here. He had no easy answers, but he knew he didn't want her to move out of his house anytime soon—which she might, since they'd left her departure date up in the air.

"I've been thinking about your labor," he said.

She looked up. "Oh?"

"I'd like to be there. To be your support person."

Emotions crossed her face. Surprise, gratification, a hint of nervousness. But where it ended was a soft smile. "Okay."

The sun touched the porch steps. A trace of vapor rose from the dew-damp boards. Ross thought of how many babies were born in the early hours of the morning. Imagined a moment, two months from now, when she might lie in bed with her infant in her arms as the sun rose on his or her first day.

"This house," he said, "would be a good place for a birth. It's quiet. It's peaceful. The hospital is nearby. And there's a doctor close at hand."

She digested this. "You're asking me to stay until after the baby is born."

Or longer, but they could work that out later. "I don't think you should be alone in your last weeks of pregnancy."

Jennifer cradled her mug, thoughtful, and he didn't press. At last she nodded.

"Okay," she said. "I'll stay."

CHAPTER SEVENTEEN

MELISSA CALLED HER in the afternoon. She had plans to take Emily to a paint-your-own-pottery place and invited Jennifer to tag along.

Inside the shop Jennifer perused the tall shelves of unfired pottery—dishes, vases, planters, salt-and-pepper shakers and more. As she and Melissa helped Emily to pick out the paint colors, she imagined returning with her own child in a few years—a prospect that made her smile. She couldn't wait to share the world with her baby.

They sat down at a low round table. Emily asked Jennifer to tie her apron for her, and then the girl set to work on the mug she'd selected as a birthday present for her grandfather. She brushed on bold streaks of yellow and orange paint, while Jennifer and Melissa watched and occasionally assisted.

"How's Frank?" Jennifer asked.

"Crazy as ever," Melissa said. "I think she had a great time with you and Ross. Thanks again for looking after her. I'd guess you were in the house with her more than Ross."

She nodded. "And when he's at work it's for pretty long stretches."

"Tell me about it," Melissa said on a sigh. "I hate

being away from Emily for more than an hour, much less twelve at a time.'' She addressed her daughter. ''It's hard, isn't it, honey, when Mama has to go to work all day?''

''Uh-huh,'' Emily said, absorbed in her work.

''But it's extra nice when I get home, right?''

''Uh-huh.''

''And the moon is made of green cheese, isn't that so, Emily?''

''Uh-huh,'' the little girl said in the same tone of voice.

Melissa grinned at Jennifer. ''The thing about being a mom is that everyone appreciates you so much.''

''Uh-huh,'' Jennifer said, mimicking Emily.

Melissa laughed. ''So you have what—ten weeks left?''

''Just under.''

''It goes by quickly. How are the preparations coming along?''

''Pretty well, thanks to you and Kyle. The baby things you lent me are amazing.''

''Glad we could help,'' Melissa said. ''The stuff wasn't doing us much good in the basement, and we're not ready to have a second child yet.''

''Well, I appreciate it.''

After Ross had left for work that morning, she'd continued the sorting and washing she'd begun the day before. Melissa had outfitted her with enough clothes for the baby to change outfits every three hours and still not wear everything. Most of the items were unisex, too. Jennifer had organized the clothes by size and season, and the main task now was to figure out where to store everything.

"We bought a giant changing station," she confided, "but I honestly don't think it'll hold everything you've lent me."

"'We' meaning you and Ross?" Melissa asked.

"Yeah."

Melissa raised an eyebrow. "Buying furniture together. Big step."

Jennifer felt herself color. "It's not exactly like that."

Melissa, thankfully, left the subject alone. "Any other supplies you could use?"

Emily dropped her paintbrush, which rolled across the table out of reach of her small arms. Jennifer rescued it and gave it back to Emily, who rewarded her with a bright smile. "I'm not exactly sure. I have lists from books and magazines but there's a lot of stuff on them that might not be necessary."

Melissa nodded. "We overbought. But I'll tell you a couple of things you should have. A bouncy-seat, definitely. That was a lifesaver in the early months, especially when I was alone with her and wanted to take a shower. And I'm a strong believer in baby slings. They're a great way to carry your baby. Easy in and out, and babies love them."

"I saw some at garage sales in San Francisco, but I didn't know how they worked."

"At first I found it a little nerve-racking," Melissa admitted. "I kept worrying she would fall out. But you get comfortable fast. I'll check again to see if I can find either of ours, and I'll see if I turn up any other goodies while I'm down in the basement.''

"Thanks," Jennifer said. "I guess what I need most of all is the baby."

"You want some practice beforehand? I thought maybe you could look after Emily from time to time in the next couple of months. She seems to like you. I could use a little free time when I know she's well taken care of. Her day care center's great, but there's something about having a friend look after her that's even better."

"I'd love to," she said, complimented that Melissa considered her a friend and that she would trust her with Emily.

"I'll pay you, of course," Melissa said.

Jennifer shook her head. "No. No money."

"I have to pay you or else I'll feel like I'm taking advantage of you."

"Uh-uh. You've lent me hundreds of dollars' worth of baby supplies. Stuff I would never be able to afford otherwise. I'd say I owe you a few hours of child care in exchange for that."

"Oh, fine," Melissa said with good humor. "Be that way."

Emily had finished painting the background on her mug, so Jennifer and Melissa helped her dip her hands in purple paint and put a handprint on each side.

As they cleaned up, wiping Emily's hands with the water and paper towels provided on the table, Melissa said, "I know this is personal, and you don't have to tell me if you don't want. But is the father at least going to contribute some child support?''

''I don't know.'' Maybe she really had gotten through to Drew last night. And maybe he would clean up his act, try to make some kind of effort—but she doubted it. ''Ross thinks it'll never happen.'' At least not the way she'd wanted. ''I guess I'm starting to agree.''

Melissa cocked her head. ''Ross is pretty involved in this whole situation, isn't he.''

Jennifer bit her lip. She needed to confide in someone. ''Have you ever met his brother?''

''Oh, dear. Is he the…?''

Jennifer nodded.

''I wondered.'' Melissa paused, her expression sympathetic. She held Jennifer's gaze. ''That must be complicated.''

''Very. Even more so than I first thought. Drew's wife…'' she stopped, losing her nerve. Not sure if Ross would want her to talk about it.

''Lucy,'' Melissa finished.

''So you know about her?''

''Ross and I started working together when he was going through his divorce. Her marriage to his brother seemed pretty hard on him, though he didn't discuss it much. He's very self-contained.''

''Just a little.''

The two women shared a smile. They finished tidying up, and as they stood Melissa gave her a hug.

''Tough stuff,'' she said.

''Yeah. If it's okay, I'm not really ready for the world to know.''

Melissa nodded. "Won't tell a soul, not even Kyle."

"Thanks," Jennifer said. Having a female friend and confidante, especially one who was also going through the challenges of raising a child, was good.

ON THURSDAY NIGHT Ross returned from dinner well after nine. After a quick stop in the kitchen, he joined Jennifer in the study, where she sat at his desk, hunched over her big belly, squinting at the screen of his laptop.

He stood watching her for a full minute, waiting for her to become aware of his presence. Finally he cleared his throat.

"Just a second," she mumbled.

He leaned against the doorway. She tapped a few keys and then used the track pad to bring up a new window. She hit a button on the window and the screen redrew itself. After peering at it for a moment she said, "Darn."

"What are you working on?"

She glanced over. "Oh, Web page stuff. I'll be done in a minute."

"No rush."

She bent over the book that lay open on the desk beside her. "I'm just trying to make it do this one thing...."

He walked up behind her and studied the page in the book, which was full of lines of code he didn't understand. "I'd offer to help, but I'm clueless."

"It's okay," she said. "I'll figure it out."

Ross put his hands on her shoulders. "You're going to kill your back sitting like this."

He began to knead the muscles, starting first at the top of her arms, then working his way toward her neck. The muscle fibers were tight under his fingers.

"Why are you doing that?" she said, still distracted.

"You look stiff."

"I am."

"Therefore the back rub." *No big deal,* he wanted to add. *It's just a massage of your sore neck and shoulder muscles.* "Relax a little," he told her.

"I'm trying."

"What's holding you back?"

She didn't answer. He figured the real answer was probably "You." But he didn't want to hear it any more than she seemed to want to say it.

After a couple of minutes she put a hand on her belly and held it there. She'd stopped looking at the computer screen.

"The baby moving?" he asked.

She nodded.

Ross bent forward and placed his palm on her. Jennifer slid his hand to the spot where hers had been. He felt the movement. Something poking out, maybe a foot or an elbow, and gliding along.

He stayed like that, caught up in a moment of overpowering curiosity, wondering what the little person inside her would be like. The baby was completely dependent on her and yet already had started to strive for independence. It moved on its own and could suck its thumb, could blink and swallow amniotic fluid.

"Do you ever get used to this?" he asked, meaning the movement, the pressing and poking against her belly.

She shook her head. "Never. And each time it's almost as incredible as the first time I felt it."

The kicking ebbed. Ross resumed the massage. He kneaded the muscles of her neck right where it joined her skull and she let her head flop forward, giving a small sound of pleasure.

When he brought the back rub to a close, he left his hands on her shoulders. "You need to finish up?" he asked.

"No, I'll figure it out tomorrow."

He watched as she shut down the computer, lowered the lid and closed her book after neatly inserting her notes into it to mark her place. She lined the book up against the edge of the desk.

"Did you eat?" he asked her.

She nodded. "More tofu and greens with brown rice. A fruit smoothie with protein powder. A lot of baby carrots." She pointed to an empty bag of carrots in the trash can.

"You're taking care of yourself," Ross observed, leading the way to the kitchen.

She shrugged. "I'd be eating something completely sinful right now if you had it."

"Like chocolate cake."

"Oh, yum. If you had chocolate cake right now…" She looked at him as if she knew something was going on. "You going to tell me I shouldn't have things like that?"

He motioned her to take a seat at the breakfast bar. "I don't think it would hurt. Your diet is pretty healthy."

"I'll say."

"You want ice cream with that chocolate cake?"

"How could I not?"

"Vanilla okay?"

She narrowed her eyes. "Are you trying to torment me or just being insensitive?"

"Neither." He walked to the fridge, opened the freezer and pulled out the pint container of gourmet vanilla ice cream he'd brought home. He read the label. "Four grams of protein per serving. Sixteen in the whole carton. For your growing baby."

"And the cake?"

"Not much protein in that, I'm afraid." He fished a plastic clamshell take-out box out of the fridge. A dense, decadent slice of cake lay within. Three layers alternating with a chocolate ganache icing.

"Oh my Lord."

"I thought you might like it." He took a fork and lifted the slice onto a plate, then put it in front of her along with the ice cream. Then he dug into a drawer and came up with an ice cream scoop. "Go crazy."

She scooped out a big mound of ice cream. "For the protein," she said.

"Naturally." He put the carton back in the freezer. "And even without the protein, ice cream is a wonderful thing."

"I know. Believe me, I know."

She had a few bites, then looked up guiltily. "Do you want some?"

"I got it for you."

"Where?" she asked. "I want to be able to go back."

He named the restaurant he'd eaten at that night. They were known for their desserts, prepared on site by a world-class pastry chef and available nowhere else. It was one of the reasons for the place's popularity.

"You had dinner there tonight?"

The question was offhand, and Ross couldn't tell if it was actually due to her lack of attention or if she was more curious than she wanted to let on.

"With my parents," he said.

"Oh." A pause, and then she took another bite. Another after that. "Are you sure you don't want any?"

No, he wasn't. Ross got a clean fork from the drawer and cut a mouthful of cake from the corner opposite the one Jennifer was working on. He scooped a dollop of ice cream from the ball sitting beside the cake and ate the two together in one mouthful. The ice cream had already begun to melt against the plate. The different temperatures and textures formed a delicious contrast.

He was glad he'd thought to get the cake for her, even though it had meant backtracking to the restaurant after saying good-night to his parents.

She finished her bite, chewing deliberately. "How are they?"

"All right. Mom's making progress."

"And other than that?" She set her fork down, the plate still half full.

"Well, Drew told my father about you. The baby."

"That I'm blackmailing him?" Her expression was wry.

"That you say the baby is his and he says it's not."

"And your mother?"

"Blissfully oblivious," he said, allaying her concern. "She was in the ladies' room when Dad told me about it."

"I assume your father believes Drew?"

"He's concerned. He doesn't know what to think." Ross suspected his father was actually closer to her side than to Drew's but didn't want to say so.

"Really?" she said.

He nodded, wondering if she would volunteer the information about his father's visit.

She didn't.

He smiled at her. "Your ice cream's going to melt."

"Oops," she said, digging in again.

"Bring it outside," he said on an impulse. "The stars are incredible." He grabbed a blanket from the hall closet and led her out, turning off the kitchen lights as they left. "Walk down ahead of me," he told her, and stayed on the porch until she reached the grass, at which point he turned off the porch light, as well.

The backyard was dark, but not so dark he couldn't see the outline of her rounded figure. He joined her on the grass, spreading the blanket and then lying down flat on his back, staring up at the sky.

She laughed. "You're serious."

"Uh-huh." He patted the ground beside him. She lowered herself, leaning onto the hand he offered for support. She set her plate of cake and ice cream on a corner of the blanket and seemed to forget about it.

The combination of crystal-clear air and no moon made for the best stargazing anyone could possibly expect in the middle of a city. He stared upward, telling himself he shouldn't be out here, shouldn't be lying next to her feeling the heat of her body in the cooling air, thinking forbidden thoughts. But he couldn't seem to help himself.

And neither could she, he realized when her hand slipped into his. They lay there, fingers entwined, staring at the hundreds of visible stars.

At last he said, "You could have told me, you know."

"About what?"

"About my father's visit."

She said nothing, just gave his hand a squeeze.

Ross raised himself onto one elbow. "A hundred thousand dollars. That's a lot of money."

"Not for what he wanted me to do."

He knew what she meant. Leave. Raise her baby alone, without any family.

And he knew what he wanted her to mean. *A hundred thousand dollars wouldn't be enough to make me go away and never see you again. A million wouldn't be enough.*

He watched her, and for a moment she pretended to watch the stars, but then she shifted her gaze to his. Her pupils were large and dark. He listened to her breathing, to the little hitch as he put his hand on her hip, settled her against him.

"I'm going to kiss you," he said.

"I know."

CHAPTER EIGHTEEN

BUT HE DIDN'T KISS HER, not right away. He raised his hand to her face and cupped her cheek. Stroked the side of her neck. Buried his fingers in her hair and skimmed along her nape.

She lay very still, captivated, with a wonderfully expectant expression on her face.

He felt like a sixteen-year-old, lying on a blanket on the grass with his first girlfriend. But he wasn't sixteen anymore, thank God, and he felt no need to rush, no desperation. He knew this wouldn't go anywhere and he liked it that way, despite the restlessness he would have to deal with later.

Every curve of her face fascinated him. In the light spilling into the backyard from neighboring houses she looked more beautiful to him than ever.

"What happened to kissing me?" she asked on a light breath.

"I'll get there," he murmured. "Be patient."

She made a little sound that didn't seem at all patient.

Thank God he *wasn't* sixteen anymore or that would have been the moment he lost all awareness of the world, of complications, of their having to face each other in the morning. If he'd been sixteen he would have been checking to make sure he had a condom.

Instead, he aligned his body to hers, taking the roundness of her belly against his stomach, his chest to her breasts, wrapping one leg around hers to lock them together from head to toe. Tormenting himself.

He felt her melt against him, breathing shallowly, as caught up in the moment as he was.

Burying his fingers in her hair again, he brought his lips to her forehead, inhaling the scent of her. He made a trail of kisses to her temple and along her cheekbone. He savored the softness of her cheek, then slowly lowered his lips to hers.

When he kissed her she moaned. Her lips were warm, slightly parted, and when he deepened the kiss her mouth tasted sweet.

The night air cooled their skin. He heard crickets and a car that passed on the street out front, and in the dark protection of his yard, on the scratchy wool blanket, he felt safe, incredibly safe.

They went on kissing, hardly breaking away to breathe. By force of will he kept his hands from wandering, from caressing her body in all the places he wanted to touch, all the places he knew she wanted him to touch.

This wasn't about satisfying their desires. It was about exploring them, testing the shape and depth and color of their feelings for each other.

And then he reached a point when he didn't need any more than he had. Kissing her was enough. He didn't think anything could be more intimate than what they were doing, but it was innocent, too.

At last they ended the kiss, as if by mutual agreement. He lay there with her, tangled with her, not saying anything, but absorbing the stillness of the night, the incredible warmth of their touching.

Slowly he released her body. She relaxed back, staring up at the stars again, a long sigh escaping her.

He wished it could always be like this, but knew it couldn't. He pushed the thought aside, not wanting to experience the sorrow, the sense of loss. Not wanting to communicate it to Jennifer, to taint what they'd just shared.

He smiled down at her. "You know," he said, "I don't think you finished your cake."

LUCY WAS OUT IN THE GARDEN when Drew called. She hadn't taken the cordless with her and didn't hear the phone ring inside or the answering machine pick up. But the message waited for her when she went in.

She pressed the play button and heard Drew's voice, familiar and yet distorted by the machine. "Lucy, I...want to make things right. Can we talk?" He left his number at the hotel.

She'd anticipated this, wondering when it would happen. Now that it had, she wasn't sure how she felt. Except that she really wanted to yell at him, demand to know how he could have done this to her.

She waited an hour before calling back, giving herself time to prepare. The hotel had an automatic phone system that saved her from having to go through the front desk. All she had to do was punch in his room number. His room was on the seventh floor, and she remembered how they'd stayed at that hotel one winter evening two years earlier, when they'd gone to a late event in Portland—a fund-raising banquet and auction—and hadn't wanted to drive home to Vancouver.

Lucy was always very careful about drinking and driving and this was a night she'd wanted to cut loose and enjoy herself. They'd both been tipsy at the end of the evening. She remembered riding up in the elevator, laughing with him at some shared joke and then spilling through the door of the suite and into bed. She remembered their lovemaking, sexy and intense; they'd been very into each other.

Now it was a bittersweet memory.

Drew picked up on the second ring, and she said, "It's me. I assume you want to talk face-to-face?"

They arranged to meet an hour later near a big fountain by the Portland riverfront. It sat in a long narrow park that ran between the downtown sky-scrapers and the water, where bridges arched across every few blocks. The park was a main spot for marches and festivals and public events in the summer, and the fountain was popular with children.

When Lucy arrived, Drew stood by a small tree, his right arm in a cast and sling. Katherine had told her he'd broken his arm, but she wasn't clear on the details.

He appeared to study the kids at play in the fountain.

She looked hard at them, too, at those who seemed to get along with the others, at those who were alone.

The scared ones and the ones who were so intent on their play that they bumped into their neighbors or splashed them without awareness or consideration.

What did Drew see when he looked at the same scene she did? She wanted to get inside his head and know what was there. Because if they had an overlap in the world they saw when they looked at the same scene, maybe they could salvage their situation. But if he saw something completely different they didn't have a chance.

She'd thought their visions matched, that they were living the same reality. To know he'd slept with some other woman... It hurt like hell. It was so wrong. She'd assumed they were both excited about creating a child together. Both committed to their marriage.

But he hadn't been. He'd been pursuing his own pleasure.

She wondered if it was because of their attempt to get her pregnant. Because he'd realized his life was about to change, his responsibilities were getting more serious, his opportunity to be a boy rather than a man coming to a forced end. And he was five years younger than she. He hadn't been listening to an increasingly loud biological clock.

Drew turned from the view of the fountain and met her gaze.

Lucy walked closer. She saw emotion in his eyes, but it appeared to be self-pity more than anything else. Had he been watching the children and thinking about all he'd put in jeopardy?

Without a word she indicated they should walk

along the river. She didn't ask about his arm as she set the pace, moving slowly as if they were a reasonably happy couple out for a stroll on a summer afternoon. The sun hung low to the southwest, its rays warm on her skin without being too hot. Lucy wondered whether people watching would see her belly and think a wonderful thing was happening between them. A time of promise. The excitement of bringing a new life into the world.

But if any observers looked closely at their faces, they would read a different story. Neither she nor Drew could hide their tension—the way they walked, the way they stared at anything but each other.

Probably they weren't the only expecting couple who'd ever had a hard time during the nine months of pregnancy. Everyone had a hard time at some point, and more than one couple had broken up before the baby was born.

She hated that they might be one of those couples. A statistic.

It was such an unbearable situation, and Drew was the one who'd put them in it. She glanced over, then away. "I'm so angry at you, I can hardly look at you."

"I know."

She waited, walking on.

"That's probably how it should be. You deserve to be angry."

Lucy didn't trust this side of Drew. He seemed too contrite, too wrapped up in his sad story about himself. She wondered what would happen when he recovered from his bout of self-pity. Wondered what would happen if he got his way and she took him back. Would he forget all about his contrition? Would he truly change, or would his old impulses resurface and lead him to cheat on her once more?

And how would that affect their child?

"If we didn't break up," she said, "and please note the 'if,' then what would our relationship be like?"

"I don't know."

"And what about Jennifer?"

"There's nothing between us."

"There's her baby. Your baby."

Drew didn't answer for a moment, looking almost as if he would admit the truth. But then he spoke. "It's not my baby."

Disappointment flooded her. She didn't let it show. She made her voice quiet and steady. "It's your baby."

He couldn't meet her eyes.

"The blood tests are going to prove it," she said. "So you shouldn't lie about it."

"She won't take any blood tests. She'll chicken out. She's trying to intimidate me, to get something out of me. She's suckered all of you onto her side, but when she realizes there's no point, she'll run back to California and we'll never hear from her again."

"Are you going to pay her off?"

"No. Of course not. That's exactly what she wants. And that's what I'm not going to give to her."

"Or she's telling the truth."

He sighed. "I want to talk about us, not Jennifer."

"We are talking about us. Because I don't believe a word you're saying."

Drew took a moment to adjust the nylon strap on his sling. He studied it as if engrossed. "I guess that doesn't bode well for us, then."

"Have there been other women?"

"There's no 'other.' Because I didn't sleep with Jennifer."

"Have you ever cheated on me?"

"No," he said.

She knew she shouldn't have asked the question. Drew wouldn't say yes; she couldn't trust his denial. It got her nowhere.

Lucy walked to the railing by the river and stood staring down at the water moving slowly below. "I don't think this is going to work out."

"Now THIS," Ross said, holding up a gray dress with a dog on it, which matched a pair of striped pants, "is very cute."

"Girl pile," Jennifer said.

Ross folded it and placed it on the pile of items suitable only for a girl. He'd never actually handled baby clothes before, aside from that sock in the laundry room, and he found them fascinating. Everything was so small. He couldn't wait to see the baby dressed in some of the outfits.

They'd been at this for an hour now, since finishing a late dinner. Earlier in the day they'd assembled the changing table in her bedroom. Now they were rapidly filling it.

The phone rang. Ross picked up the receiver on Jennifer's nightstand.

"Drew called," Lucy said at once, sounding somewhere between annoyed and frantic. "He's drunk and he's being a jerk. We talked today, argued, and I told him I'm not interested in taking him back anytime soon, if ever."

"And he reacted badly," Ross said.

"I can't trust him anymore. I don't know how many other women he's slept with and he won't be honest about Jennifer. He won't admit he slept with her and won't admit the baby might be his."

So he'd gone back to being Drew, Ross thought. Jennifer hadn't gotten through to him, after all—not in any lasting way. "You don't think there's a chance he's telling the truth." He had to float it out there.

"No. I believe Jennifer. She wouldn't lie."

"I'm glad you see that about her. What do you want me to do about your husband?"

He regretted the choice of words as soon as they were out. The reminder that *he* was no longer her husband and Drew was, that he'd been left and she'd chosen her second spouse unwisely.

A moment of silence followed. He heard her begin to speak, then stop, the word half formed in her mouth, the nature of it unknown to him forever.

He didn't hold any ill will toward her, not anymore. But he didn't love her anymore, either. Not romantically. More like a brother and sister now, which was just as it should be. He wanted her to be happy, but he didn't necessarily want to be involved in any substantial way. She'd made a choice to live without him and he recognized her reasons as valid, but to have someone walk away from you was still difficult. It didn't feel good, even if you agreed with their reasons.

He said, "I'll go to the hotel."

"He's not there. He called from a bar on Second."

"He called from a bar?"

"All I can say is, I hope he had a little privacy. But I don't think he did."

"Which bar?"

"The Del Raye."

Ross knew of the place. "I'll go see if I can talk some sense into him. At least keep him off the road."

Half an hour later he found his brother in a booth at the bar. Drew shared the table with a slim woman in a revealing dress, but didn't seem to care that she was there. She, for her part, seemed to be there mostly for the presumably free alcohol and wasn't paying Drew any more attention than he was paying her.

Still, Drew was a good-looking guy, even with his arm in a sling, and who knew where the evening might end. If not for Ross, who decided his brother didn't need another notch on his belt at this time in his life.

He stood beside the booth, arms crossed. The woman was the first to look up. She had hair like Andie MacDowell's and a lot of cleavage on display.

Ross said, "Would you excuse us?"

The woman glanced at Drew, who shrugged. She took her drink and unfolded herself from the bench, twisting sideways and then rising onto her long legs to walk back to the bar on her black high heels.

Ross waited for Drew to look up, to acknowledge him, to invite him to sit. Drew didn't. Ross let a moment go by, then sat. A circle of light shone on the dark wood table from a low-hanging fixture.

"Asshole," Drew muttered.

Ross signaled to the waitress, who came over and took his order for a beer. He didn't want to risk being sanctimonious by having mineral water or some other nonalcoholic beverage. Of course, it wouldn't really have mattered, because Drew was already pissed.

Once they were alone again, Ross spoke. "You're mad because I asked your lady friend to leave?"

No answer.

"You wanted to sleep with her?"

"Screw you."

"Don't seem to be in a very good mood tonight."

"Don't seem to be any less of a supercilious jerk than usual," Drew retorted.

So this was the game they were playing. "Tell me more."

Drew muttered something into his glass, which by the look of it held hard alcohol. Something clear on the rocks. He set the glass on the table, aligning it with a water ring left on the varnished wood.

Since Drew wasn't going to answer, Ross tried another tack. "How's the arm?"

"Hurts like a son of a bitch. What do you expect? You're the doctor. You know how these things go."

Drew had his arm inside his suit jacket, leaving

one sleeve empty. Ross wondered if the injury was what had attracted the woman. Some women went for men they could fuss over. Not that she'd been fussing over his brother when he'd arrived.

"You take the painkillers for it?"

"Yeah."

Ross paused before replying. "They don't mix well with alcohol."

Drew gave him a hostile look. "I read the bottle."

"It had that sticker on it, right? Little picture with a bottle and a line over it?"

"You always do everything right, don't you."

"No."

"My brother, the saint."

"Stop it."

"My brother, the hero. The virtuous doctor. The one who heals people. And I'm the slimy divorce lawyer."

"That isn't all you do."

"It's the lucrative part. It's the part I like best."

"Okay."

The waitress came and dropped off Ross's beer. She took one glance at their faces and backed away fast.

Drew glared at him again. "Even the way you say that. Condescending. Belittling. And the things you're thinking."

Ross tasted his beer. "You don't know what I'm thinking."

"But I do. I've lived with it for so many years. I know exactly what's going through your head. The way you look down on me, on my choices. Well, the law is what I like. It's what I do well. And I'm good at divorces. Damn good.''

Ross remained silent.

''Even now I know what you're thinking. That it's fortunate I'm good at divorces because I'm going to get one of my own. Well?''

''You're right,'' Ross admitted. Their turns of ironic humor were the same—proof they were brothers.

''Well, I'm not sure I'll make out so well in this one. Lucy's going to hire a good lawyer. As good as I will. And she's got something on her side that I don't. Namely, the fact that I'm a cheating bastard.''

Ross waited.

''Unless I can dig up something on her. Hire a private investigator. Find out she's been screwing the mailman for years. A total cheating bitch. I could believe it. How about you?''

Ross didn't give Drew the reaction he wanted. But hearing his brother speak of Lucy that way pained him. ''No.''

''And I'm goddamn kidding, but you'd never stop to consider that might be the case, would you? No, you believe I'd really have my wife investigated. The mother of my child.''

''One of them.''

''Bite me.''

''Just stating a fact.''

''So am I. Christ, I *hate* you.''

The words came out with a venom Ross hadn't expected. It nearly made him recoil.

He watched as his brother took a swallow of his

drink. "That stuff must be hitting you hard," he said at last.

"I haven't had that much. This is just my second."

"On top of the narcotics."

Drew gave him an innocent look. "Is that what they are?"

"You know damn well they're narcotics. Just as you know damn well you shouldn't be drinking if you're on painkillers."

"Yeah, well, I'm pretty good at doing things I know I shouldn't."

"And why is that?"

"And why is that?" Drew mocked, his voice harsh. "Because that's who I am. I'm a screwup. I always have been."

Ross took a swallow of beer to keep himself from agreeing. "So how long have you hated me?"

"Forever."

"Since the bike accident?"

"Before that. I hated you for being older than me, for knowing everything I didn't. For being such an insufferable prig. For being so goddamn perfect. For everything about you. You were a hard one to grow up in the shadow of."

Ross suspected that might have been true at one time. He'd been his parents' first child, their star, and he'd gotten more attention at times than his brother. He'd had privileges as an older sibling that would have driven Drew to jealousy and anger.

But that had changed with the accident. In one afternoon he'd gone from favorite son to the cause of the family's suffering.

CHAPTER NINETEEN

Eighteen years earlier

We're in the park down the hill from our house. I've got my new BMX bike—new for my twelfth birthday, just a month ago—and we're doing jumps. "We" means me and my friend Grant and, of course, my brother. Drew always tags along when we go biking. He can barely keep up and he whines *a lot*.

We only let Drew take the little jumps, the ones any dork could do blindfolded.

Today Grant shows me a new jump, up and over a fallen log. It's pretty intense, but I can tell by the way the ground is packed hard that a lot of kids have done it. Grant takes it first, pedaling like hell and then shooting up over the log and landing hard on the other side. He skids his bike to a stop and gives a *whoop*.

It looks cool so I go for it. I know I need a lot of speed so I really stand on the pedals, and as the jump gets closer I realize there's no way to back out. It's too late to brake and if I veer away I'll go straight into a nasty clump of dead branches. But it's kind of a rush.

The jump throws me up into the air and I

sail over the fallen log, working hard to keep the bike upright. I nail the landing, though, even better than Grant did. When I skid up beside him, he has a grin on his face.

"That's so cool," he says.

We do it again. Drew stands astride his bike up where we start, watching us. "I wanna do it," he says.

"You can't," I say. "You're too young. And you're not good enough."

He pouts and looks like he wants to cry, but we ignore him and keep doing the jump. After six times my hands are starting to get sore from the impact. Grant and I are just past the landing area, talking about how cool the jump is, when Grant glances over my shoulder and says, "Oh, shit. Your weenie brother's trying it."

I turn around and, sure enough, Drew is on his bike, pedaling as fast as he can. "Drew!" I yell. "Don't! Don't do it!"

But he doesn't stop and I can tell he's not going fast enough, and when he takes the jump he doesn't get enough air. His back wheel skims the fallen tree, knocking the front wheel straight toward the ground. Drew yells in sheer terror. When the wheel hits he smashes onto the handlebars and then gets tossed forward onto a patch of hard, rocky soil.

I hear the bones cracking, and Drew lies totally still on the dirt, not making a sound. His legs are caught on the bicycle, the front wheel is mangled and the back one still spinning.

He's dead. He must be dead. If he wasn't dead he'd be screaming. I know he would.

"Oh, shit," Grant says. "Oh, shit."

We both run over to my little brother. He's lying facedown on the ground and there's blood on his leg and then I see a piece of bone sticking right out of his thigh.

Grant sees it, too, and bends over to hurl.

"Go get help," I tell him, even as a string of puke still dangles from his mouth. "You've got to get help."

He rides off on his bike, and I'm alone with my brother. He's not dead, I realize, because I can see his back move as he breathes, but he's unconscious. I'm completely freaked out, but I can't do anything to help him, and for all I know he's going to die right in front of me while I sit here, powerless.

It takes fifteen minutes for the ambulance to arrive. It feels like hours. Even the ambulance guys look a little pale when they see Drew's leg. As they get him on the stretcher he wakes up for a second and screams like you wouldn't believe, and then he passes out again.

At the hospital I learn the broken leg was the least of it. He's got broken ribs and internal injuries from smashing against the handlebars—and he's in surgery for hours.

My parents practically live at the hospital for the weeks it takes Drew to recover. They blame me for what happened and it's hard to deal with, even though I know I should have been watching him better.

A few weeks later, when Drew should be getting out of the hospital, he comes down with an infection and almost dies before the doctors

can fix it. It's a lot longer before he leaves the
place and it's almost a year until he's totally
recovered. And all the time my parents are
thinking they're going to lose him, that he'll
keel over from some mysterious complication
before they can get back to the hospital.

ROSS SAT IN THE BOOTH with his brother, remembering the accident and how responsible he'd felt, how
responsible his parents had made him feel. As a child
of twelve he hadn't been able to understand that his
parents blamed themselves, as well.

Edward and Katherine had spoiled Drew after the
accident, no doubt telling themselves they were just
making up for what he'd suffered. They'd failed to
set appropriate limits. Drew had responded by becoming selfish and manipulative.

Yet he'd always been smart enough to hide those
qualities from people he wanted to charm or im-
press—people such as Lucy. Had she truly known
the kind of person he was, Ross doubted she would
have married him. But she hadn't known, thanks to
his own complicity.

Ross looked across the table at his brother. Saw
the lines of tension around his eyes, the defeat and
anger there. The set of his mouth.

He'd often tried to tell himself they had an average
prickly relationship. No love lost between them but
no vicious animosity, either. Nothing that extreme.
Nothing that intense. But apparently he'd been
wrong.

"You hate me."

Drew scowled into his drink. "I'm jealous, is all."

"Of what?"

"You're so steady," Drew said, almost snarling. "You know who you are. You always have. You just walk through the world with a presence I'll never have. I've been jealous and angry about it for years. Everything's always so easy for you. You sail through medical school, have your pick of residencies. You do this...you do that."

The person Drew described didn't correspond to the person Ross felt he was. He'd never thought things came easily for him. He'd worked hard to get where he was and he'd endured setbacks along the way. Lucy's abandonment, for example. "You've had too much to drink."

"Even that."

He lost his patience. "Tell me what I'm supposed to say that's not going to piss you off."

"Nothing you can say won't piss me off. You broke my damn arm."

"This is ugly."

"And everything always has to look good for you."

"For me?" Ross asked, incredulous. "For *me?* I'm not the one who left Jennifer a fake phone number. I'm not the one who needs a brand-new BMW and a seven-hundred-thousand-dollar home."

"Oh, whatever."

He stared across the table. "You and Jennifer made a baby together. And instead of stepping up to the plate, you're trying to make her out to be a gold digger. Jennifer deserves better and you know it. Better than your lame and insulting attempt to buy her silence."

Ross took a sip of beer, trying to cool off. It didn't

work. "You know what the real problem is?" he asked, clenching the beer glass. "You know you don't have to do right by her because you know that if you don't take care of her, I will. And you hate me for that. Because I know what's right and can do what needs to be done and you've never been able to do that."

"Shut up."

"You started this, Drew. And I'm not in a mood to back off. Your little moment in the sack with Jennifer is going to change the course of my life and I want you just once to look me in the eye and admit you did it, that you lied to her and slept with her and got her pregnant."

Even as he said it, he knew it would never happen. He gave Drew a chance to respond, but he didn't.

He glared at his brother. "With all your money, the only thing you can offer her is a slap in the face."

Drew glanced away, then back, straight into Ross's eyes. "I don't have any money."

Ross laughed. "Yeah, right."

"It's all gone. I had to take out a second mortgage on the house. I'm behind on my car payments. What I offered is a lot more than I can afford. So don't talk about things you don't understand."

They'd each gained control of substantial inheritances on their twenty-first birthdays. He couldn't imagine how Drew could have burned through his already. "Where did it go?"

Drew was sullen.

"You hate me because I'm not in debt, don't you." Ross sighed. "Because I didn't blow my money on fast cars and exotic trips. But you did, and you don't have any choices left. And you can't depend on Lucy's money to bail you out. Was that the plan? Get her to underwrite your lifestyle? Spend her money when yours was gone? You can make a decent living practicing divorce law, but that wouldn't be enough, would it? Where else did the money go—up your nose?''

''Bastard.''

''Am I right?'' The thought was distressing, but it also explained a lot.

Drew reached for his wallet. He opened it and threw some bills down on the table. ''I don't have to listen to this.''

''But we have to clean up after your messes.''

''Go to hell.''

Ross rose, too. ''If you think you're driving out of here, think again.''

With his one broken arm, Drew wouldn't present much of a challenge. And he seemed to know it.

''Ever the guardian of public morality,'' he taunted. ''Wouldn't want me driving under the influence. Couldn't have me getting myself killed, now could we?''

''Honestly, tonight I'm not sure I'd care. It's the other people on the road I worry about.''

''Yeah, you always say that. Never fear.'' Drew extracted his keys from his pocket. ''I'll take a taxi home. I think I've still got money enough for that.'' He dropped the keys onto the table with a clatter.

Ross took them. ''You need a twenty?''

It was the wrong thing to say. Drew's expression closed.

''Good night, big brother.'' He turned and left the bar.

DREW SLAMMED OUT THE DOOR to the street. It was dark and cars whipped by, headlights on. He looked for a cab but didn't see one. Then he remembered that his Beemer, which he'd picked up from Ross's house a couple of days before, was parked on the street and would be towed if he didn't move it. What a hassle. What a goddamn pain in the ass that was going to be. And it wasn't like he had spare cash for the towing fee.

Good thing he carried an extra key tucked into his wallet. Ross could go to hell. Self-righteous bastard.

He walked around the corner to his red BMW. In the dark he retrieved the key from his wallet, where he kept it behind his frequent-flier cards and a Visa that was supposed to be for emergencies but that he'd maxed out several months ago.

He settled behind the driver's seat. Everything seemed fine, and if he concentrated hard, he didn't feel he'd had much to drink. After all, he'd only had three vodkas. He should be fine, whatever saintly Ross had to say.

Not bothering with his seat belt, he pulled out of the parking place and joined the traffic flowing down the street. He headed home.

It wasn't until he got onto the freeway that he remembered he wasn't going home. That he didn't have a home to go to.

He'd missed the last exit for downtown. Damn. He didn't know where his brain was, except replaying his conversation with Ross, wishing he'd hung on to his patience, wishing he hadn't been such a hothead while Ross kept his cool. As the jerk always did.

Amazing that Drew hadn't reached across the table

and strangled him. Or smacked him in the face. Ross could be so damn smug.

He checked the dashboard clock. It was just after ten. Still early. Maybe he should drop in on Lucy as long as he was headed this way. See how she was. Come clean. Apologize—for all the good an apology would do him.

This was such a mess. Everything was going to hell.

Ross had been right; if not for Jennifer, he would have hoped to skate out of his financial difficulties without Lucy's knowledge. Okay, so Ross hadn't said exactly that, but he'd seemed to understand that point. And Drew could have pulled it off. Could have scraped by, making his debt payments and eventually set things right, stopped making mistakes and started living within his means.

Of course, that would entail changing his behavior, but he'd started to do that. Started to realize what it meant to have a family, what was required of him now.

And knowing that Lucy had money of her own in case things ever reached a truly difficult point had been reassuring. Oh, having to ask her for help would have been embarrassing, but not the end of the world as long as they were in the game together.

Which they no longer were. He didn't think Lucy would be sympathetic to his money problems now. She would probably just consider it a further sign of his lame-ass nature, of his unfitness for marriage to her. More ammunition in the battle that had started between them.

And he didn't know how to keep the information

from coming out. Not if Jennifer needed money. Money he didn't have to give her.

He'd crossed the bridge over the Columbia by now, into Vancouver, and began to realize the foolishness of coming up this way. Ten o'clock was late, not early, and Lucy wouldn't want to see him. He took the exit for their house, but turned around immediately and got back on the freeway heading south.

Cursing himself, wondering why he couldn't make a damn decision today to save himself. Why he couldn't do a damn thing right in his whole stupid life.

Everything had unraveled. Everything was crap.

The words echoed in his brain as he drove down the freeway to Portland, picked up the 405 across the Fremont Bridge and dropped back toward downtown. There was a knot of traffic across the bridge and he came up on two big gasoline tankers slowing things down in the right-hand lane at the end of the bridge. Traffic from northwest Portland was merging on the right. He needed to take the first exit to get to his hotel but didn't want to wait behind the tankers, so he zipped around them on the left and then cut back into the far right lane ahead of them.

He hadn't seen the old Chevy in the other lane, fast and heavy, the driver drunker than he was and more reckless. The car hit him from behind, jolting him forward. In a reflex action he put his foot on the brake and the car spun.

Drew caught a glimpse of the tankers bearing down on him and knew he had to get out of the way, not only to save himself but to avoid a gas explosion on the downtown freeway.

Frantic, he gunned the engine and tried to steer
into the spin, but he had no real idea where he was
going and his broken arm prevented him from con-
trolling the wheel. He shot to the right, hit a retaining
wall, but bounced off it, back into the path of the
Chevy.

"Oh Christ," Drew said as the heavy vehicle
struck his car. He felt the door smash against his side
and then everything went dark.

ROSS DROVE DIRECTLY HOME after leaving the bar.
He'd been back about half an hour, working in his
study, trying to ignore the emotional repercussions
of the conversation with his brother, when the phone
rang.

Jennifer sat across the room from him, doing her
Web design exercises. They'd said little to each other
when he'd returned. Just her asking how things had
gone, him saying it had been challenging.

He picked up the receiver, surprised to hear the
familiar voice of Jackie, one of the triage nurses at
the hospital. "Ross?" she asked.

Her tone was serious instead of joking, and he
snapped to attention. "Yes?"

"There's been an accident," she told him. "Your
brother…he's here. The ambulance just brought him
in."

Ross found he couldn't draw in a breath. "An accident?"

"Bad one." A pause. "It doesn't look good."

"Shit," he said. "Shit, shit, shit."

CHAPTER TWENTY

THEY WERE IN THE CAR two minutes after the call. Ross handed her his cell phone and recited Lucy's number.

"I've never used one of these before," Jennifer said. Her pulse hammered and she felt nervous and unsteady. She couldn't believe Drew was back at the hospital.

"Punch in the number and push the send button," Ross told her.

She made him repeat the number, then dialed it into the lit keypad. When the phone started to ring, she handed it over.

Ross put it to his ear. "Lucy, it's me," he said. "Drew's had an accident. He's at Northwest. Jennifer and I are on the way there."

He waited. She watched him.

"They didn't say. I think it's pretty serious."

Another pause.

"Okay. Be safe."

He pulled the phone from his ear and pressed a button as he handed it back to her, all without taking his eyes off the road. "My parents are speed-dial two."

"How do I do that?"

Ross told her, then had a brief and terse conversation with his parents. He hung up, saying "Shit" to no one in particular.

"This doesn't feel real," Jennifer said.

At the hospital he helped her out of the car and walked at her pregnant woman's pace to the emergency room entrance, though she could tell he was impatient. She went as fast as she could and was out of breath by the time they reached the automatic sliding door.

This time Drew hadn't been left to sit in the waiting room. The nurse at the triage station looked up as they approached, held Ross's gaze for several seconds.

"He's in surgery," she said, but didn't supply any other information.

Ross led Jennifer to the closest row of molded plastic chairs. "I'm going back there," he said.

She watched as he disappeared around the corner. Dazed, Jennifer stared after him.

Katherine and Edward arrived and headed straight to where she sat.

"Tell us what you know," Edward said, looking tense. "How's Drew? Where's Ross?"

Katherine had been crying. Her eyes were bloodshot, her lips tight, her expression bleak. Jennifer wondered how this night would affect her health and hoped it wouldn't be too much for her. To imagine anything more stressful than having your son in a car accident was hard.

"Ross went to see what happened. Drew's in surgery. That's all I can tell you."

Ross's parents sat down a few seats away. They talked to each other in hushed voices. Katherine started to cry. Jennifer could hear Edward urging her to stay calm.

Lucy came in just as Ross returned to the waiting room. Ross was pale. Katherine and Edward stood, and so did Jennifer.

"Tell us," his father said. "How is he?"

Ross took a deep breath. "He's pretty banged up." His voice was tight, as if he had to struggle to control his emotions. "There's a lot of internal damage. And a head injury."

"He'll be okay, won't he?" his mother said.

"He's got a good team working on him. Dr. Srinivasan is the best."

Jennifer noticed he hadn't answered his mother's question. She wondered what he'd seen in the operating room, how bad it really was.

Lucy appeared numb. Ross put his arm around her and gave her a reassuring squeeze. The gesture seemed to release something inside Lucy. She leaned against Ross, burying her face in his shoulder. She sobbed, and Ross murmured something in her ear, stroking her back to soothe her.

Seeing the connection between them despite their divorce, Jennifer felt unexpectedly raw, unexpectedly jealous.

Finally Lucy straightened and stepped away, brushing at her eyes. "How did it happen?" she asked.

Ross shook his head. "I don't know. When he left the bar he said he was going to his hotel. He'd been drinking, but he gave me his car keys." He pulled them out of his pocket and stared at them, as if to prove to himself this couldn't have happened, couldn't be real. "I have his car keys."

Lucy spoke quietly. "He always carries a spare key in his wallet. In case he gets locked out."

Ross shook his head. "Idiot," he muttered. "Damn idiot."

"We don't know that his drinking caused the accident," Edward said.

Ross didn't buy it. "He told me he was going to take a cab. He said it flat-out. He lied."

He always lies, Jennifer wanted to say, feeling incredibly sad. *Why does it surprise you that he did so tonight?*

"Was anyone else involved?" Lucy asked. "Another car?"

"Apparently, yes. The driver walked away. Also drunk, and the police arrested him for driving under the influence."

"Was it his fault?" Katherine demanded.

"I don't know," Ross said. "I don't know whose fault it was."

"If it was his fault…" she began, angry.

Ross put a hand on her shoulder. "Mom, you should try not to get worked up. It's not good for you."

She paused, taking a deep breath. "I just wish someone here could tell me what's going on," she said, her voice quieter. "I can't stand not knowing."

"They're doing their best for him," Edward said.

"As soon as they can tell us anything definite, they will."

"But I want answers now. He's my son."

"I'll see what I can find out." Ross led his mother to a chair, motioning for Lucy to sit with her, then disappearing back into the guts of the hospital. His father crossed to the window.

Sitting alone for several minutes, Jennifer watched Lucy and Katherine grip each other's hands, supporting each other. She felt superfluous, again an outsider in the family.

She stood and walked over to a corner of the waiting room, to a table with magazines on it. Staring blankly at the covers, she felt the baby start to move inside her. She put her hands on her belly to feel the kicks, the bond with her child.

Behind her she heard Ross return and tell his parents and Lucy that he couldn't give them any more information.

A moment later he came over. He stood behind her, resting his hands lightly on her shoulders. "Hey," he said, voice soft.

She turned and met his gaze. "How are you holding up?"

"So-so. You?"

Jennifer shrugged. "Okay. I just can't believe this is happening." She hesitated. "Maybe I shouldn't be here. For your father. For Lucy. So they aren't reminded of... So they can focus on your mom."

Reluctantly he nodded. "Do you want to go home?"

"I think that's the best thing."

"Have you got enough cash for a cab?"

"Yeah," she said. "I'll see you at home."

"Do you want me to call with news?"

She nodded. "I probably won't be able to sleep."

"Try."

"Okay. Will you say good-night to your parents and Lucy for me? I don't want to interrupt them myself. It's better this way."

"Your choice," Ross said. "I'll see you out."

They walked together through the late-night quiet of the hospital and out the E.R. entrance. As luck would have it, a taxi idled at the curb, having just dropped off a passenger.

Ross opened the door for her. She didn't get into the car right away, but stopped to put her arms around him.

He held her. "At the bar tonight. I said some things…"

She could feel his regret and his pain. She wanted to tell him everything would be okay, that it would all work out. But she didn't know if it would, so all she did was hug him.

Ross helped her into the back seat. He gave the driver his address through the open window.

"I'll call," he said as the taxi pulled away.

AT HOME Jennifer couldn't manage to settle down and go to bed. She was too restless and keyed up. She tried to eat but couldn't, then took a cool shower with the cordless phone in the bathroom so she could answer it if Ross called.

He didn't.

After dressing, she went downstairs to the living room, where she sat and tried to read her Web design book. She couldn't concentrate on it. Finally she put the book aside and sat in the circle of light thrown by the single lamp she'd turned on.

An hour passed, and another. The phone didn't ring.

Then she heard Ross pull into the driveway. His car door opened and shut. A moment later she heard his key in the lock.

Jennifer rose as he walked into the front hall. He looked incredibly tired, beaten down, the skin of his face slack and colorless.

She opened her mouth to ask how Drew was, then closed it again.

Ross stared straight at her for a moment, silent. And then he just shook his head, the motion barely perceptible.

Jennifer felt a hole open up in her chest. "He's…?"

"He didn't make it." Ross's voice was thick with restrained emotion. She saw that his whole body was trembling.

He didn't make it? *How could he not have made it?*

She went to Ross. Stepped close and put her arms around him, her belly pressing into his. "Oh my God," she said. "Ross."

He held her tightly. He made a sound, a deep, grieving sound, and she knew no matter how angry he'd been with his brother in the past few weeks, no matter what tension had filled their relationship all their lives, they were still brothers, Drew was still their parents' only other child and the loss was incredible.

She leaned into him and cried. For Ross and his family and for her baby, who would never know its father.

Ross clung to her. She looked up and saw his tears. She reached up with the pad of her thumb and brushed one of them away.

"I thought I'd be able to hate him for the rest of my life," he said.

Their eyes met. His gaze was intense; he was hungry for something to hold on to.

They stood like that for a time, frozen, and then he kissed her. Nothing like their kiss nine years before. Nothing like the one the other night. No romance, just raw need, and her body responded instantly.

"Jennifer," he said.

A statement and a question rolled into one, and she knew what he was asking, knew what he needed. She knew she needed it, too. In the early-morning hours she wanted to lose herself in the physical, to push away thought and emotion.

Yes, she said, not with her voice but with her hands and lips.

He took her upstairs and undressed her. Made love to her slowly and reverently, worshiping her. And when they both came, he held her and wept.

I love him, she thought. *I always have.*

SHE WOKE UP in Ross's bed. It was wider than the one in her room, the sheets pale-gray and soft.

She lay belly to belly with him, their limbs touching but not tangled. Over his body she could see the clock showing six in the morning. Three hours of sleep. Three hours since they'd made love.

Reality rushed at her. The reason for their loss of control. Drew's accident. The hospital. Ross coming home.

She observed his face in sleep. He appeared peaceful and relaxed. Calm. She took advantage of his closed eyes to look her fill, to trace the contours of his face with her gaze.

He was beautiful, but then, she'd always known that. Beautiful and fascinating. Sometimes she felt she hardly knew him at all. And other times she felt she knew him far better than she should, considering the amount of time she'd spent with him.

She let her breathing match his and she didn't turn away when he finally opened his eyes. She'd thought of getting up, running away, but she'd known she wouldn't be able to lumber out of bed without waking him, and she figured she could just face up to what had happened.

She had made another mistake. She'd slept with the other brother now, and he might think less of her for it.

Ross didn't move as he watched her. Neither smiled nor frowned, gave her no hint of what he was thinking.

At last he said, "How long have you been awake?"

"Not long. A few minutes."

He smiled then, a half smile that reached his eyes

but didn't live there. His brother had died. "Good morning."

"Good morning." She reached out to run a hand along his shoulder, the top of his arm. A consoling gesture.

He took her hand and kissed it.

She felt a little trip of desire inside her, but fought it. "Ross," she said. "Last night…"

"Was not a mistake," he said. But he gave her hand a squeeze and put it down on the gray sheet.

He seemed to pick up on her mood very well, she thought. She was glad of that.

"Did you plan to scurry out of my bed and pretend this never happened?"

"It crossed my mind."

"But it did happen. And I think we've both been wanting it to happen."

"Not like this." She closed her eyes. "Drew is dead."

"I know," he said. "I know. And we're not."

"What happens now?"

When he didn't answer, she opened her eyes, watched him roll onto his back. He stared at the ceiling.

Jennifer pulled the sheet around herself. She worried he thought she was cheap. That she'd been nothing but a convenience to him, that he would have sought comfort with any woman. That he was more like his brother than he wanted to believe, than either of them wanted to believe.

But maybe he was just mourning Drew's death.

Ross didn't look at her. "I don't know. We'll

work it out. Right now, I need a shower. And then I need to see about burying my brother.''

THE DAY OF THE FUNERAL dawned clear and mild, but by ten o'clock clouds had filled in over the coast range. The sun and clouds traded off constantly from then on, as if the sky couldn't decide whether it should be a nice day or a grim one. And the wind blew, too, riding in from the west over the deep forests that separated Portland from the ocean.

They held the service in an old stone church, not far from the site of Drew's accident. The air inside was cool and still. Jennifer sat in the back, alone in a pew. Ross had asked her to join the family in the front, but she hadn't wanted to encourage gossip. Better to be an anonymous mourner, remembering the scene so she could describe it for her child someday in the distant future.

Buck up, honey. Time to be strong.

They were old words, familiar words from her childhood. Comforting. And they were the last ones her mother had ever spoken to her.

After Drew's funeral, they gathered at Katherine and Edward's home. Relatives and friends of the family came, as well as colleagues from Drew's law firm. They ate and talked in hushed groups around the house and out on the deck.

Jennifer recognized many of the people from the Fourth of July picnic. She spoke with Ross's aunt Lenora and with several others, knowing she wouldn't remember a thing they said to each other.

She thought back to high school. To dating Drew

and the time she'd spent in this house—never conceiving that, nine years later, she would come here the day of his funeral.

Eventually everyone left and only the caterers and the immediate family remained. Ross spoke with his father in a corner of the living room. Lucy went to keep her mother-in-law company while she took her medication and got ready for a nap.

Drew's death had set back Katherine's recovery. She seemed weaker now than she had a week earlier at her party.

Jennifer stood by herself in the dining room while the catering staff cleared the buffet from the table behind her. A large window overlooked the city and she stared through it, thinking of everyone living and dying and being born out there.

After ten minutes Ross came up behind her. They were very isolated in the big house. The caterers had finished in the room and left, shutting the doors behind them. The muted clatter of their cleaning in the kitchen was the only sound.

She felt his body heat against her back. "Your parents okay?"

He made a noise that meant they were, as much as could be expected, but not really, because they'd buried their son that day. "Dad went for a walk."

"My presence here was probably hard for him."

She hadn't been involved in the arrangements for handling Drew's body and the memorial service so she hadn't seen Edward since the night at the hospital. Though he'd been perfectly polite when she'd paid her respects today, it had been the politeness of a stranger. And she'd tried to stay out of his way. And out of Lucy's.

"I wish," Ross said, "we'd been able to acknowledge you more. You're carrying Drew's child. A part of him."

"It's all right. I know it's impossible. And I can only imagine how your father feels. How your mother would feel if she knew. Their son's life unraveled when I showed up. He died in an accident probably caused as much by stress and lack of concentration as anything else."

And now she wanted to disappear again. Ross and his family were paying too high a price.

"Drew was drunk," Ross said. "He mixed alcohol and painkillers and shouldn't have been on the road. He could have killed someone."

"He did kill someone."

"He could have killed someone else. Like that driver in the other car. It was completely selfish and irresponsible."

"You've never driven after getting tipsy?"

"Have you?" he demanded.

"No."

"Neither have I."

"You can see how it might be hard to have an older brother like you," she said.

He exhaled. "What I can see is that he did whatever he wanted, all the time, without regard for how others might feel. Which is one way to live, and I can almost respect it. Except in his case he also wanted people to like him, so he had to lie all the time. Saying he would take a cab, for instance. He lied to get me off his back and then did what he wanted, anyway.''

Jennifer knew, despite his words, that Ross blamed himself for believing Drew's lie. But he wasn't the only one who hadn't always seen through him. ''Do you think your parents understood what he was really like?''

He pulled out a chair from the dining table and sat, shoulders slumped. ''I don't know. They didn't want to. They had a lot invested in their image of him.'' Ross gazed at his hands, clasped between his knees. ''They were his parents.'' He was silent for a long time. And then, as if he'd read her mind, he said, ''I don't want you to leave.''

''Why not?''

''Because you should be here. Everything is different. Your child needs a family. And a father.''

She stared down at the top of his head. ''What exactly are you saying?''

''That you shouldn't be on your own.''

''I can handle being on my own.''

''You came up here,'' he said.

''Yes?''

''To give your baby a father.''

''And he's dead. And I'm afraid the grandparents won't want anything to do with me and my child, not after what's happened. I'll be stuck with a family that can't stand me.''

''I can stand you.'' He pulled her toward him until she stood between his thighs. ''The other night...''

Making love. They hadn't discussed it since the morning two days ago—hadn't had the emotional energy. Yet they'd collapsed into bed each night, exhausted, beside each other. Taking solace from the nearness. And awakened in each other's arms—but not had sex again.

"It was just comfort," she said. "We both needed reassurance. To be with someone... Life."

"You know it was more than that. Don't cheapen what happened by regretting it." He wrapped his arms around her and rested his head against her stomach. "Things are different now. We have to be different."

They stayed that way for a long while. The sounds from the kitchen subsided.

Finally he eased her away. "Let's go home. We'll talk more later."

CHAPTER TWENTY-ONE

AFTER DINNER that evening they went upstairs to unpack two more boxes of baby things from Kyle and
Melissa. The activity felt good after the stresses of
the funeral. To focus on the future rather than the
past, on a joyful event rather than a tragic one.

Among the clothes and toys was a black-and-white
geometric mobile. Ross stood beside the changing
table, choosing a spot to clamp it where it would
provide maximum diaper-change entertainment. He
glanced out the window, observing that dusk had
gathered over the grass and flowers in the backyard.
He saw the quick dim shapes of two bats wheeling
above the grass, harvesting insects before they disappeared for the night.

Turning back to his task, he attached the arm of
the mobile to the upper portion of the two-level
changing table. After he tightened it, he stepped back
and gave the mobile a spin with his finger. Such a
short while ago they'd talked about her moving out
after the baby was born, possibly before the baby
would even be interested in an item like this. Now
he hoped that wouldn't happen.

They'd only buried his brother a few hours ago. It
might be too soon to discuss the future. But he'd let

three days go by, three days since everything had changed. And they would have to tackle the issue sooner or later.

He turned and looked down at her. "We need to talk about what we're going to do. About your baby. About us." Because they definitely had an "us." The past few days had proven that. Making love, even if it was only once. Sleeping beside each other.

She sat cross-legged on the floor, unpacking more items from a box. A portable breast pump, a wool changing pad. She looked up. "Okay."

"I want you and your child to have security. A place to call home. Someone to help you." He walked over and sat down, mirroring her posture. Half a foot away. He was filled with the need to experience everything in this child's life. The birth, the first time crawling, the first step, the first word. To share the triumphs and lend his support after the inevitable disasters. "I think we should get married."

At first she said nothing, her expression almost carefully blank. And then she raised an eyebrow.

"Get married?"

"Yeah, get married."

Jennifer reached into the box again. Pulled out an unfinished maple rattle and a ring of colorful beads.

She glanced at him, and what he saw in her eyes gave him hope. A glimmer of longing as if she wanted to say yes. As if she wanted all he could offer her and her child. Not just the house and financial security, but him, too.

But it only lasted an instant. She picked up the wooden rattle, turning it in her hands. "Ross, I—"

He waited for her to finish the sentence, but she didn't continue. So he gently said, "You think it would be a bad idea."

"I just don't know."

He thought of their lovemaking, their hunger for each other. He thought of how it felt to lie side by side in the night, to hold each other. Her face next to his, peaceful. She couldn't fake that. It was intimate, real. They had something together and she was too smart not to recognize it.

"This situation," he said. "It is what it is. Messy. You're carrying my brother's child. So is my ex-wife."

She winced, head down.

He reached for her, resting his hands on her knees. Waited for her to meet his gaze. "But it's how we handle it that counts. If Drew were still alive," he said, "then maybe this would be too much."

And for her child's sake, he could have let go of her. Watched her walk away. Helped her get settled in an apartment of her own. Been the uncle and nothing more. A steady, stable adult presence in the kid's life, silently longing for Jennifer without ever revealing even a hint of it.

But that wasn't necessary.

He'd been so determined to do the right thing. And he'd thought that included resisting his feelings for Jennifer. But his guilt from the past had clouded his thinking about the present. Certainly Drew's actions during the last years of his life had made any brotherly loyalty unnecessary. Ross had been too busy punishing himself for things he'd done long ago to let himself truly accept it.

And now Drew was dead. And Ross and Jennifer had made love. And they couldn't go backward, only forward.

He squeezed her knees. "I know it will be difficult when your child finds out the truth about Drew, but with two of us there to help..." He gave her a moment, then added, "Your child deserves a father."

"That's all I wanted," she said, her voice soft.

"And I will love your child as if I were the real father." *Maybe more so,* he thought.

She chewed on her lower lip. "There's more to marriage than child rearing," she said. Tentative. A little embarrassed.

"Yes..." Sex. "I think we'll do okay with that." And talking about it made him want her again. But this was definitely not the time. "I don't make love with a woman unless I want to," he told her, remembering the concerns she'd raised that afternoon. "Even if the circumstances are difficult. Even if I'm upset. Even if my brother has just died."

He saw the pleasure and relief in her eyes.

"We could have picked a better time to make love for the first time," he said, "but I'm not sorry we did. I hope you aren't, either."

"I'm not."

Ross reached for her hands. "I have feelings for you. And I believe you have feelings for me."

"Ross..."

He could have told her he loved her. And perhaps he should have been ready to do so. But he didn't want to say anything now, or for Jennifer to say anything now, only to realize later it wasn't true. To realize perhaps they'd just been affected by the intensity and trauma of the past week.

Nor did he want her to say she loved him if what she really felt was gratefulness for his support, for the security he could provide. She might not realize that was her reason until later—and he wouldn't have been able to stand that.

They should marry as soon as possible, though. To protect themselves and the baby. To get her on his health plan. So he could be her legal husband in case any complications arose when she went into labor.

"Will you consider this?"

Jennifer released his hands and picked up the wooden rattle again. Contemplated it.

"You have reservations," he said. "Do you want to share them with me?"

She paused before replying. "If we got married, Ross, I'd be placing a lot of trust in you. I'd be depending on you and so would my child. Right now you think it makes sense. But life changes. If you back out five years from now, it'll be so much worse than if you were never involved."

"I won't back out."

"I don't want my child to be thirteen and try to go looking for you, and have you say she's not important to you and you don't want anything to do with her."

He leaned forward and took hold of her shoulders. "Your father said that to you? *Your father?*"

She gave him a weak smile. "Not those exact words. But close."

His heart ached for her. For the girl she'd been. He gave her a long, serious look. "I would treat your child better than that. And I won't back out."

"You really want me to marry you."

"It's the best thing for you and the baby."

"And you?"

He heard the seed of doubt in her voice. "I wouldn't have suggested it if it wasn't the best thing for me, too."

"You know I'm going to have to think about this."

"Of course."

"I need to make sure we're not crossing a line we shouldn't cross… This whole situation is so confusing to begin with. I want my child, when he or she grows up, to know I did my very best to look out for his or her well-being. I wouldn't want him or her to feel I'd made a bad situation worse—wouldn't want to have made it harder to understand and accept— by marrying you. That's why I have to be careful, why I have to think this through."

What she said made sense. Their decision to marry, if they made it, would have lifelong consequences. Ross believed it was the right decision. He felt surprisingly confident that she would, too.

"Okay," he said. He reached into the box of items from Melissa and pulled out a little wooden car. He placed it in the pile of toys. "Take all the time you need."

LATER THAT WEEK Ross drove to Lucy's house in Vancouver. He pulled into the circular drive and parked behind her car. No one answered the doorbell, so he walked around to the garden. He found her sitting on a chair in the shade. She saw him coming and rose.

"Doing okay?" he asked her.

"Hanging in there."

"You're on your own."

"Yeah."

"Seeing friends?"

"A few. People drop by. It can be awkward."

Gossip spread quickly and stories got around. *And did you know she'd just kicked him out? Poor man. He must have been devastated….*

Lucy seemed hollow, somehow. At the funeral she'd been more distraught than he'd expected. But she'd been through a hard couple of weeks. She'd lost her husband twice. Her grief might be as much for the marriage as for the man, but it was still strong.

She'd told him she hadn't revealed the reasons for her actions to anyone, out of concern for Katherine's health. So she had to bear this without the support she might have otherwise received.

Ross said, "I'm sorry to bring bad news, but I've spoken with Drew's lawyer. Did you know he was in debt?"

"In debt?"

Obviously she hadn't. Another unpleasant surprise for her. "His life insurance will cover the payments on the house, but that's about all there is. Everything else was on credit."

She stared up into the trees that lined the backyard. "Was anything real?"

Dark-green leaves shivered in the wind. A crow squawked from a high branch.

"He loved you," Ross said, believing it was true.

"Did he?"

"As best he was able."

Lucy started to cry. Ross took her in his arms, offered reassurance. She cried against him, sobbing that she'd made so many mistakes. He stroked her back until she quieted but was unprepared for the way she pressed herself to him, turned her face up, kissed the corner of his mouth.

"Ross," she said, her voice hoarse.

She moved to kiss him on the lips. He tilted his head so her lips landed on his cheek.

He stepped out of the embrace, his motions gentle but the message firm. "You're upset," he said softly. "And right now, it's hard for you to see how you're going to get through this. But you will. I know you will."

"Without you," she said, her voice faint.

"I'll always be a member of your family, Luce. I'll always be your child's uncle. But I can't be more than that."

She absorbed his words. Gave a watery smile. "I'm so embarrassed."

"Don't be."

She stepped away, averting her gaze. "Can we forget this ever happened?"

"Yeah. We can do that."

They shared a smile. Sad, for what had been and what might have been.

He said, "Take care of yourself."

She walked around the house with him. "This is partly about Jennifer, isn't it?" she asked, questioning but not challenging.

"Partly."

"But you love her?"

He didn't answer.

She studied his face and nodded, as if what she saw made it easier for her to take his rejection. "Be happy with her," she said, and headed for her front door.

ON SATURDAY MORNING ROSS went to his parents' house for brunch and to tell them about his proposal to Jennifer. He let himself in and found his mother in the kitchen. She sat on a stool pulled up to the counter, folding egg whites into her waffle batter. The kitchen was large, built for entertaining. Clean and white, it had acres of counter space and the latest appliances. It could handle a group of fifty for a full dinner without any problem, and often did.

The morning newspaper lay open on the kitchen table beside a cup of coffee.

"Your father's on the phone," his mother said, resting her spoon against the side of the bowl and sliding off her stool. She came over to give him a hug. It wasn't such an unusual gesture from her, but today she hung on longer, as though to absorb his strength as fully as she could.

"I'm not going anywhere," he said in a soft voice.

She pulled away first. He saw her eyes were damp. She turned back to her batter.

Ross leaned against the counter. "I have something I want to tell you. I've asked Jennifer to marry me. I think she'll say yes." He paused. "I know it's not an easy time to consider a wedding but I hope you'll be happy for us."

For a moment his mother simply took in the news. Then she tried to smile. "Of course I'm happy for you."

He saw the concern on her face, even though she tried to hide it. "But...?"

Her baking supplies lay on the counter. A bag of flour. A tin of baking powder. A measuring cup and spoons. The bowl in which she'd melted butter.

She reached for the bag of flour, then folded down the top. "I've asked you this before, but—"

"You know it's not, Mom. You know it couldn't be."

"I just thought maybe. If something extraordinary had happened. And this is just your way of trying to break the news gently..." she said. "So you don't give my poor heart a shock."

Ross stepped to the sink and began washing the measuring spoons and cups his mother had used. "It's not my baby."

"Then, are you sure you understand what you're getting into?"

He smiled. "She's pregnant. And will no doubt give birth to a perfectly healthy baby. I'm going to help her raise her child. So yes, I understand what I'm getting into."

His mother put away the dry goods in the cupboard. "What about the father?"

"He's not in the picture anymore."

"You know who he is?"

"Yes. And he's not interested in being a father."

Ross put more soap on his sponge and washed the bowl in which his mother had beaten the egg whites. He washed the beaters, then dried his hands and put away the electric mixer.

"What if he changes his mind, Ross? It's so easy to get attached. I wouldn't want you to get hurt, if he decides to claim his child."

"He won't."

"You sound very sure of that."

"I am." He took a mug from the cabinet and poured himself a cup of coffee from the automatic coffeemaker. "As sure as I am that this is the right thing for me."

"You're not—" She hesitated, then spoke again. "I'm your mother. I just want to make sure. You're not doing this—taking on Jennifer's problems, her baby with another man—just because of…because of what happened with you and Lucy?"

He shook his head. "Not at all."

His infertility had dealt the killing blow to his marriage to Lucy. They'd had their difficulties, anyway, wanting different things from life, and her willingness to compromise hadn't been stronger than her need for a family. Her desire for children who were related to both their parents.

He'd wanted a family, too, and had been shattered to learn he could never have one the traditional way.

But now he didn't want just any family. He wanted Jennifer and her baby.

His mother checked her waffle iron and spooned in batter for the first waffle. She smiled at him. "Then, it seems as if you're making a good choice. The child will be lucky to have you as a father."

The waffle iron steamed gently. A glass pitcher of orange juice sat on the counter next to three glasses, and he picked it up to fill them.

"Thank you, Mom."

Someday, he thought, he would tell her the truth. Introduce her to her grandchild. Make her happy, he hoped.

Ross's father came in just as Katherine opened the waffle iron to reveal a perfect golden-brown waffle. Over the meal he told Edward about his proposal to Jennifer. Edward betrayed no response other than happiness on his son's behalf. When Ross left the house his father walked him out.

They were silent as they went down the steps and to the car. Ross unlocked the Camry and opened the door. His father, he thought, looked haggard, as if he hadn't slept since the news of his son's death.

"You're okay?" Ross asked.

His father shrugged the question away. "The baby," he said.

"It's his."

Edward nodded. "A matter of weeks will prove it, anyway." He sighed. "What a mess he made of things. Poor Lucy. I wish I could know what he was thinking."

"It doesn't matter anymore."

His father looked thoughtful. "Drew told me his financial situation was complicated. It'll take a while to sort out. But I imagine we can all figure out a way to split things among his children."

Ross shook his head. "There's nothing to split. Drew was in debt. Everything's gone."

"Another lie."

"I'm sorry, Dad."

"It doesn't actually surprise me. I kept trying to believe him long after I should have." He looked away. "I've been thinking a lot since his death. I suppose I never gave Drew the limits he needed. I failed him in that respect and I'm as much to blame for his death as anyone. He was my son, and I didn't hold him to the high standard he deserved to have to meet." He held Ross's gaze. "We were very scared, your mother and I, by nearly losing him. We made mistakes as a result. I'm not sure we did our best by you, either."

"I turned out okay."

Edward nodded. "So you'll provide for his child?"

"As if it were my own."

"And is that your only reason for marrying her? To make up for your brother's failings?"

"No."

His father nodded again. Smiled. "You're a fine man."

A FEW NIGHTS LATER Ross was lounging with Jennifer on the sofa in the living room, watching a comedy he'd picked up on the way home from work.

Take-out cartons from the Mediterranean restaurant near the video store littered the coffee table. After eating, he sat with his arm on the back of the sofa behind her.

Five weeks had passed since she'd arrived on his doorstep, and Ross couldn't bring his previous life into focus. He'd thought himself reasonably happy, content, but now he knew he'd been more lonely than he'd wanted to admit.

And if she turned down his proposal, he would be so much more than lonely. Which might be why he hadn't mentioned the proposal during the seemingly endless days since he'd made it. She would give him an answer in her own time, he told himself. He didn't want to pressure her.

Tonight she wore a necklace, a simple silver chain she'd told him had belonged to her mother, and as the movie unfolded on the screen he toyed with it, enjoying the way his fingers brushed the soft skin of her neck. And he wondered if he planned to seduce her.

They'd made love in the past week, but soon she would probably be too far along in her pregnancy to welcome his advances. And he expected at least a couple of months to go by after the birth before she might be interested again.

He thought about the birth. She'd almost decided on a midwife and had given him her two final names. He'd asked around to find out what the medical community knew about them. Both of them had checked out well, as he'd told her over dinner.

When the movie ended, he turned off the television with the remote control but didn't move from the couch. He rested his hand at her nape, feeling the closeness, the warmth from her body along his side, the weight of her head on his shoulder.

"Can I get you anything?" he asked, speaking softly in the dim room. "More water? A snack?"

She shook her head. "I'm fine." She paused, long enough for him to notice the house's gentle creaking and the small noises of the night outside. "Maybe I should get *you* something."

"Not necessary," he said.

She turned toward him, placing her hand on his chest. "You're very good at helping people. At doing nice things for them. You can be very self-sacrificing." Her voice was husky. The kind of voice that made him want to do things other than discuss his altruism.

"You're going somewhere with this," he said, slightly suspicious.

"I'm just wondering how you react when someone does something for you."

"I'm grateful," he said.

"So you don't have any trouble accepting other people's generosity?" she asked, a smile in her voice.

"Of course not."

"Uh-huh," she said. Not believing him. "We'll see about that."

"Jennifer, what's going on?"

"Shh." Her hand drifted slowly down his body.

He felt himself begin to harden. "Jennifer," he said.

She put her hand on him, cupping him through his jeans, and he pulled in a breath. She'd initiated a seduction before he'd had a chance to do anything himself, which was fine by him. He drew her toward him for a kiss, seeking her mouth. She let him kiss her briefly, then pulled back.

Slowly she unbuckled his belt, undid the buttons of his fly. "You're very considerate in bed," she said. "But this is just for you."

"You don't have to do this." But he didn't want her to stop.

And she didn't seem to want to stop. "You said you could accept generosity," she murmured.

"Mmm," he said, a sound that was half agreement, half pleasure.

"I think you'd better prove it."

"Anything you want."

"Then, I want you," she said, lips to his ear, "to lie back and let *me* take care of *you*."

And so he did.

CHAPTER TWENTY-TWO

ROSS'S FATHER called Jennifer and asked her to join him for lunch at his club. When she hesitated, he said, "I understand you might not be eager to accept after my visit to the house. One of the reasons I want to have you to lunch is to apologize."

So Jennifer agreed and met him downtown. Inside the club, the heavy drapes and dark-wood paneling gave a severe, private feeling to the rooms. She knew it had once been a men's club but was now open to both sexes.

Edward was already seated at a table when she arrived. He rose as she approached, saying he'd taken the liberty of ordering her a soda water since that was what he'd seen her drink on previous occasions. It surprised her that he'd been so observant, with everything else going on.

"As I mentioned on the phone," he said as they both sat, "I'm sorry for my behavior at Ross's house. I shouldn't have offered you money and neither should I have asked you to leave. It's clear to me you were telling the truth."

"Thank you." Jennifer didn't know what else to say.

"Long overdue," Edward said. He handed her a

menu. "Now, take a look at this and see if there's something on it you might like."

They ordered, and while they waited he kept the conversation going with seeming ease. Somehow, in the forty-five minutes until they finished eating, they managed to avoid completely any serious topic or discussion of family matters. Jennifer couldn't figure out how he did it.

At last Edward brought the subject back around. "You've been very brave through this whole ordeal," he commented, after their plates had been cleared and he'd ordered coffee for himself and herbal tea for her. "And I'm speaking not merely of the time since my son's death but of the time before, as well."

"It's been difficult," she admitted.

"I'm sorry Drew acted as he did. God knows he put himself in a difficult situation, but he didn't handle himself in the way I would have wanted." Edward was quiet for a moment. Then he said, "I understand Ross has asked you to marry him."

"Yes." She wondered if he would try to talk her out of it.

"Do you plan to accept?"

"I haven't decided yet."

Edward watched her steadily, his eyes intent. At last he smiled. "Well, I suggest you do."

She felt relieved, and realized Edward's approval meant more to her than she'd have thought. It gave her hope that Katherine would also respond well and that her child would be welcomed by the extended family. Perhaps she'd been too quick to expect their rejection.

"I didn't think you would be happy about this."

"I am. I'm happy my grandchild will have a stable home and financial security. And I'm sad to have to say Ross will make a better father than his brother ever could have." He paused. "Do you love him?"

Jennifer wanted to say yes, but she knew it wasn't right to tell his father something she didn't have the courage to say to Ross himself. "We...have feelings for each other," she said, borrowing Ross's words.

Edward was silent. He reached into his breast pocket and withdrew a folded slip of paper. A check, she realized, as he laid it flat on the table and pushed it toward her. He'd made it out in her name, the amount substantially larger than the check he'd tried to write her at the house.

She looked up at him, not touching the check. "Why?"

He interlaced his fingers. "I don't want you to marry my son if you don't love him. If all you need is the security he can provide, then I want you to take this check and raise your child on your own. On the condition, of course, that you allow grandparent visits."

Jennifer didn't hesitate. She pushed the check back across the table.

Edward pocketed it. "Please try to make him happy. I would like to have at least one son who lives a good life."

THE NEXT DAY Ross's volunteer hours at the clinic overlapped with her full-day shift. She liked to have him there while she worked at the front, knowing he would come to check in with her between patients.

They had lunch together at Buddy's, and when he walked her back to the clinic, Melissa had arrived to replace him for the afternoon. She'd brought Frank with her.

"Hey, sweetie," Jennifer said, scooping Frank up into her lap. The little three-legged dog stuck her tongue out and licked Jennifer's face.

"Frank," Melissa said, "try to behave."

Frank let her tongue loll about, but stopped trying to lick Jennifer.

Melissa offered Ross her condolences, and the three of them talked for a few minutes before Ross left. Then Melissa gave Jennifer a sympathetic look. "Are you doing okay?"

"Yes and no," she answered. "It's pretty complicated."

Melissa nodded her understanding. "If you need to talk, I'm free after my shift here. We could pick up Emily and take Frank for a walk."

"I'd love that," Jennifer said. She needed a friend right now, and she particularly needed someone who knew Ross and could understand what was happening between her and him. Someone with whom she could discuss Ross's proposal.

The rest of the afternoon went by quickly. Kyle came out during a lull to check on her progress on the Web page. She'd brought the design with her on a disk, and showed it to him on the computer at the office.

"It'll look better on a more modern system," she told him. "But I tried to design it to look decent on almost any computer. I kept it very simple—I figured some people might access the page from old equipment."

Clients came in steadily after that, with appointments and without. Jennifer was busy answering the phone and pulling records and calming down one person who arrived quite distressed because she'd taken some kind of foreign substance, probably illegal, and was seeing small gnomes who kept pulling down their pants and revealing their gnome-size privates. After consultation with Barbara, the woman was directed to a detox facility.

"You handle your job really well," Melissa said a short while later as they walked to her car, which was parked a few blocks away in a garage.

They passed some people on the street. A woman sitting in the doorway of a boarded-up convenience store said, "Hey, Doc," as Melissa walked by.

"It's not so hard," Jennifer replied.

"We've had other people in that job. You make it seem easy. You're good at multitasking. That's a good skill for a mom to have."

"Am I supposed to feel prepared for motherhood?" she asked. "Because I don't."

Melissa laughed. "You're never going to feel prepared. And if you do, it'll just be an illusion."

"Uh-oh."

Melissa looked over at her. "Nothing can prepare you for how hard it is, how little sleep you'll get, how overwhelmed you'll feel."

"Stop now," Jennifer said. "I'm freaking out."

"But nothing is going to prepare you for how much love you'll feel, either," Melissa added. "Nothing."

"Okay."

"I'm serious. You think you love your baby already. Right?"

"I adore my baby." Jennifer held her stomach, which got bigger every day. She'd started to feel, along with the anxiety about being ready, an almost desperate need to see her baby.

"What you feel right now—it's like ten on a scale of ten, right? So much love for that little baby that you think you're going to fall apart."

"Yeah." That was exactly how it felt. It was overwhelming and beautiful and scary. Unlike any experience she'd had in her whole life.

"Well, that's nothing. On the scale of loving your child you're at *one* out of ten. You're going to look back on this time, and what you feel now will seem like lukewarm fondness compared with what you'll experience. It's going to blow you away."

They drove to Emily's day care center across the river in southeast Portland, about ten minutes from Kyle and Melissa's house. When they parked they saw Emily on the porch, looking like a puppy quivering at the prospect of being able to fetch a stick. As soon as they were out of the car, Emily scampered down the porch steps and dashed across the lawn. Melissa scooped her up in a hug and spun her around in a circle. Emily squealed with happiness.

"So, what did you do today?" Melissa asked.

Emily rattled off a list of activities, talking so fast Jennifer couldn't keep up.

Melissa laughed happily. "That sounds marvelous," she said. "I'm glad it was so exciting and I'm glad you enjoyed seeing the bunnies. Jennifer wants to come on a walk with us. What do you think about that?"

Emily smiled up at Jennifer. "Yay!"

"Okay," Melissa said. "Off to the park."

They bundled her into the car seat in back. "Do you mind sitting next to her?" Melissa asked. "She loves having someone to interact with when we're driving."

Jennifer didn't mind at all, and settled herself into the back. She found a stack of books on the far side of the car seat. "Okay if I read to her?"

"She'd love it."

As they drove, she read to Emily from her picture books, first a story about some monkeys playing drums and then one about a voracious caterpillar. Emily grinned hugely at the stories, her eyes fixed alternately on the pages of the book and on Jennifer's face.

"You've made a friend for life," Melissa observed as they got Emily out at the park. Melissa retrieved a small backpack from the trunk and looped it over her shoulders. She snapped a leash around Frank's neck.

They headed off to explore the park, which was a few city blocks in size. It held a couple of tennis courts and a ball field near the parking area. Both courts were full, and a group of kids played a game of pickup baseball on the diamond.

Emily took Frank's leash and toddled along with her, while Melissa and Jennifer strolled behind. Emily was absorbed in her dog-walking duties, which left the two women free to talk.

"Things must be different now," Melissa said, starting the phase of the conversation Jennifer had been waiting for, had been needing.

"They are," she agreed.

"The few times we talked about it, I got the impression you didn't feel too friendly toward Drew. How has his death hit you?"

"I was angry at him, but I'm not happy he's gone. I wanted my child to know its father."

They walked in silence for a few minutes. Then Melissa said, "Would he have come around?"

"I don't know," Jennifer answered. "Maybe. Then again, I'm not sure I could have trusted him to be the kind of dad I'd want my child to have."

"A lot of men," Melissa said, "like a lot of human beings, just can't do what's right."

"That's depressing," Jennifer said, giving Melissa a wry smile.

"But some men can. Kyle can. So can Ross."

"He's stood by me."

"Of course he has. He's a good man."

They paused in their conversation to look at some dandelions with Emily, who seemed fixated on the yellow flowers beside the path and wanted to wear one tucked behind her ear. Then they resumed their walk.

"What's going to happen next?" Melissa asked. "Will you keep living with Ross?"

"At least until after the baby's born. Maybe a lot longer." She paused. "He asked me to marry him."

Melissa stopped in her tracks. "He *what?*"

"Asked me to marry him," Jennifer repeated, though she knew Melissa had heard her the first time.

Melissa grinned. "Oh my. Oh my goodness. That's great news." She gave her a hug. "Ross is a great guy."

They started to walk again.

"I know he is. It's just that…"

"You don't want to marry him?" Melissa said it as if the possibility were inconceivable.

She hesitated. "That's not really the issue."

"So what's holding you back?"

"Well, he's Drew's brother. My baby's uncle."

"Sure. And in an ordinary situation that might be a little weird. But your circumstances are different."

"Are they?" Jennifer wanted to believe they were, but didn't trust her own motives.

"For one thing, and correct me if I'm wrong, it sounded like you and Drew were together just one time. It's not as if you were involved in a long-term relationship when you got pregnant, right?"

"No…but we did date each other in high school."

Melissa gave her a startled look.

"Yeah. See?" She took a few minutes to fill her in on the past—all of it. How she'd gotten to know Ross when he came home from college and began to feel closer to him than she did to Drew. The kiss they'd shared. "I had a pretty big crush on Ross back then, and I can't tell you how guilty I felt when I gave in to it.''

"But it was just a kiss. And you were just a couple of kids. I can see how it's all a little complicated now. Still, you've behaved ethically. Drew's behavior, the way he lied to you about being married, his refusal to take responsibility for your child... He's the one who made the mistakes. You shouldn't have to spend the rest of your life paying for them. Do you love Ross?''

It was the second time someone had asked her the question. She figured she might as well own up. "With all of my heart.''

Melissa nodded. "Of course you do. So you should marry him. The two of you are good people, Jennifer. You deserve to be happy.''

Ahead of them Emily and Frank spotted a water fountain and trotted toward it. Frank danced in a puddle of water that had formed at the base. Emily asked to drink, so Melissa held her up and turned on the water for her.

As they walked farther, the path curved gently back toward the parking lot. Jennifer asked, "But what if it's not the right thing for my child?''

Melissa shook her head. "Ross is going to be a terrific dad. You don't have anything to worry about.''

She had to say it again. "The fact that he's the uncle, too...?''

"You want to know what I think is the most important thing for children in a two-parent home? Aside from being loved? To have the parents love each other. At one time I thought the other things were enough—things like financial security and shared responsibilities. But I've learned a lot since then. I've realized a loving environment is what matters—to have that model of a healthy relationship so your children can feel like the world is a safe and supportive place, and someday forge good relationships of their own. The rest of it, they can sort out. And you'll both be there to help them understand. I honestly think you should do this.''

"It means a lot to me that you think so."

"But?"

"But there's one more thing..."

Melissa gave her a questioning look.

Jennifer hesitated. It wasn't easy to admit, even to someone as understanding as Melissa. "I'm not sure he loves me."

"He won't say it?" Melissa asked, not sounding at all disturbed.

"No." Telling someone you had "feelings" for them wasn't quite the same.

Melissa smiled at her. "I have a bit of experience with people who are afraid to admit they're in love. But it's obvious Ross loves you. I've seen the way he looks at you. Kyle has, too. And I can understand why Ross might have a hard time talking about it after his last relationship." Her smile turned mischievous. "Maybe you'll just have to force the subject a little."

ROSS WAS GLAD he'd bothered to change out of his scrubs, when he emerged from the hospital and found Jennifer behind the wheel of her car.

She tilted her head toward the front passenger seat. "Get in. I'm taking you to dinner."

He complied. "This is a surprise."

"We need to talk."

At the restaurant the hostess seated them at an outdoor table far from other diners, with a view of a nearby park. Across a wide green field, some toddlers played and an older couple walked arm in arm.

Jennifer unfolded her napkin and placed it over the curve of her big belly. She opened her menu. "I hear the fish is good."

He peered at her. The only reason he could think of for this impromptu dinner was that she'd decided to marry him. But she wasn't acting like a woman about to get engaged.

"Jennifer, do you have something to tell me?"

She shrugged. "Maybe it's more that you have something to tell me."

"Really."

"Yes." She placed her menu on the tabletop. "Ross, we're friends. You don't have to keep secrets from me. I want you to be able to tell me the truth."

"And that would be…?" he asked, genuinely puzzled. And disappointed—but maybe she still planned to accept his proposal.

The busboy, a young guy with extremely black hair and several piercings, arrived to fill their water glasses.

"Thanks," she told him when he finished.

She sipped her water. A lemon slice had been

placed over the rim. She squeezed the juice into the glass and gave the water a stir with her spoon. Taking her time. Driving Ross slightly crazy.

"You invited me to dinner. Are you sure you don't have something to tell me?"

"Oh. Well, Melissa and I took Emily and Frank for a walk yesterday."

He waited, expecting more. Nothing came. "And?"

"It had to be something interesting?"

Their waitress cruised by. "Do you folks need another minute?"

"I'm ready," Jennifer said. "Are you?" She ordered grilled salmon and a large salad, with chocolate cake for dessert.

"The same," he told the waitress, since he'd hardly glanced at the menu.

The waitress left, taking their menus with her.

Jennifer said, "Will you excuse me a sec? I've got to go to the ladies'. Pregnancy, you know."

Ross sat, not quite patiently, while she was gone.

"There *was* something else," Jennifer said when she returned. "Melissa thinks it wouldn't be all that much of a bad idea for us to get married."

Not exactly a ringing endorsement. He'd expected better from a friend as close as Melissa. Weren't good friends supposed to help you out, instead of undercutting you?

"She thinks it might actually be good for my child to have you as a parent."

"I agree."

"And she doesn't think a relationship between us would be inappropriate."

"Okay," he said, drawing it out. "And how do *you* feel?"

"She's really not worried about any of the complications. She says they'll all take care of themselves."

He was starting to get tired of hearing Melissa's opinions. "And how do you feel?" he repeated.

"Well, I think she makes a lot of sense."

"Good."

She folded her hands on the table. "But the other thing she said—"

He couldn't help it. He groaned.

"The other thing she said was that the most important thing for children is that their parents—if they have two of them—love each other. Because that way the children have a good model for adult relationships."

"Very sensible."

"I know," she said, with just a hint of sadness in her voice.

Where the hell was that coming from? He leaned forward and covered her hands with his. "She's right. So why are you sad?"

"Because I can't marry you."

If a man could feel his heart stop beating, Ross did. "You can't marry me."

"Uh-uh."

He could think of only one reason. "You don't love me." God, he'd been such a lovesick fool. Thank goodness he hadn't said anything when he'd proposed. Having someone tell you they loved you out of some kind of obligation would be bad. Having them say it out of pity would be worse. But now he knew that not hearing it at all was infinitely more horrible.

"Of course I love you."

He took a second to put his train of thought into reverse. "You do?"

"Of course I do." She said it with warmth and a loving smile.

"Then, what in the world is the problem?" he asked, almost testily.

She raised an eyebrow. "You tell me."

Ross prided himself on his cool head in difficult situations. No matter how chaotic things got in the E.R., his brain always performed as he needed it to, as it had been trained. He never choked. He never got flustered.

Except now, when the woman he loved told him she loved him back and yet there was still some problem.

"You know what Melissa said?" she asked him.

No. And he didn't really care.

"Melissa said any man who loves a woman but proposes marriage to her without even *mentioning* that one, somewhat significant fact deserves to have his chain pulled a little."

She grinned. A big, wide *gotcha* grin.

"Oh, hell," Ross said. "I didn't—I never—"

She put a hand over his. "Hold that thought." With her free hand she signaled the busboy, who reached for an item on his station and carried it over.

"Best I could do," he said, offering a plate draped with a red napkin. He set the plate down beside Jennifer. "Hope it fits," he said as he backed away. "And congratulations."

Ross stared at the napkin, wondering what it concealed.

"You were saying?" Jennifer prompted.

Focus, he told himself. He took her hands in his, stroking the tops of them with his thumbs, feeling the warmth and softness of her skin. "I was saying," he said, "that I never told you how much I love you. I was afraid to pressure you into saying it too soon. But that was the wrong thing to do. I should have told you a long time ago. I'm madly in love with you."

"So you'll marry me."

"Is that a proposal?"

Jennifer smiled. "Mmm-hmm."

"Yes. I'll certainly marry you. As long as I can find out what's on that plate."

"A ring," she said. "No engagement would be complete without a ring."

She lifted the red napkin, revealing a bed of lettuce and, lying on it, a fork with one tine bent back into a circle.

Jennifer looked at it and laughed. She picked it up. "It's a fork."

"Yup," Ross said. "It's a fork."

She turned it in her hand. "I guess now is when I find out if you truly love me."

"Oh, I truly love you," he said. "But I'm only going to wear *that* if you wear *this*." He reached into his pocket for the jeweler's box he'd been carrying for what felt like half a lifetime now. From it he took the engagement ring he'd picked out after his proposal to her. A single diamond set among sapphires.

Jennifer drew a breath. "It's beautiful."

He met her gaze. They stared at each other for what felt like a very long time. With his eyes he promised he would love her for the rest of his life, and love her child, too.

"Shall we?" he said at last.

She extended her hand. He slipped the ring into place on her finger. She smiled. "Now you."

He held out his hand. She threaded the rounded tine of the fork onto his finger. The handle and the three remaining tines branched out sideways from his hand.

"It fits," she said, surprised.

He looked down at it, then up at the woman he loved. "How are we ever," he asked, grinning, "going to explain this to the grandkids?"

HARLEQUIN *Super*ROMANCE®

Montana Dreaming
by Nadia Nichols

**Lack of money forces
Jessie Weaver to sell the
ranch her family has owned
since the mid-1800s—and
creates a rift between her
and her boyfriend,
Guthrie Sloane, that's as
big as the Montana sky.
But a grizzly on the loose,
a crazy bear-hunting U.S.
senator and a love that
neither she nor Guthrie
can deny soon make
selling her Montana ranch
the least of her worries!**

*Heartwarming stories
with a sense of humor,
genuine charm and emotion
and lots of family!*

*On sale starting
September 2002.*

Available wherever
Harlequin books are sold.

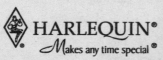

HARLEQUIN®
Makes any time special ®

Visit us at www.eHarlequin.com   HSRMD

HARLEQUIN *Super*ROMANCE®

CREATURE COMFORT

Creature Comfort, the largest veterinary clinic in Tennessee, treats animals of all sizes— horses and cattle as well as family pets. Meet the patients— and their owners. And share the laughter and the tears with the men and women who love and care for all creatures great and small.

Listen to the Child
by Carolyn McSparren

Dr. Mac Thorn—renowned for his devotion to his four-legged patients and his quick temper—is used to having people listen to *him*. But ex-cop Kit Lockhart can't hear him—she was injured on the job. Now Mac is learning to listen, and Kit and her young daughter have a lot to teach him.

Coming in September to your favorite retail outlet.

Previous titles in the Creature Comfort series

#996 THE MONEY MAN (July 2001)

#1011 THE PAYBACK MAN (September 2001)

HARLEQUIN®
Makes any time special ®

Visit us at www.eHarlequin.com

HSRCREAT

If you enjoyed what you just read,
then we've got an offer you can't resist!

Take 2 bestselling love stories FREE!

Plus get a FREE surprise gift!

Clip this page and mail it to Harlequin Reader Service®

IN U.S.A.	IN CANADA
3010 Walden Ave.	P.O. Box 609
P.O. Box 1867	Fort Erie, Ontario
Buffalo, N.Y. 14240-1867	L2A 5X3

YES! Please send me 2 free Harlequin Superromance® novels and my free surprise gift. After receiving them, if I don't wish to receive anymore, I can return the shipping statement marked cancel. If I don't cancel, I will receive 6 brand-new novels every month, before they're available in stores. In the U.S.A., bill me at the bargain price of $4.47 plus 25¢ shipping and handling per book and applicable sales tax, if any*. In Canada, bill me at the bargain price of $4.99 plus 25¢ shipping and handling per book and applicable taxes**. That's the complete price, and a savings of at least 10% off the cover prices—what a great deal! I understand that accepting the 2 free books and gift places me under no obligation ever to buy any books. I can always return a shipment and cancel at any time. Even if I never buy another book from Harlequin, the 2 free books and gift are mine to keep forever.

135 HDN DNT3
336 HDN DNT4

Name	(PLEASE PRINT)	
Address	Apt.#	
City	State/Prov.	Zip/Postal Code

* Terms and prices subject to change without notice. Sales tax applicable in N.Y.
** Canadian residents will be charged applicable provincial taxes and GST.
   All orders subject to approval. Offer limited to one per household and not valid to current Harlequin Superromance® subscribers.
   ® is a registered trademark of Harlequin Enterprises Limited.

SUP02   ©1998 Harlequin Enterprises Limited

HARLEQUIN *Super*ROMANCE*

A Baby of Her Own
by Brenda Novak

She's pregnant. And she's on her own—or is she?

One night, one baby.
Delaney Lawson wants a baby more than anything in the world, but there are absolutely no prospects in her small Idaho town of Dundee. Then one night she meets a handsome stranger in Boise—a stranger who doesn't plan to stay a stranger long....

Another gripping and emotional story from this powerful writer.
Brenda Novak's "books are must-reads for the hopeless romantics among us."
—Bestselling author
Merline Lovelace

Available in September wherever Harlequin books are sold.

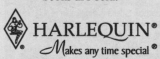

HARLEQUIN®
Makes any time special®

Visit us at www.eHarlequin.com

HSRBOHO

HARLEQUIN Super ROMANCE

**If you fell in love
with Heathcliff...
you're sure to fall for
Niall Maguire
in**

The Man on the Cliff
by Janice Macdonald

A Harlequin Superromance
novel by an exciting,
brand-new author.

Niall Maguire lives in a
castle high atop the rugged
cliffs of west Ireland. A
mysterious, brooding man
with a dark secret he's sworn
never to reveal—even though
it means he can't defend
himself against village gossip
and accusations.

Then he meets Californian
Kate Neeson who's determined
to uncover the truth.

THE MAN ON THE CLIFF is a
hero you won't soon forget...

*Available in August 2002
wherever Harlequin books are sold.*

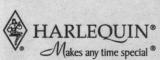

HARLEQUIN®
Makes any time special ®

Visit us at www.eHarlequin.com

HSRMOTC